Twilight HEIST

KATHERINE MCINTYRE

HOT TREE PUBLISHING

ALSO BY KATHERINE MCINTYRE

REHOBOTH PACT

CONFINED DESIRES

OPPOSED DESIRES

RESTRAINED DESIRES

CHESAPEAKE DAYS

STRONGER THAN HOPE

STRONGER THAN PASSION

STRONGER THAN LONGING

OUTLAWS

MIDNIGHT HEIST

TWILIGHT HEIST

TWILIGHT HEIST

OUTLAWS
BOOK 2

KATHERINE MCINTYRE

HOT TREE PUBLISHING

For information, contact the publisher, Hot Tree Publishing.

WWW.HOTTREEPUBLISHING.COM

EDITING: HOT TREE EDITING

COVER DESIGNER: BOOKSMITH DESIGN

E-BOOK ISBN: 978-1-922679-39-0

PAPERBACK ISBN: 978-1-922679-40-6

To my husband, who always encourages more stories about these murder hobos.

CHAPTER 1

"When you've seen the elephant, son, there's not much left to surprise you."

Tuck crept along the pitch-black corridor, the scents of furniture cleaner, the crisp night air, and polished metal filling his nose.

One step, two step, one step, two.

His father's words resurrected themselves at every job, as if the man himself were haunting him along the way. Dad had meant the mantra to carry the world-weariness of someone who'd seen too much. Except then he'd died of an embolism, which left the hollow tang of irony to his oft-repeated phrase.

Tuck liked to remember it for one reason alone. No matter how much you'd seen, no matter how perfect a plan you had—life was a fickle bitch, and she would always surprise you.

As he crept down the hallway, he didn't make a sound. Instead, the hum of the air conditioning broke through the vacuum of noise, and he continued with an even tread. They'd spent a week casing this place that might as well be a history museum with how many rare and unusual artifacts littered the rooms. Because having gold diadems from the late Hellenistic period lying around on display was common. Royal Egyptian overseer statues? Pah, commoner fare.

Elijah Whittaker could go cry into his bags of money after they robbed him.

The asshole had been strong-arming people for years to get the collector's items he wanted, and they were simply returning a rare Persian dagger to the rightful owner.

Scarlet's voice sounded over the comms. "Who ate my beef and broccoli?"

Tuck bit down on his lip to keep from snorting out loud. He crept past a few bedrooms, heading toward the study. Alanna had snapped some pictures from the outside windows the other night, and they'd analyzed them to figure out the dagger's location. But they only had a small gap of time on the internal alarm that coincided with Mr. Whittaker and most of the staff being off the premises. Once the personal chef had packed it in for the night and Elijah drove off, Tuck had slipped in.

The groundskeeper remained on-site, but last Tuck checked, he'd retired to his small cottage nearby.

The quiet ached with potential—for either opportunity or danger.

"Why don't you just order more, Scar?" Alanna

murmured into the comms. She was waiting outside the house for him, lingering near their getaway car.

"Spoken like the traitor who ate my leftovers," Scarlet responded. Their resident hacker possessed a long fuse for most of their insane shenanigans, but he drew his line in the sand at food thievery. Alanna was the constant culprit, a black hole for anything in the fridge.

Tuck shook his head with a grin as he approached the open door of the study. Already, the rich scent of wood polish reached his nose. Tuck made sure to keep away from the walls or brushing against anything along the way. He wouldn't be leaving any physical evidence behind. He stepped up to the entrance and peered into the study.

Moonlight spilled through the arched windows, gleaming across display case after display case. While a large mahogany desk and leather chair sat on one side of the room, instead of bookcases, artifacts on shelves took up the wall space. Apparently, Elijah fancied himself a museum curator. How many of these crowns, fossils, and old weapons had been coerced from the original owners? Tuck shook off the flare of irritation.

That was why they'd jumped on this job in the first place.

He took note of the shut-down security system in the room, one Scar had disabled remotely. Without being given notice, he'd only be able to keep it offline for a half hour, so Tuck had been keeping active watch on the time. Shadows cloaked him as he slipped across the room without so much as a creak. Thankfully, this asshole kept his displays organized by type of artifact, so Tuck sidled over to the glass cases of daggers, bow heads, and ceremonial knives.

John's voice came over the comms. "Did you seriously eat my pork fried rice too?"

Tuck was half tempted to turn the goddamn comms off.

"No, dickbag," Alanna hissed.

"Don't need to lie to me, baby," John flirted. "If you're hungry, I've got something else to feed you."

"If you're referring to what I think you are, I'd starve," Alanna sniped back.

Grif jumped into the conversation. "Kids, stop squabbling on the comms," he said, the leader of their outfit bringing order in as usual. Alanna and John's argument ended, and Tuck enjoyed the return to quiet as he focused on the task ahead.

He'd found the case of daggers and scoured row after row, searching for the Persian one from the client's picture. Not like he'd have to try very hard. Museum wannabe had each individual one labelled. The air possessed a velvet quality that was normal at the late hour, post evening but not yet midnight. Tuck moved silently as he skimmed through a collection worth millions.

His gaze zeroed in on the grey dagger on the bottom row. Persian. Had the three-line markings in the exact right spots. Bingo.

He leaned over to the base of the display case. This

one hadn't used wireless alarms for Scar to hack, so it was guaranteed Elijah employed either an electrical or seismic alarm system. The front part of the display case looked smooth, but Tuck brought out a small flashlight to examine the sides. He caught the slight rectangular imprint on the right one and crouched in front of it. With a few pushes, he got the flap open and brought the flashlight down to find the base of the alarm system mere inches away.

Tuck reached into his sling bag and plucked out the wire cutters. He didn't bother restraining his eye roll when he saw the model. These ones were old news, but the guy had probably bought it at top-of-the-line prices. He lowered himself onto his chest, arms outstretched as he teased out the yellow wires and gave them a snip.

Disarmed.

Time to nab this dagger and get the fuck out. Tuck brought his gloved hands up to the case and worked quickly. The air hummed around him with the resonant silence. There was something about thieving that lit his veins on fire in a way he hadn't felt since he used to slip on his leather shoes and step onto the tightrope, high, high, high above the ground. There had been nothing like the deafening quiet so high above, how worries and thoughts drained away, and his world narrowed to a pinpoint.

To one foot in front of the other.

He slid the display case glass open with nary a sound, and a moment later, he was slipping the Persian dagger into his sling bag. Tuck grabbed a few extra daggers, not bothering to pay too much attention to what he stole—guaranteed, the items in this collection were worth serious money, and this was their payment. With caution, he began to bring the glass back to its previous position. Any stray hairs, snagged threads, or smudges could be traceable, and Tuck preferred his invisibility. If he was lucky, Whittaker wouldn't notice that the dagger was missing for days.

"Fuck, he's back," Alanna's voice crackled over the comms.

Of course, because the Outlaws were never lucky.

"I'm in the study," Tuck murmured. "Is my exit clear?"

"He's coming in through the entrance," Alanna responded, her voice terse in the twitchy way she got when she couldn't just muscle her way through a problem.

Right, so the planned exit was out.

"There are a few windows in the study," Dan jumped in over the comms. Grif's boyfriend was their newest addition, but the sweet man had proved himself ten times over, and his quick thinking had pulled them out of a few pinches already.

"Are they scalable?" Grif asked.

Tuck stepped up to the nearest window and peered down. Three floors and a stone exterior. It'd be a challenging climb.

Alanna jumped in again. "He's heading inside."

No time to deliberate. Tuck pulled out his climbing gloves and swapped the pair at lightning speed. His shoes would suffice—he wore flats that worked for every type of mission. After years of tightrope, flats were always his first choice. His heart thudded harder, the burst of adrenaline infiltrating his veins as he tried to listen for any rustling from farther inside the house. Whittaker wouldn't be making any attempts at quiet.

A slight shuffle and creak came from below.

He cracked the window open and pulled himself onto the ledge. Tuck waited for a moment, listening to the sounds from inside. Another creak followed by another—steady, like someone was scaling stairs.

No more time to wait. He glanced down the stone face of the wall he'd be descending a moment later. In the dark. Great times.

Tuck brought the window shut behind him and then dragged his ass to the edge. His feet dangled there, three stories up, and the heights felt like home. His heart fluttered with a cocktail of adrenaline and antici-pation, and he gripped the ledge tight. He swung over the side in a fluid motion, his toes seeking the cracks between the stones.

He and Alanna had dealt with heights much higher than this, though most of the time with a practice round and equipment.

Who needed safety nets anyway?

He'd never used them on the tightrope—wouldn't start now.

With one last glance toward the study, Tuck began to descend.

He dug his fingers into the holds he found, and he

swept his gaze inches down with each move as he descended. His back was to the open night, and the breezes whirled around a little more briskly up here.

"Hope you're already out of there," Alanna mumbled on the comms. Tuck didn't bother responding. With the challenge that spread out before him, a puzzle of bumpy stones, cracks, and divots, he couldn't afford to lose focus for a moment.

A few minutes into the climb down, his muscles burned from some of the holds he'd attempted, straining his arm sockets' capabilities. The air smelled sweeter tonight, like gardenia mixed with granite, his deep inhales drawn in an even tempo as he ignored his racing heart and the temptation to keep looking up, down, or behind him. Years of discipline had him focused in the moment, on taking one step at a time.

He squinted, trying to discern if that was a deep crack in the stone beneath his right foot or just a shadow. Sweat prickled on his brow, the whirling wind quickly turning it to paste. Had to attempt it.

He swung his foot down and dipped his toes forward, only to slam them against solid rock. His balance shifted off-kilter.

His arms strained, and he swept his leg from side to side. He needed to find something, anything. Panic flared through him like an alarm.

A moment later, his toes dipped into a deeper crack. His deltoids screamed from holding his entire weight up like that. He swallowed hard as he settled. Perpetual joyride, this was. Tuck cast a glance down at last. He'd gone farther than he thought—two stories down, one left to go. Tuck sucked a deep breath in and continued his descent, finding another crevasse to rest his feet on, another bit of stone that jutted out as his handhold.

Out here, only the sounds of the surrounding forest infiltrated his awareness—the hum of insects and the rustle of branches and leaves. The inside of the house remained quiet of any loud noises, and Tuck kept that as his baseline of calm as he continued to climb down the wall.

He cast another glance toward the ground and then at the first-floor windows for reference.

Jumpable.

Tuck didn't hesitate—he pushed off from the wall and soared to the ground, landing with a practiced thump onto the earth.

To his right lay the path to the woods and the back of the mansion, and to the left was the entryway.

"Am I clear?" Tuck murmured into the comms.

"Lights are on in the front of the house," Alanna responded at once. "Tree line should be out of view."

Tuck leaned against the wall for a moment to catch his breath. His shoulders still heaved, and the burn in his muscles was the sort he reveled in. A slip of a grin stole his lips. Left it was.

He started out at a light jog, but the moment he reached the tree line, he ducked behind the cover of the thick trunks and hit a steady run. His soles padded along the precision-trimmed grass, and the breeze he kicked up pasted the remaining droplets of sweat to his face. A minute later, he'd reached the end of the driveway.

Each job was like this—walking the line—and the same anticipation thrummed through him as the end loomed in sight. Alanna's car was hidden farther down the street, lights off and in Park. Tuck slowed to a casual stroll, slipping into every shadow along the way like he was melting into them. The night air was tinged with opportunity, and Tuck loved being one of the lucky few who seized it.

The day he'd joined the Outlaws, his life had started anew, but he never regretted this path. He'd always been an adrenaline junkie, and this job gave him the outlet to do something worthwhile with it. Tuck reached the Honda Civic and slipped into the passenger's side.

After he'd left the circus, he'd felt aimless—like he'd never find a close family again.

And then Grif had claimed Tuck as one of his own, and the rest was history.

Tuck shut the door behind him, far too sweaty and out of breath to be inside this quiet car.

"Fucking took you long enough," Alanna said with a smirk as she turned on the car engine. The woman's features were even sharper in the shadows, her dark eyes twinkling with amusement. "Let's get back. I'm apparently facing an interrogation over goddamn takeout."

"Should've just cannonballed out the window, right?" Tuck responded dryly, an amused grin on his lips. Alanna peeled the car forward, heading down the street—away from Elijah Whittaker's mansion. Within a few minutes, they were zooming along the roads in the direction of home sweet home—Chicago.

Tuck settled back in the seat and pulled out his phone to check any messages he might've missed. Alanna set her music on to blare, some swoony female-vocalist pop that she dared the rest of the crew to make fun of her over. John was the only idiot who took her bait.

Tuck glanced down at the screen, and his heart stopped.

A number flashed there—one he hadn't seen in years.

When the circus came a-callin'…

CHAPTER 2

Out of the multitude of reasons Leo could've and should've stayed home, two compelling ones had him hopping out of the Uber in front of Polished Knives.

First, Dan asked him to come, and he was a sucker for his best friend on most days.

Secondly, he needed to get dicked down in a bad way. It'd been weeks, and he was sorely lacking in the stress-relief department.

He slipped a hand into the pocket of his navy blazer and headed for the front door.

Polished Knives wasn't his scene—a bar that collected more heavyweights in the underworld and shady deals than he liked to linger around. Leo preferred hitting up Thirst when he wanted to pull. At the gay club, the only thing he'd get stabbed with was a cock, unlike here. But now that his best friend had gone and started dating one of those underworld elements and joining his ragtag group of Merry Men, they congregated here.

Leo stepped inside, and the overwhelming scent of pine and cleaner wafted his way, which was better than sweat and Sauvage that reeked from the rafters of his usual haunts. The place preached class from the cream-and-obsidian bar displaying backlit bottles of liquor along the far wall. The dangling Edison bulbs contributed to the dim lighting of the place and gave it more of a seductive vibe, but Leo didn't miss the furtive glances shot at any newcomers or the way hands moved a little too fast in this joint.

The bouncer, a big, muscled guy with more than a few scars marring a hard face, checked him before he stepped toward the booths. Leo passed him a flirty wink before continuing forward, but the guy just rolled his eyes.

His loss. Leo had been stuck in a vortex of mind-numbing drudgery at Torres Industries this week, a company he'd been trying to leave ever since Dan Torres did. Once Grif and the Outlaws ousted their corrupt-as-fuck CFO and Dan stepped down from CEO to join the do-gooder band of thieves, the place buzzed with paranoia and uncertainty. On top of that, Leo kept hitting dead ends with the latest pursuit in his morally questionable side gig.

Which meant he would be leaving with a guy tonight.

Preferably one who was bossy in bed because he was in a mood to get shoved around.

He zeroed in on the group in one of the back booths. Not like he'd need to look too hard to find the rest of the Outlaws. Grif was a mountain of a man, all hard muscle with a murderer's glint in his eye, which was hilarious considering the way his teddy bear of a best friend was curled up against the guy. And if Leo hadn't been able to find them on sight, Alanna was arguing loud enough to wake the dead with some Urban Outfitters type of brunette beside her.

Leo's gaze wandered until he locked and loaded on the guy he'd been flirting with for the past three months, ever since he'd been involved in a little old heist to take down the company he worked for from the inside.

Tucker Hennings, aka, the fine-as-fuck former tightrope walker who worked as the stealth guy for the Outlaws. Tonight, he was looking extra broody from the sloping shadows in here that highlighted his long face and gorgeous glossy black curls. The light bit of scruff on his chin, the expressive brows, and that tight, muscular body all had Leo salivating on a normal basis, and the simple tight black T-shirt with jeans he was wearing now amped that up even more.

Leo didn't bother hiding his trajectory as he made a beeline for the empty spot beside Tuck.

"Saved this seat for me?" Leo said as he slid into the booth next to Tuck.

Tuck glanced his way, his upper lip curling with wry amusement. Those dark eyes were banked coals glimmering with the sort of lust Leo was looking for tonight.

Even though they'd been teasing each other over the past few months, Leo seemed to only end up at the Outlaws HQ when they needed help, so the timing to get bent over and fucked hard hadn't been right. He might be easy, but he wasn't enough of an exhibitionist to want to have sex in the living room of the Outlaws penthouse where all six of them lived.

"You're welcome to sit wherever you like," Tuck said, dripping with insinuation. He opened his legs a little wider as Leo sat down so their thighs pressed together. Leo didn't mind in the slightest. All that hard muscle brushing up against him was enough to get his cock hard.

"Is that Leo Kennedy here in the flesh, or is it an apparition?" Dan's voice drew his attention up and away from the eye candy. "It's been so long since I've seen my damn best friend that my guess is hallucination."

Leo rolled his eyes, stretching his legs out so they tangled right up with Tuck's. He flashed the guy a "Fuck me, please" grin before returning his attention to Dan. "Heaven forbid we don't see each other daily, due to work. I just went to lunch with you last week, drama queen."

"Are you trying to say I'm needy?" Dan asked, an amused grin playing on his lips. His best friend looked even smaller next to Grif—slender and adorable, his business casual clothes always neat and his black hair tamed.

Leo arched a brow and shot a glance at Grif. "I think your boyfriend can answer that one."

Grif let out a snort. "Please, Kennedy. What sort of idiot do you take me for?"

John leaned against the side of the booth. "When it comes to Danny boy over there, a pretty big one."

Grif flipped John off and took a smooth sip of his whisky. Leo skimmed his gaze over the man. He could see why Dan had lost his mind and morals for the guy. Big-ass bruiser with scars and muscles for days and intelligent blue eyes. John wasn't a slouch in the looks department either—depending on the day, the guy came across like a muscular farm boy or slick CEO with a brawny frame and charming smile that'd lure in anyone.

Leo wasn't insanely picky—both of those guys were fuckable, but he gravitated more toward men in the tall, dark, and elegant category. Something about the liquid way Tuck moved had snared him from the start, and with those dark curls and sarcasm to spare, the guy always pinged Leo's radar.

"Where's Scar?" Leo asked, looking around for the resident hacker of the Outlaws. He'd been admiring Scarlet's work for a long time, well before he and Dan had ever met Grif and the crew.

"She's on her way," Dan said, taking a sip of his old fashioned. "Had to tie up some loose ends of some project she was working on."

That piqued his interest. He and Scarlet were cut from the same cloth of hacker, mostly under gray hat, flipping between white or black as the day or situation required.

"Why?" Dan asked, his eyes twinkling with amusement.

Leo rolled his eyes. Dan seemed to think flirting with anyone meant Leo was interested, but his best friend was too honest and sweet that way. Which was exactly how big bad Grif Blackmore had gobbled him up.

"Because I've been working on a few projects of my own," he responded, tapping his fingers on the surface of the table. His skin itched at the thought of the ones he'd be tackling next, a deep dive into something akin to touching a live wire, which was necessary in this circumstance, but he knew it'd zap. "But tonight, I'm less work and all pleasure." Leo railroaded over those memories before they could emerge.

"You came to the right place, then," Tuck said, his voice a velvet rumble. He traced a finger around the rim of the aviation he was drinking, the crisp scent of gin fragrant in the air. Those dark eyes flashed his way, and Leo couldn't help the smirk rising to his lips.

"Fucking women," Alanna spat as she yanked over a chair which screeched against the floor all the way over. She huffed into the seat and leaned forward, her pointy elbows looking more threatening than some of the heat the denizens of this bar were packing.

"Do I want to know?" Leo asked. Already, Dan was shaking his head no, and Grif licked his lower lip, clearly hiding his own grin.

"She said she understood the score with my work." Alanna scowled hard enough to set the table on fire. "I. Don't. Talk. About. It. Yet she was all—you're always disappearing, why can't you say anything, blah, blah, blah."

"How dare she have feelings," Dan said, his lips twitching with the light sarcasm.

John shrugged. "I agree on this one. She knew the score."

Alanna swung her scythe glare his way. "Ew, don't agree with me. That just makes me feel filthy."

Leo sank back in his seat. He needed a drink if he was going to keep up with any of this.

Tuck set his glass on the table with a clink and nudged his knee against Leo's. "I'm grabbing a refill. You want anything?" He didn't move away from the point of contact, and Leo couldn't help but push back a little, greedily drinking in the sight of the man beside him. Tuck's eyes flared with renewed heat.

"Yes, to escape to the bar," Leo said, his lips curling into a flirty smirk. "Take me with you?"

"Sure thing, Kennedy," Tuck said. At that, he pushed up from his seat and slipped his palm against Leo's. The man's competent grip and the skin-to-skin connection flicker-flared through him, and he couldn't ignore the shiver that ran down his spine. Leo hopped out of the booth, and Tuck swept past him, directing him toward the bar. Leo half expected Tuck to drop his hand, but instead, the man kept a fierce hold on him as he maneuvered through the throngs of people glutting up the bar area until they stood in front of two empty stools.

Leo slid into the nearest one, not hesitating to claim them. While he might've shown up at Dan's request tonight, there was only one man in his sights. Tuck snagged the other and leaned forward, his elbow digging into the bar. He caught the eye of the bartender, who zipped over at once. The looming guy wore all black with the sort of broody scowl that vacillated between hot and dangerous.

"What can I get you, Hennings?" he asked.

"Cole, I'll have another aviation and whatever he's having," Tuck said, a curl of possession in his tone and in the sizzling look he directed Leo's way. Leo's lips twitched with his grin, and he shifted in his seat. His body had been scorched from the moment his gaze landed on Tuck tonight. The flirty attraction that had zinged between them before was now blaring, like someone had cranked up the volume. Leo wasn't sure if the intensity was due to his own desperate need for stress release, Tuck riding on a post-heist high, or a combination of the two, but the potency couldn't be denied.

"Sidecar, thanks," Leo responded, and the bartender slipped away to go take care of the drinks. Sitting this close to Tuck had his temperature raging, and he slipped out of his blazer, folding it over his arm. He didn't miss how Tuck's hungry gaze traced the movements. Leo arched a brow. "Waiting for me to remove the rest?"

Tuck's grin widened. "I wouldn't be opposed."

The clink of ice cubes against glass drew his attention as Cole set their drinks on the smooth hardwood bar in front of them. Leo snagged the orange-and-amber drink in front of him and took a sip, letting the delicate citrus taste wash down his throat.

"How are things going at Torres Industries?" Tuck asked, casting a casual glance at the surface of his drink.

"Oh, you mean the company you lot gutted mere months ago?" Leo responded, his lips quirking in amusement. "Complete restructuring is peachy."

Tuck lifted a shoulder as he glanced up, those chocolate eyes dark and arresting. "I'd apologize, but I'm not sorry."

"Nor should you be," Leo said, taking another sip of his drink. "Those assholes got what they deserved. I'm already casting nets to work elsewhere anyway." He had options, but the best application of his skills wasn't at his job—the work he did as Polonius not only kept him entertained but gave him the control he'd been searching for his entire life.

He'd never be helpless again.

An itch crawled under his skin that had been bothering him all week. It was stronger than normal and was the exact reason he'd landed here, chasing a distraction. His knee brushed against Tuck's since they sat in close proximity, and he caught the whiff of vetiver, the scent sparking his adrenaline.

"How's your aviation?" Leo asked. A steady thump, thump, thump pulsed under his skin.

"Want a taste?" Tuck asked, lifting the drink in his direction.

Leo's lips curled.

Caution had a time and a place, and it wasn't tonight, nor was it here.

He leaned in, closing the distance between them. Leo brushed his lips against Tuck's, the tip of his tongue slipping out to run along the seam. He could taste the crisp juniper of the gin, could feel those firm lips quirk against his, and pleasure shuddered through him at the contact. Fuck, this man was delicious. He'd wanted him from the moment they met—running on nerves in the middle of planning a heist against the company he worked for. Before Leo could pull away, Tuck's hand wrapped around his nape, his grip tight enough to turn him on, and the man deepened the kiss.

A rumble came from Tuck's throat, one that purred through Leo like the rev of a motorcycle. Heat licked through him at the touch that grew firm and demanding with a deliberateness that couldn't be denied. Each of Tuck's movements had purpose, and in this case, they were designed to make his knees tremble and his cock hard. Leo melted into the kiss, lapping into Tuck's mouth as the man drove his tongue in long, languid sweeps that had his arms tingling to the tips of his fingers.

Leo reached between them to grip the flimsy fabric of Tuck's tee, needing the grounding lest he float away on the heady bliss pumping through his veins at the sensual way this man kissed. If he'd known how sinful his mouth would feel, how tender and commanding his touch would be, there was no way in hell Leo would've waited this long for a spin in the sheets.

Tuck slowly pulled away from him, and their breaths puffed through the air, thick and heavy.

Leo ran the tip of his tongue over his lower lip. "Aviations taste delicious."

Tuck brushed his thumb along Leo's chin. "Fucking hot as hell, computer boy. Please tell me I can take you somewhere private."

Leo's eyes danced. "You mean you're not going to just bend me over the bar and take me here?"

Tuck let out a low swear, the heat in his eyes searing at this point. "Let's go to the penthouse," he said, not waiting for an answer from Leo. "With the rest of the crew here all night, we've got plenty of privacy."

Leo lifted his sidecar and proceeded to drink the rest of the contents of the glass in a few quick gulps. The liquid burned down his throat, bolstering him as he flashed a cocky grin in Tuck's direction.

"Lead the way, gorgeous."

CHAPTER 3

Tuck's blood was burning hot tonight.

High on the successful burglary, he'd been looking to lose himself in a good time, and Leo Kennedy showed up, looking fine as hell.

They'd slipped out of Polished Knives before the rest of the crew could disrupt them and hopped right into the cab for a quick ride. The air in the back seat had been explosive, one shared glance away from igniting, and Tuck had all but bolted to the entrance of On the Park, the high-rise their crew lived in.

"Trying to impress me with your big… high-rise, Henning?" Leo quipped as they approached the entrance. The man's eyes danced, and his lips were upturned in the flirty smirk that had snared Tuck's attention from the day they met. His chestnut hair was coiffed and carefully tamed, and the live-wire cleverness in his gaze amplified the adrenaline coursing through Tuck right now.

"Don't tell me you're a size queen, Kennedy," Tuck shot back, unable to help the quirk of his lips.

Leo arched a brow. "Yes, I fucking am, and you better deliver."

A slow grin rolled over Tuck's lips. Something about the direct way this man teased pressed all his buttons. "I think I can handle that."

Leo kept pace with him, those long legs carrying him forward in a fluid stride, and Tuck couldn't help but devour the man with his gaze. Business casual wasn't a style Tuck ever donned himself, but the way Leo looked, slipped into the fitted slacks and tight button-down—Tuck was dying to unwrap him.

They headed straight to the elevator, the tension climbing, climbing, climbing higher than the floors of their high-rise. The doors clicked open, and Tuck led the way, stepping on first.

Once the doors closed, he struck.

He crowded Leo against the mirror-paneled wall until their chests bumped and their mouths were a breath apart. Tuck placed one palm on the wall, bracing himself there, and with his other hand he drew his fingertip down Leo's chin until he tipped it up. His mouth closed over Leo's a moment later, and he didn't waste time before devouring the man. He could still taste the sweet alcohol on his tongue, and the heat of his mouth, the press of their bodies together, sent the headiness buzzing through him, better than any high.

The moment Leo had first kissed him back at the

bar, their chemistry had exploded like a spark to flash paper. He wasn't a stranger into getting men or women into his bed, but he didn't need to hook up with the urgency John did or Grif had before Dan. However, the way his skin buzzed right now, how Leo's taste imprinted on his tongue, and those pitched moans vibrated through to his marrow—once wouldn't be enough.

The kiss only confirmed the stirring in his core that he'd felt from the day they met, and their collision stripped them both down even while they were still fully clothed. Leo's fingers curled into the fabric of Tuck's shirt, and he bucked his hips forward, his erection brushing against Tuck's thigh. The faint bing, bing, bing of the elevator surging past floor after floor echoed in the background, but all he could hear was their heavy breaths, a low whimper from Leo that vibrated between them, and the slight swish of their clothes brushing together while Tuck longed for skin on fucking skin.

The elevator wall was cool on his palms as he pressed Leo harder against it, their hips connecting and clothed erections grinding against each other's. Leo nipped on his bottom lip, the damn minx, and Tuck found his heart pounding faster at the teasing way he moved even while they made out.

Tuck pulled back for a breath before leaning in so his lips brushed against the shell of Leo's ear. "I need to get inside you."

"And here I was about to beg," Leo responded, his eyes wicked and his voice a little breathless.

The elevator settled into place, and the doors cracked open. Tuck pushed up from his lean against the wall and slipped through, holding them for Leo who scrambled to step out. Even though Tuck led the way to the penthouse, Leo wasn't a stranger—he'd been here often enough to either help the Outlaws with the occasional consult or visit Dan. He couldn't deny the lure of someone he shared this crackling chemistry with who already knew what they did, but Tuck tamped down those tendrils of yearning before they ruined his night.

Tonight, he needed the distraction more than ever. The message he'd gotten earlier had burrowed into his mind to the point of obsession, and this was the one surefire way he could think to excise it.

Tuck unlocked the door to the penthouse and clicked the lights on. Their swanky place was one he could've never imagined living in growing up a circus rat—all modern chic with a view of the Chicago skyline some would kill for. However, the Outlaws made this space feel like a home filled with a large, bickering, often infuriating family he loved. That was familiar, a holdover from his troupe days.

"Lead me to your room," Leo said, sliding in beside him. "The last thing I want is the untimely interruptions the rest of the crew are notorious for."

Heat bloomed inside Tuck. "Trust me—once we get started, nothing is interrupting this."

"Don't know," Leo teased as they strode down the hall toward his bedroom. "The penchant for explosive arguments and shootouts with you lot has me questioning that."

Tuck reached over and gripped his chin so their gazes locked. "Nothing," he promised, his voice coming out husky and low.

Leo's pupils dilated, and he let out a shuddering breath. "Well, fuck."

Tuck's lips curled at the side, and he took a step past Leo to push open the door to his bedroom. With a flick of the switch, the dim amber lights flooded the room, giving the space a more relaxed vibe.

He didn't miss how Leo's gaze zipped right past his bed, freshly made with a black comforter and black sheets, and the spartan furniture to the crowning highlight of his room. One of the things Tuck adored their high vaulted ceilings for—his aerial silks rig. He stayed limber for their climbs by practicing with these, and he didn't miss the undivided attention Leo gave those purple silks right now. His cock had already grown hard from making out with the gorgeous man, but he needed to reach down and adjust himself at the thought of getting Leo anywhere near those naked.

Leo wandered past them to skim his fingers along the edge of his bed. "Looks cozy. Think we should test it?" The pointed look in his eyes and the impish curl of his lips had Tuck's blood heating right up.

He prowled toward Leo one purposeful step at a

time. The sheer lust brimming from the man's expression had him craving, and with the way his veins howled with need tonight, he couldn't deny those urges. Tuck gripped the front of Leo's shirt and tugged him closer, licking along the smooth length of his jaw all the way up to his ear. He sank his teeth down on the lobe.

"Not there," he murmured in Leo's ear. "Do you trust me?"

Pressed close against him like this, Tuck could almost feel the corners of Leo's lips kick up.

"Not in the slightest," he responded, his tone wry. "But if this plan involves getting your dick in my ass, I'm game for anything."

Tuck drew in a deep breath, inhaling the man's scent, which was all dark rum and rosewood, before pulling back. He grabbed Leo's hand and tugged him in the direction of the aerial silks, their strides automatically synching up.

"Gonna tie me up?" Leo asked, eyeing the hanging silks as they stepped in front of them. Based on the way Leo's pupils flared with desire and the lurid fascination there, Tuck would have his hands full with this one. He couldn't fucking wait.

"Tonight? No, but you can bet that if I'm lucky enough to land you in my bed again, we're going to explore *that* a bit more," Tuck purred as he nudged Leo in the side to station him right in front of the two hanging silks. The man was pliant in the best sort of way, moving with Tuck's guided touches to the point that his mind reeled with the possibilities. He'd worked with partners in the circus long enough to know their body chemistry couldn't be fabricated.

Tuck slunk behind Leo and reached around his chest to begin unbuttoning his shirt. His cock had grown so hard, he could barely think, and he thrust his hips forward, grinding against Leo's pert ass. The friction sent a pulse of pleasure through him. Fuck, he needed deep in that ass as of yesterday. He got the shirt unbuttoned in seconds, dragging it down Leo's arms and watching the fabric drift to the floor. He pressed up against him even tighter, enjoying the hitch in Leo's breath as the man faced obediently forward.

Tuck brushed his thumb across the tip of one dusky nipple, and Leo bucked his hips back, grinding harder against Tuck's cock. Tuck bit on his lower lip until he tasted blood in the attempt to restrain himself. His fingertips drifted over the smooth skin of Leo's chest, across the slight definition of his slender abs, and the sharp divot of his hipbones in the delicious V that disappeared into his slacks.

"Never expected this sort of obedience, sweetness," Tuck murmured in his ear, amusement and a delicious thrill thrumming through him. "Not with that mouth of yours."

Leo's lips quirked up. "Excuse you. People adore this mouth."

Tuck couldn't help the sharp laugh that escaped him as he reached around Leo to brush his thumb across the man's lush lower lips. "I can see why."

Leo's full-body shudder rippled against him, and Tuck couldn't help but thrust his hips forward again, needing the friction, bad. He unsnapped the button to Leo's slacks, the zipper coming down with a *shiiick*. A second later, those slacks were pooling on the floor, and Leo was stepping out of his shoes and then his socks.

"You've got me naked, gorgeous," Leo purred, tossing him a flirty look. "Now what do you plan on doing about it?"

Tuck ran his hands along Leo's slender waist, enjoying each shiver and light breath and how the man shuddered at his touch. He reached for one of the silks and wrapped the fabric around Leo's hand, repeating the action with the other length of silk.

"Clutch onto these," Tuck murmured against Leo's ear.

"Goddamn, that's hot," Leo responded with a low groan. He thrust his ass back, temptation fucking incarnate.

Tuck slipped over to his bedstand to grab supplies before returning to the pretty-as-hell picture splayed out in front of him. Leo had gotten the idea real fast, clutching the lengths of silk wrapped around his palms as he thrust that tight, luscious ass back in invitation. The fluid curve of Leo's spine mesmerized Tuck, and the low amber light cast enticing shadows along the creamy expanse. The man bared himself without shame, which Tuck found hotter than anything.

He stepped behind Leo again and hiked his pants

down to midthigh, taking a moment to draw a couple of lazy strokes along his cock. Pleasure shuddered through him, amplifying his need to bury himself inside this gorgeous man. His sharp intake of breath echoed around the quiet room, mingling with Leo's shallow pants.

Tuck clicked open the top of the bottle of lube, and Leo glanced back, his blue eyes nearly glowing with lust. The purple silks trembled as his grip tightened on them—they'd betray every delicious movement. He squirted some on his fingertips and then ripped open the foil packet of a condom with his teeth before rolling it along his cock.

"Are you going to fuck me, or do you plan on keeping me in suspension?" Leo teased him, a far too amused grin on his face.

Tuck let out a groan and slapped Leo's ass, the smack echoing around the room. "I hate that I liked that pun," he responded.

A shiver ran down Leo's back, causing the silks to tremble again. "Fuck, do that again."

Heat flared through Tuck. "Goddamn, babe, you've been holding out on me. If I'd known you were this fun in bed, I'd have fucked you ages ago."

"Come on now—the chase is half the fun," Leo said, glancing back again. "Except for now, when you better get your goddamn cock inside me."

Tuck reached down and brought his fingertip between Leo's crease to circle around the man's perfect pucker. Pink and enticing, he couldn't wait to bury himself deep in that tight hole. "Look at you, gorgeous. Think you're ready?"

"Screw prep," Leo huffed out, thrusting his ass back as he clenched his hands tighter around the taut silks. "I want to feel you now."

The tip of Tuck's tongue snuck out to wet his lip, and he couldn't help the amusement that rushed through him. He continued to rub circles around the man's pretty hole, watching the way his breaths quickened and how his ass kept shifting up as if seeking his fingers. "Why would I do that when you're so fun to play with?"

Leo opened his mouth as if preparing to launch into another demand, but when Tuck slipped the first finger into his tight heat, a whimper came out instead. Tuck's cock was harder than ever as he began to thrust his finger inside that gripping channel. Leo clutched onto the silks, and Tuck braced him at the hip with one hand while tunneling a finger inside him slow and easy, enjoying the way Leo's breath hitched, how he desperately tried to spear himself on Tuck's finger. He slipped another one inside and drove them in deeper, crooking his fingertips.

"Fuck." Leo lunged forward, the silks drawing him back. He spread his legs, stabilizing his stance. "Do it again, but this time with your cock."

"Bossy," Tuck responded, continuing to fuck his fingers in and out of that tight hole. He added a third, enjoying the way Leo trembled, how his lithe body almost vibrated with need.

"What are you, a monster?" Leo gasped out, finding a rhythm with Tuck's thrusts. His cheeks were flushed, and when he glanced back, the glossy look in his blue eyes dosed Tuck with lust. The chestnut strands of his hair splayed across his forehead, all that smooth, creamy skin, and the open expression on his face—so different from the sharp-witted and closed-off normal one—Leo Kennedy made an imprint on him without even trying.

"Just a little sadistic," Tuck murmured, finally drawing his fingers out. He squeezed some lube over his cock and lined the tip up with Leo's hole. "Better hold on tight, gorgeous."

He began to push inside Leo, who bore down at once, accepting him with ease. The easy glide had him letting out a low moan as the feel of that firm heat squeezing his cock coasted over him. He gripped the man's hip with his other hand, finding the way his hipbone jutted out like the perfect handhold a massive turn-on. Tuck sank in until he was buried to the base inside Leo's scorching channel, and a shudder rippled through him.

Flings didn't scare Tuck, but he knew when he'd found a connection worth chasing. The internal click once he sank deep inside this man, the way their bodies melted against each other's, and how their breaths turned synchronous—this was that connection. A spark of potential. A glimmer of starlight to chase.

Leo let out a choked breath, drawing Tuck into the moment.

Determination sank into his bones as he began to move inside Leo. Pulling back, then pushing forward, Tuck started out easy at first, small movements that had the silks above swaying while Leo gripped onto them tightly. His body was bent over, displayed like a feast before him, the long, sloping back, his ass presented, and his even longer legs bracing him on either side as Tuck rocked into him.

"You're tight as hell," Tuck murmured as he gripped both hips now, starting to thrust in harder, driving his length deep into that tight, hot hole. It gripped his cock each time, the rasp of their skin meeting and the wet, sloppy sound of fucking echoing through the quiet air of his bedroom. The amber light mingled with the pronounced shadows, highlighting every dip and hollow in Leo's body, the slight perspiration that broke out on his shoulders, and the dusting of dark hair along his legs. Tuck rammed in harder, causing the silks to buck and Leo to go surging forward.

"Holy hell," Leo cursed, scrambling to keep hold of the silks.

"I've got you, gorgeous." Tuck kept one hand gripped on Leo's hip while he wrapped another around one of the aerial silks Leo was holding on to. With his better control, he drove in deep again.

"Fuckkkk, you feel good," Leo slurred out.

"So do you," Tuck grunted, finding a rhythm as he enjoyed the sway of the silks, the tension of their muscles, and the interplay of their bodies, a careful dance he longed to memorize. As Tuck rammed into him harder and harder, they were swinging forward with each thrust, Leo lifting himself up onto his tiptoes as he bucked forward again and again.

"Fuck, I need to come," Leo panted, the words sharp and desperate.

Not like the man had his hands free.

A wicked little thrill rose inside Tuck at the realization. "Tough, gorgeous," he said, and he increased his pace, his body snapping forward. Leo's moans grew louder at this point, needier as Tuck ruthlessly rammed into that sweet spot over and over. Drops of sweat beaded along Tuck's brow, and the moisture from his palm imprinted on the silk he gripped. His breaths came in faster as he reached a crescendo that had his balls drawing up, had him so close to soaring.

"Guuuh," Leo groaned out, his legs full-out shaking at this point. "Please."

Tuck buried himself deep, the friction enough to send him over the edge.

His orgasm rocked through his entire body in one dominating wave. His cock pulsed as he unloaded into the condom, and his knees turned to jelly in the wake of the sheer bliss radiating through him in such a fierce sweep. He rode out those sensations until they tapered away and he settled back into his body.

Tuck sucked in a sharp breath, bringing himself back to the man who full-out trembled in his arms with the need for release. With care, he drew himself out of Leo's ass and a second later had pivoted in front of him and dropped to his knees.

In one quick motion, he took Leo's cock into his mouth. The silken length rested heavily there, the burst of salt from precum on his tongue. Leo let out a choked gasp as Tuck began to suck him down. He didn't hesitate, drawing him to the back of his throat hard and fast. Leo's hands clenched hard on the silk, and his thighs tensed.

A moment later, Leo was coming in thick spurts, his seed spilling down Tuck's throat.

Tuck swallowed it all, relishing the taste of him, the musky scent of him here. His legs were still a little shaky from his own intense orgasm, and he leaned back to rest on his heels before brushing the back of his hand over his mouth.

Leo sagged forward, holding on tightly to the silks as if they were embedded in him at this point. He'd never let go the whole time, and hell if that didn't give Tuck *ideas*.

Tuck pushed up on his shaky legs to wrap his hands around Leo's, facing him at last. He dipped in to press his lips against Leo's. The man's mouth was hot and sweet, and he sank into the headiness of those feelings after the explosive way they'd come together. He carded his fingers through Leo's sweaty strands, loving the way the man leaned into the touch—so responsive, so sweet, so utterly perfect. Tuck unwrapped the silk from around Leo's palms, feeling the divots that remained from how tightly he'd gripped. Leo sagged against him, still kissing him back with sweet, lazy strokes of his tongue that had Tuck mesmerized.

Tonight might've started as some much-needed stress relief to distract himself from the upcoming troubles tomorrow. However, throughout the night, a single truth had become startlingly clear.

Once would never be enough.

CHAPTER 4

Leo lay staring at the ceiling while Tuck snored in bed beside him.

Even after they'd both come like champions, they'd gotten frisky again in the shower and then had finished off in the bed. Tuck had passed out almost at once in a cascade of snores, probably from expending all that energy into being a goddamn sex god. Leo hadn't slept a wink, but then again—he hadn't been planning on it.

He didn't do sleepovers. Ever.

Still, he could admit to himself he'd enjoyed basking in the afterglow, curling up next to this furnace of a man and feeling a bit too comfortable. Everything about his night with Tuck had been a little too much like lingering by a bonfire—alluring, enticing, and so scorching hot.

Yet he'd been burned by fires before and carried the marks.

Time to bounce.

Leo slipped out from under the sheets and began to collect his clothes from where they'd been flung across the floor. His palms still stung from the way he'd gripped those aerial silks, but the sway and feel of them as Tuck had fucked into him hard and fast? Worth every second of discomfort. He zipped his pants back on and lazily buttoned up his shirt in the dark, working on autopilot at this point. Leo patted himself down for his essentials—wallet and keys—and then made his way to the door.

He paused at the doorknob, casting a glance at the gorgeous man who'd fucked him into next week. Tuck Hennings was the sort of sexy he didn't come across often—not just in looks, though that crooked smile, the muscles, and his luscious smooth skin, fuck—but he carried himself with a confidence beyond bravado.

It had transferred into their night together, a heady, mesmerizing thing—how he moved his body and the way he knew who he was and what he was about. Tuck seemed steady, rooted to the earth rather than getting upheaved by it. Goddamn, Leo had found himself spellbound. And watching the man slumber, the steady rise and fall of his chest, the heat that had been pressed up against him, and those protective arms trying to curl around him, Leo's mind couldn't help but drift to forbidden places.

What it might be like to be worthy of someone like that.

To be more than a quick fuck and a useful friend.

The sex must've screwed with his head real good.

Leo twisted the knob and slipped out of the bedroom. The penthouse was quiet at the late hour since most of the Outlaws had trickled in around the time the bar closed. He and Tuck had burned hours away in his bedroom, and then Leo had just lay there in his bed for a while, listening to the ruckus of the crew settling into their different sections of the penthouse, readying themselves for bed.

Despite the darkened hallway, dim lights glowed from the main rooms, so Leo walked carefully. The last thing he needed was to get held up by one of Dan's nosy new roommates while he attempted to make his escape. The second Dan and Grif had gotten together, Dan slept over here so much he'd just moved in, despite the fact that six of them now lived in the place. Still, it was large enough that they each had their own space even if they shared the main ones.

Leo bit back a shudder. Thanks, but no thanks. He'd gotten a taste of the crowded family life at the Kennedys' house, and while the foster home had been better than the fuck-all nothing Gerald and Carol Thatcher had provided, he wasn't about to wax poetic on the joys of all those people up in his fucking business.

He tiptoed past the living room and into the main area with those breathtaking views of the Chicago skyline.

"Didn't want to stay for the walk of shame?" Scarlet's voice pierced through the air. He sat hunched over in the curved chair in front of their computer rig, several of the screens lit up.

Leo resisted the impulse to jump in surprise as he stopped mid-stride. Scar swiveled around in his chair like some James Bond villain, only missing the purring cat on his lap. His lips were twisted with wry amusement, and his warm eyes danced. The resident hacker for the Outlaws was handsome on a bad day with an ear-length pixie cut he always kept sharp and styled.

"And risk getting suckered into your family breakfasts?" Leo countered. "That sounds like my personal form of torture."

"Don't knock it until you've tried my burnt bacon and rubbery eggs," Scar teased, tapping his fingers on the arm of the chair.

"Really selling it there." Leo swept his gaze over the screens on display that provided glimpses of what Scarlet was working on. Leo couldn't help his curiosity —it was compulsory and what got him into trouble the most.

A knowing look glittered in Scar's eyes when he caught Leo looking. "The offer still stands."

Right. Collaborating with Scarlet as part of the team. Grif hadn't made mention, but Dan had, as well as Scarlet.

Except Leo wasn't meant for teams. The work he did kept him isolated for a reason. He'd built his self-reliance from the ground up, and he wouldn't sacrifice it for anyone.

"Tease," Leo shot back, switching to flirting because he found it easier.

"Pretty sure that's all you," Scarlet responded with an arched brow. "How long were you and Tuck fucking in there?"

Leo's lips upturned in an impish grin. "That man has *stamina*."

Scarlet's nose wrinkled like a bunny's, which was an amusing expression on the man. "Nasty. Tuck's like a brother to me. I can do without hearing about his sex life."

Leo snorted. "Come on, like the lot of you don't hear way too much as is."

Scar tapped at the headphones wrapped around his neck. "These are lifesavers."

Leo tipped his fingers in a lazy salute. "Good luck on those mystery projects, Scar. I'll see you around."

"Guaranteed," he said with a nod before swiveling around to face those glowing screens. "Night, Kennedy." Some shuffling sounded and then the clack of fingertips onto keys as Leo turned and headed for the door.

He made his way to the elevator in record time, unable to hide the stupid grin on his face at the memory of the intense ride up with Tuck. All those sex hormones were addling his mind tonight. The elevator dropped down with a whoosh, and all too quickly, it was already settling in the lobby right as he finished nabbing an Uber.

Leo strode out of the lobby of On the Park and into

the night that had started to grow thinner with each hour closer to dawn. The sky had turned gray and looked even paler with all the lit-up high-rises that cluttered this area. Some days he wondered why he stayed in Chicago. Sure, his foster family lived in the suburbs, but he spoke to them once a year on Christmas, if that. No boyfriend, and his only real friend was Dan Torres.

However, sometimes when the nights stretched on too long, when the distant silver stars got snuffed out by all the ugliness that Chicago brought, Leo thought about packing up and running as far and fast as he could manage.

Still, his past would catch up. It always did.

His Uber driver pulled up in a silver Toyota Camry. Leo allowed himself one more look toward the top of the building where he'd left one memorable-as-hell fuck.

Tucker Hennings had caught and held his attention more than anyone had in a long, long while, but like all things in Leo's life, he had to be transitory. Hopefully, their filthy night together would be enough to get the man out of his system.

The driver rolled his window down to gesture, and Leo hopped into the back seat. The guy was blaring 90s R&B loud enough to drown out any conversation, so Leo settled back and began to skim through his phone.

A notification lit the screen.

Another set of bodies had washed up in the old drop site.

Leo's stomach plummeted. He kept tabs on all of the

old drop sites in the city, the deaths, and just who operated where. He wasn't naïve enough to think they'd stopped running, but he'd been hoping they might've shipped out or found a different city to haunt for a while. But if the site by the warehouse was getting utilized, that could only mean one thing.

He swallowed hard, looking at the picture of the bloated corpses along the banks of the Chicago River.

The Stockyard was active again.

CHAPTER 5

Tuck strode up to the familiar entrance of Windy City Grill. He jammed his hands into his pockets to shield against the chill, taking the lead here since Sophia would recognize him but not Grif and John. The two hulking guys trailed behind him like bodyguards. Tuck might not be a slouch in the muscles department, but he didn't have massive frames like they did.

The neon red lighting stood out against the black signage, and those wide windows placed the interior of the diner on display. The place was crowded with the morning rush—a mix of young couples trying whatever new special was on the menu and groups of the sixty-and-older club out for their cups of decaf. The Outlaws had rushed through their own family breakfast back at the penthouse to get here on time. Fine by him—in that short time, he'd already gotten his fill of wink, wink, nudge, nudges from Dan and Scar about spending the night with Leo.

Though, spending the night would've required the man to stay.

Tuck had known Leo's M.O. before they hooked up —no strings, no attachments—so he shouldn't have been surprised to wake up to the empty bed after their marathon of fucking. However, Leo hadn't just been memorable—he'd struck the match of Tuck's interest in a way no man or woman had in years, enough to make him imagine what it'd be like to pursue something more.

The last time he'd felt a spark like that had been with the woman he was preparing to meet with now.

"Just how flexible is this ex of yours?" John asked from behind him. "She was a contortionist, right?"

Tuck flipped him the middle finger. "And she's happily married, jackass. Don't start trying to work your charms on Sophia. She'll eat you alive."

"Maybe I'd like that," John responded, amusement lilting his tone. "Fuck, I'm hungry. They better have eggs."

"Best in town," Tuck responded. "After Scar's rendition of scrambled sadness, I'm starving."

"Surprised you can manage anything after all that dick you choked down last night," Grif said, smugness in his tone. After all the flack Grif had taken during the Torres Industries heist when he'd lost his mind over Dan, he had been on the front lines, doling out shit this morning.

"I'll take that meal any day of the week. Fucking delicious," Tuck shot back as he reached for the door and dragged it open. No lie there either—every second of his time with Leo had been goddamn perfection.

As he entered Windy City Grill, the familiar scents washed over him—the salty bacon, the jet fuel coffee, and the same orange cleaner they'd been using for years. The fluorescent lights cast everything in the place in sharp relief and the classic black-and-white floor tiles, red vinyl booths, and glossy white walls screamed vintage diner. The stools along the bar were full, and chatter flowed through the tight space, the mirrors and chrome casting reflections with each step he took.

It only took him seconds to locate Sophia. She sat tucked in a corner booth, looking as pretty as the day he'd left her. With her plush scarlet lips, pristine olive skin, and thick shoulder-length raven's hair styled artfully in waves, the woman belonged in a classic place like this. When she caught sight of him, her eyes crinkled with her genuine smile, and Tuck felt something settle inside him.

The Outlaws might be his family now, but Sophia and the rest of the Twilight Circus had been his family first. He'd grown up with the other circus kids—getting into trouble at the different fairgrounds they'd spirited to throughout the season, playing on equipment they weren't supposed to, and sneaking drinks between shows. The other circus workers had been like parents too, especially after Dad had passed. Tuck's gut squeezed tight.

If the Twilight Circus was in trouble, he needed to help.

"Hey, sweetheart," he said upon reaching her booth. He didn't miss how her gaze flickered to both Grif and John behind him. "Figured I'd bring a few friends along to help with your problem."

At that, Sophia's shoulders relaxed. He reached down to wrap her in a hug, and the way she clutched him a little harder than normal with a tremble through her body told him everything.

"It's good to see you, Tuck," she murmured against his neck before letting go and settling back down in her seat.

Tuck slid in beside her, and Grif and John squished into the other side of the booth together.

John offered a hand, as friendly as ever. "John Smith, nice to meet you." Tuck hadn't missed the extra-flirtatious note he'd layered on there, and he shot him a pointed look.

"Grif," their ever-verbose leader said, lifting his chin in acknowledgement.

Within seconds after they'd gotten settled, a young brunette waitress slid over to take their orders. Tuck didn't miss the way her gaze rotated between himself, Grif, and John.

"What can I get for you?" she asked him, her voice coming out breathy.

He bit back a grin, and Sophia rolled her eyes. "Coffee and a sausage omelet. Thanks, sweetheart."

The woman blushed prettily as she turned her attention to Grif and John. Sophia leaned in. "I see you haven't lost your charm in the slightest," she murmured.

Tuck arched a brow. "If I remember, that was one of the things you liked most about me." As much as he and Sophia had clicked for a long time, he'd broken her heart in the end. An itch had sprung up, one that grew consuming after a while, demanding he leave the circus behind and find a new life. Sophia might have called him for help, but she would never have been comfortable with the direction he'd ended up taking. Unlike him, she was loyal to the troupe for life and had found someone who fit that path better. "Where's Asher? How come he didn't join you today?"

Sophia's gaze darkened, and her lip trembled. The realization slammed into Tuck at once.

"Oh fuck," he whispered. "I'm so sorry, Soph."

The waitress had already departed from their table to place the orders, and with the distraction gone, Grif and John were looking their way. Sophia seemed to notice with a glance, and she sucked in a steadying breath. "That's the reason I reached out," she said, her voice surprisingly steady.

Tuck fell quiet, and Grif and John were tuning in as they gave Sophia the space to speak up. Her text hadn't been clear—just that the Twilight Circus needed his help. Out of all of his old circus family, Sophia was the only one who knew what he did—and even she had only a vague idea at that.

"Reynauld's been bleeding us dry for years, but

written into our contracts with them, there's the option to buy ourselves out," Sophia started.

"Reynauld Industries?" Grif interrupted. His blue eyes had turned intense, predatory. They weren't just a random company to him, clearly.

Sophia nodded. "We'd finally saved enough to get out from under them at the contract renewal, but the night before the meeting, armed guys showed up at our caravan and killed Asher and Mugs." She paused for a moment as words abandoned her, her eyes growing glossy, and Tuck placed a hand on her back. His heart lurched at the news—he'd known both of those guys. Had spent summers wrestling with Asher and stealing chocolate from Ninabella's stash with Mugs.

She sucked in a shuddering breath. "They said if we showed up to the meeting, they'd kill more of us. That we'd sign the contract renewal and continue on as is." Sophia gave a hopeless little shrug as she clutched her mug of tea tighter. "What can we do? They're taking more and more from us each year, but it's clear the company's not ready to let us go, and they're willing to pay to ensure we can't leave."

Tuck's pulse thrummed with rage. He remembered the way Reynauld's overheads made everything harder —getting new supplies, keeping up on safety standards, even basic housing and food needs. Getting out from under them was the dream, so Javier and the rest could own the Twilight Circus outright.

This. This was why he had joined up with Grif and the Outlaws in the first place. Because he understood what a toll some of these corporations took on the people under them.

"So, if I'm understanding correctly," Grif interrupted, his voice the sort of low that demanded attention. "Your goal is to own your circus outright, and you need the impediments to the process smoothed out."

Sophia chewed on her lower lip and cast a nervous glance at Tuck. "I'm not quite sure what you do, but I've got the gist from Tuck that it's not strictly… legal."

"It's all right, doll. You can call us criminals," John said with an amused smirk.

Tuck placed a hand on Sophia's arm, drawing her gaze to him. "You're not alone in this, okay?" he said, hoping the confidence in his voice transferred over even as his mind still whirled. Truth be told, while Grif had a personal vendetta against a lot of their large-scale targets, a sense of injustice had never burned inside Tuck with the same rising flames that consumed him now.

The waitress swung back to plunk several coffees in front of them, and the omelet Tuck ordered with hash fries looked the same as it had for years now—buttery, golden, and cheesy. While Twilight Circus had traveled all over the country, Chicago had always been his home base, and this spot had been a favorite of all the circus brats in their troupe. They'd find a corner of the city and busk for some quick cash to spend around town and gorge themselves on deep-dish pizza and ice cream. All those fond memories fueled the anger piping through him at the thought of what Reynauld Industries had done.

His people were in an impossible situation.

"And I'm concerned that even if we find a way to handle the hitmen the company sent to us...." Sophia trailed off, spearing her fingers through her glossy black waves. She sucked in another sharp breath, those eyes glossing with tears again.

"They'll just send another," Grif filled in the blank, his voice grim.

Tuck nodded. The reality settled in his veins. The Twilight Circus would be trapped under these bastards if they didn't step in.

"Unless we find a way to force Reynauld Industries to let you out of the contract," Tuck said, meeting Grif's gaze.

Grif nodded, a simple gesture, but that was all Tuck needed. He understood. He swallowed hard, the gratitude welling in his chest.

Sophia's eyebrows drew together, and she glanced between them. "Is there a way you could do that? We'll pay whatever we can."

"Please, impossible situations are our specialty," John said, a charming grin on his face. Tuck resisted the urge to roll his eyes. Their resident conman was always on the sales pitch, smoothing every situation over even when it wasn't necessary.

"And don't worry about payment right now," Tuck reassured her. Alternate streams of revenue were their specialty, and guaranteed, if they dug deep enough with Reynauld, they'd be able to extract something to make the situation worth their while.

"You've got our help, Sophia." Grif sealed the deal, reaching across the table to offer a hand.

Her jaw dropped, and tears welled up in her eyes as she shook his hand. "But how?"

Tuck rested a hand on her shoulder. "Leave that to us. We may need to come talk to the troupe, but it'd do me some good to see everyone."

Sophia threw her arms around him and buried her face in his neck. He could already feel the hot imprint of her tears. Not only had she lost her husband in this, but their entire troupe was under threat. He might've walked away from the circus, but they'd always be family to him. Nostalgia filtered in like morning fog, consuming and effortless and heavy with the regret that he hadn't been there to protect them. Tuck squeezed her back, trying to offer whatever comfort he could.

"Thank you," she murmured, her shoulders shaking from emotion.

Tuck's throat tightened as he held her, overcome with a fierce, hot rage that she had been put through this, even though the bitter tang of guilt lingered. Maybe if he'd stayed, if he hadn't run off to chase a future....

Except he had.

Circus money wouldn't have paid Mom's medical bills, and the big tent had been feeling smaller and smaller with each subsequent show. He'd needed to break free, and he'd needed roots, two things which didn't seem like they should've lined up—however, he'd found them both when he joined the Outlaws. Still, he couldn't help but wonder from time to time what life would've been like if he'd stayed.

Sophia's phone started buzzing, and she extricated herself from his embrace. When she glanced at the screen, she heaved a sigh.

Tuck knew the sigh intimately. "Javier's calling you, isn't he? Big show today?"

She passed him a grateful smile as she wiped beneath her eyes, smudging the tears away. "Mama Orlov isn't feeling good, so I'm going on longer."

Tuck shook his head, a rueful grin rising to his lips despite the chaos brewing inside him. "Never a dull moment, is there?"

Constant shows, constant movement from one city to the next, constant practice, practice, practice. While he'd seen the entirety of the country from Twilight's caravan, performing show after show eventually felt like shackles during circus season. Sure, he might slide from one heist or burglary to the next as an Outlaw, but no two jobs were ever the same.

"You won't be upset if I head out?" she asked, placing down cash for her tea.

Tuck shook his head. "Go. We've got to discuss all this anyway. I'll come to the caravan in a few days, and we can talk then, okay?"

Sophia slipped her purse over her shoulder, and Tuck pushed up from his seat to let her out. She brushed a quick kiss on his cheek before she turned to

Grif and John. "I can't thank you enough," she said, clutching the strap of her purse.

"Save the thanks for when we've got the job done," Grif responded, as cool and collected as ever. John winked at her to offset Grif's seriousness, and she blushed prettily while Tuck just shook his head in amusement. At that, Sophia took off toward the door, and Tuck slid back into the booth.

He sank against the seat, the information he'd just learned crashing down on him. Ever since he'd left the circus, he'd been moving forward, forward, forward. The violent yank back into his past had left him with whiplash.

"Look, if you want me to follow this up on my own —" Tuck started.

"We're taking the job," Grif interrupted.

"I get why Hennings here is jonesing for some revenge, but what's personal in this for you?" John asked Grif, jostling elbows with him as he tried to get comfortable in the small booth. Tuck sprawled out a bit more as he took a bite of his omelet. The explosion of fennel sausage and salty cheese on his tongue was pure bliss as he waited for Grif's response.

"Guess whose parent company owns Reynauld Industries," Grif said, taking a sip of his black coffee.

Tuck's eyes widened. "Robert Davies? Goddamn."

Grif Blackmore had one white whale—Robert Davies, who was one of the wealthiest men in the country, with a silenced history of bloodshed to get where he had.

He was also the man responsible for making Grif an orphan.

The Outlaws had gone on jobs for years that circled around this man and his properties, but taking down one of his direct subsidiaries? That would be a massive blow.

Even if the Twilight Circus didn't have that connection, Tuck hadn't doubted for a second that Grif would back him. The man had proved himself in blood, time and time again.

However, if saving his circus family also meant cracking a dent in Davies' armor?

The Outlaws would stop at nothing to take Reynauld Industries down.

CHAPTER 6

Leo had promised himself he wouldn't get involved with the Outlaws again.

Polonius was a lone wolf, not a team player.

Except Leo found himself listening more intently than planned to Dan's spiel over lunch at Costa's anyway. Mention of Tuck's past in the circus, of his old troupe's plight, and the reappearance of his ex-girlfriend held Leo's attention whether he wanted it to or not. And that interminable curiosity that got him into trouble as his hacker alias, Polonius, welled up.

He should be turning his brain off to all thoughts of the hot ex-carnie who'd fucked him like a goddamn freight train a few nights ago, but the more he tried to suppress them, the more they bubbled up like really sexy daydreams. He tapped a spoon against the ceramic mug of coffee he'd barely touched. Didn't help that it was his fifth? sixth? cup of the day.

"Scar looked into the group who attacked Tuck's old

troupe," Dan said between bites of his ham-and-cheese croissant. His best friend was too pure sometimes.

Leo crooked a brow. "Are you sure you're supposed to be blathering all of the Outlaws' secrets to me?"

Dan shrugged. "Grif said I get one person to tell this shit to, and you're my person."

Leo swallowed hard. Dan dropped bombs on him like this and then wondered why Leo would do anything in the universe for his best friend. Leo had never been anyone's person. Not his parents' or foster parents'. And he'd avoided boyfriends for a reason— after all, who wanted to pour all their time and energy into something that would leave them lonelier in the long run? No fucking thanks.

"But yeah, Scar has some bad blood with this group —the main guy knows her from a run-in, so she's out for any on-site hacking that might come up." Dan stared at him with those puppy-dog eyes, and Leo heaved out a sigh.

"And I suppose you want me to take Scar's place?"

"If not for me, you could do it for Tuck," Dan said, feigning innocence.

Leo rolled his eyes. "When have you known me to do anything besides bend over for a guy? And even that's a one-and-done deal."

"I swear, these underground groups sound ridiculous though," Dan continued, sipping at his coffee that was mostly cream and sugar. "The leader runs some operation—the Stockyard? The Outlaws have pissed them off in the past, so we've got to tread carefully."

Leo froze.

Out of every damn hitman or gang organization in Chicago, of course it'd be this one. Of fucking course.

He drew his coffee to his lips in an effort to disguise the shock that pattered through his system. If Dan was going to be fighting the Stockyard, he couldn't stay out of this. Not with the chance of running into said leader —Craig Baldwin—again. He'd been searching for a way to cut the organization off at the knees, to knock Baldwin out of the picture once and for all, and the Outlaws might just be handing him a solution on a silver platter.

Apparently, he was getting into bed with the Outlaws again… and not in the fun way.

"You're involved in this one, right?" Leo asked, his tone coming across casual even though his heart raced a thousand miles a minute.

Dan flashed him a crooked smile, a knowing look in his eyes. "Yep, thrust into the throes of danger. Does that mean you'll join us?"

Leo heaved a loud, affected sigh. "First off, you know Grif wouldn't toss you into danger he couldn't get you out of. But yes. I'll help."

To help his best friend.

To put a dent in the Stockyard's armor.

And if he were being honest with himself, for Tuck.

TWO DAYS LATER, LEO FOUND HIMSELF AT THE FRONT DOOR of the Outlaws' penthouse, which looked quite different when he wasn't crashing into Tuck's mouth for swollen kisses every five seconds. This visit reminded him more of the first time he'd come here—with Dan, when his best friend still worked as the brand-new CEO for Torres Industries and they were going to confront the criminal who'd later become his boyfriend. Crazier things had happened.

Leo hooked his thumb in the pocket of his slacks. He was still wearing his work attire after another long day at the company he had been actively trying to leave ever since Dan stepped down from being the CEO. No offense to Vanessa, Dan's sister and his current boss, but he was over the whole organization.

The door creaked open, and Leo swallowed his tongue.

Tuck stood in the entryway, his black tank stretched tight over the defined muscles of his chest and a pair of black sweats low on his hips. With his dark curls glossy and wet because he'd clearly come from the shower, Leo couldn't help but salivate. Those coffee-colored eyes sparked with banked heat, and the long lashes framing them along with the dark scruff along his slender chin had Leo standing there like an idiot, staring at the guy.

Get it together, Kennedy.

"Heard you were joining our little entourage for this," Tuck said, leaning against the doorway, the casual confidence sparking Leo's bloodstream to life.

"What can I say? You guys always find the most interesting jobs," Leo responded dryly. Truth be told, he was eager for any more scraps of information about Tucker Hennings, and that in and of itself created a problem. "Planning on letting me in?"

Tuck's gaze scorched as it traveled his body from head to toe. Leo's cock responded to the perusal at once, even though he should've been forgetting about him and moving the hell on. "Any time you like," he said, his tone dripping with intent.

Leo swallowed. Well, shit. He hadn't expected that in the slightest.

It wasn't just the insinuation that Leo hadn't anticipated—Tuck came across as a toppy bastard, especially considering the way he'd bossed him around the other night—but also the fact that his body was still having a serious reaction to his flirtation.

"Don't tempt me," Leo responded, keeping his tone level even while his pulse jumped all over the place. He could flirt on autopilot any day of the week.

Tuck pushed up from the door in a fluid motion and pivoted on his heel to stride into the penthouse. Leo couldn't help but watch that ass sway as he walked behind his tight, muscled perfection.

The main computer setup glared from the opposite end of the room, except no one sat behind it this time. Still, Leo couldn't help but glimpse the screens, soaking in the information. His curiosity would eventually be his downfall, but until then, he'd peek into everything he could.

"Everyone's waiting in the living room," Tuck said as he turned the corner. "Takeout just arrived—you're welcome to whatever you want."

"That's a bald-faced lie," Alanna shouted from the other room. "If you touch Scar's beef and broccoli, he'll complain about it into the next century."

"While we're at it, no one's touching my sweet-and-sour chicken either," Dan called out. "Last time I put my leftovers in the fridge, they disappeared into the abyss."

"Known as Alanna," John added. Leo bit back his grin as they approached the entryway. Dan and Grif were curled up on one of the navy corduroy couches together while Scar sprawled across the cream carpet with his laptop in front of him. John lounged in one of the armchairs, but Alanna was already striding toward him.

"Fuck you." She stabbed a finger in his direction.

"You wish," he leered.

Alanna snorted. "Not unless you want it the other way around."

"Don't tempt me." John's grin widened.

Tuck glanced back at him. "Unless you want to get dragged into this mess, just split my meal with me."

Leo tried to ignore the stupid way his heart stumbled. Tuck was a hot piece of ass, that was it. And he'd been there, done that.

"I'd share too," Dan offered.

"He says, having already finished most of the chicken," Grif responded, tossing Dan an affectionate look that melted the iceberg of a man. "What were you going to do, offer him your container of white rice?"

"Watch out for your white rice when Vortex Alanna's on the roam," John called out.

A low curse came from Alanna, and a second later her fist smacked hard into his shoulder.

"Want to grapple, babe?" John said, his eyes sparking.

Holy hell, five seconds in this place was like downing an entire bottle of Ritalin. Who needed speed with the way these motherfuckers amped each other up? "It's a miracle you get anything accomplished," Leo murmured in Tuck's ear. Tuck snorted as Leo followed him to the spot on the floor where Tuck had set up camp by the sliding glass doors that led out to the balcony. A few hand weights were lying next to a stack of containers and chopsticks.

Leo settled down, and within seconds, Tuck was passing him a pint of sesame chicken and Leo was wondering how the fuck he'd ended up glued to this guy's side. One-night-stand protocol dictated he go sit by his friend, that he stop flirting with the sexy, sexy man, but in a few quick strokes, Tuck had bypassed his defenses and drawn him in. Leo chewed a piece of sesame chicken, enjoying the sweet burst on his tongue and telling his concern to go fuck itself. Accepting the guy's Chinese food didn't mean he'd be walking to the chapel with him.

"So, you're finally agreeing to help us, Kennedy?" Scar mentioned, his eyes dancing with amusement. Leo didn't miss how his gaze swung back and forth between him and Tuck. Better Scar think his change of heart was due to some fixation with Tuck than the actual reason. He couldn't have any of the Outlaws knowing about his connection to the Stockyard—they'd take him off of this job at once, if not something worse.

Leo finished chewing another bite of sesame chicken before responding. "Dan wore me down," he said, casting a look toward his best friend while trying to ignore the heat radiating from the man beside him. Tuck's calf brushed against his, an explosion of sparks following in the aftermath.

"We're just glad to have you on board," Tuck responded, his voice smooth, deep, and steady.

"How do you feel about ground infiltration?" Grif asked, his gaze sharp. The man looked every inch the leader here, a knowing look in his eyes that made Leo shiver, feeling as if Grif could see through his façade at once. Thank fuck he wasn't actually omniscient.

"I've only hacked on-site at my jobs," Leo responded. "But as long as you're not expecting me to go in firing guns and pulling off acrobatic stunts, I'm not opposed." He tried to play his statement off as cavalier, but if he wanted to ruin Craig Baldwin, he needed to get into the Stockyard's warehouse. He couldn't pass up the opportunity.

"Tuck'll do all the shooting for you," John said, casting him a lazy-lidded look. "Just hide behind him."

"Thanks, stud," Leo said with a wink in Tuck's direction. Going alone to the warehouse? Suicide. Going with Tuck Hennings? He might stand a chance at finding something to take Baldwin down. "Care to share what it is I'm actually going to be doing? Besides looking pretty?"

"We'll be infiltrating Reynauld's main offices downtown after-hours," Tuck said before biting an egg roll in half.

Leo's heart sank. Of course they weren't heading straight for the Stockyard. They'd want to play it safe and handle the business end of the job, which meant he might be dangling himself into danger for nothing. Unless he could somehow pivot them in that direction like a total fucking asshole. He tapped his fingers on the floor, a nervous habit that could easily be interpreted as nerves from the new kid.

Little did they know he'd dealt with dangerous situations since he was a kid. It was a goddamn miracle he'd lasted long enough to make it to a foster home.

"I'll be running the comms, and Scar will be handling disabling alarms from here," Grif said, leaning back in the seat, his arms stretched out along the top of the couch.

"Apparently, the rest of us will be sitting around with our thumbs up our asses," Alanna complained, tugging on the end of her ponytail.

"Don't be jealous, sweetness," John drawled, one leg lazily resting over the other. "Can't help that the rest of us are better suited for this job."

"You're a dead man," she shot back, her eyes flashing. John loved toying with his life.

"John and I will be checking the perimeter in the getaway car," Dan offered with a genuine smile, the attempt to reassure Leo clear.

Leo's chest twisted. His best friend looked so earnest about him coming on board, and guilt crawled out from its hiding place. He had one goal in taking this job on with them, and it had nothing to do with their objective and everything to do with the man he'd sworn revenge against years ago. The little dents he'd made in the Stockyard's business hadn't been enough—funds drained here and there, fabricated notices, system shutdowns when he got a pulse on one of their locations.

None of them were enough.

And if the Outlaws happened to solve their sticky situation with Tuck's old troupe and Reynauld Industries without involving the Stockyard, he'd have to find a way to bring the two together.

Tuck nudged at his side again, and Leo's attention flicked to him at once. The man was next-level gorgeous with that prominent nose, intense brown eyes, and expressive lips. And Leo couldn't forget their night together if he tried—and he'd tried.

"Hey," he murmured, his voice low, gruff. "I know you didn't have to help us with this. I just wanted to say thank you."

Those words drove a dagger through his chest.

Leo pasted a smile on his face that felt light-years away from sincere as his fingers numbed. "Save the thanks for after you see how terrible I am in the field. Guaranteed, you'll be eating those words."

Tuck shook his head, but the amusement and warmth twinkling in his eyes made Leo feel like he'd just reached the top of the rollercoaster to see the nauseating drop.

Fuck. He was such a goddamn bastard.

And yet, he couldn't stop his vendetta from reaching its inevitable collision.

CHAPTER 7

Dusk descended over the horizon, the lengthening shadows settling over the line of maroon-and-gold caravans parked along the campgrounds where the Twilight Circus had set up on the outskirts of the city. The sight struck him square in the chest with nostalgia—he could feel the talcum powder, the sharp sweat in the air, and the residue of smoke. For a moment, the ghost of the old live-wire electricity coursed through his veins, the pre-show energy that had filled him again and again.

Until the shows had lost their glitz.

Until the final accident that pushed him to leave.

He headed toward the one at the end where Sophia told him to find her. Chances were, she'd returned to staying in her family's caravan after losing her husband. Tuck let out a low curse as he approached, one hand jammed into his pocket. A quick stop and then he'd be off to Reynauld Industries to infiltrate with Leo.

Goddamn Leo Kennedy. The man was full of surprises, and the more Tuck got to know him, the more he wanted him again. Beneath him, beside him—fuck, any way he could get the damn man.

He reached down and adjusted himself fast before taking a deep breath. Showing up to his ex-girlfriend's caravan with a hard-on wouldn't give off a great impression. Tuck knocked, and a moment later, the door creaked open.

A familiar face came into view. Tall, broad-shouldered, and as well-groomed as ever, even with a few more lines around his eyes, Javier, Sophia's father, was every inch the ringleader he'd always been.

"Well, if it isn't Ace," Javier said, sweeping his arms open wide with a broad smile. "It's damn good to see you, boy."

Tuck swallowed hard and squeezed Javier tight in a hug. After he'd lost his own father, Javier had stepped in when he'd needed a parent the most. Just the timbre of his voice and the presence the man emanated brought him back to those younger years. Javier was a force to be reckoned with, and he'd kept their family together for a long time. The scent of his English Leather cologne hit Tuck with a hefty dose of comfort.

"Good to see you, Javi," he murmured before pulling away.

"How's your mother?" he asked, his expression fading to a more serious one.

Tuck tried to ignore the aerial flip his stomach took at the mention. He'd known they'd ask—after all,

Felicity Hennings had been an integral part of this troupe once upon a time. "She's surviving."

That was the most he could say. The last time he'd visited, she'd been the same mental black hole as before, reeking of Jim Beam, lidocaine cream, and grief.

Javier frowned, but the expression quickly softened as he placed a hand on Tuck's shoulder. "Come, my daughter tells me you're going to solve our current problems. Let us know what we can do to help."

"I'm just here to pick up the copies of the contract you signed with Reynauld Industries," Tuck said. "Otherwise, don't worry about what we're up to. The less you're involved in, the less danger you'll be in."

"Oh." Sophia's voice chimed like a bell as she stepped into view. "I didn't realize you were already here."

"She's been in the bathroom, dolling herself up," Javier said with a knowing gleam in his eyes.

Tuck scratched the side of his neck, uncomfortable with the comment. It'd been no secret that Javi hadn't approved of Sophia with Asher—especially considering the way Javi and Asher had clashed—but, fuck, he'd still been a part of the troupe. Besides, Tuck might've loved Sophia when they were kids, but they'd both grown in very different directions. When he saw her now, he felt the affection of family, but nothing that sparked his veins any longer.

The last time he'd felt those embers ignite… wasn't all that long ago with a certain flirty hacker.

"Dad," she hissed, smacking Javier on the arm. He

let out a loud, booming laugh and stepped over to the plush red benches accented by emerald-green pillows. Everything inside here was bright and patterned and larger than life, fitting Javier's personality perfectly.

Sophia slipped up to him and wrapped her arms around him in a tight hug. Tuck patted her on the back before they broke away. She was lonely and mourning the loss of her husband, not pining after their old relationship.

"I've got the paperwork right here," she said, heading over to where her father sat on the benches in front of the slender coffee table parked in the middle. Tuck had been spoiled by living in the penthouse with the other Outlaws—even with all of them crammed into one place, it was spacious compared to the days of families living in cramped caravans.

Tuck took a seat at the bench and accepted the thick bundle of papers Javier passed to him.

"Can I get you tea? Coffee?" Sophia asked, brushing her fingertips along his shoulder.

Tuck flashed her a smile. "Nothing for me, thanks. I don't drink any caffeine if I'm going to be out."

"Out where?" Javier asked, crooking an eyebrow. "Sophia's informed me you're something of a private detective now?"

Tuck bit back a snort. "Something like that." He glanced down, skimming the contracts in his hand. These were dense, but if anyone could make sense of them, John could. Their resident conman had been a defense attorney in a different life, and those skills still served them on jobs.

"You're going to handle things tonight?" Sophia asked, her brows drawing together in concern. "That seems awfully quick."

"Just getting a lay of the land," Tuck reassured her, running his fingertips over the lines of the contract. "But I need you guys to tell me if anything changes here. If Reynauld starts putting pressure on you again or if you see any suspicious men lurking around."

Sophia bobbed her head, and Javier offered a grim nod.

"Not that this life is peril-free, but we've never encountered anything like this before," Javier said, his voice resonant and weighted. "If you're somehow able to help… well, we can't thank you enough, Ace."

Tuck's throat tightened, and the guilt crept in on him. Maybe if he'd been here, they wouldn't have gotten hurt in the first place. Except he would've never lasted with Twilight Circus—at least that was what he told himself on the nights when he missed the crowds, the bright lights, and the centering bliss of crossing the tightrope. "No need to thank me," Tuck murmured, his hands tightening on the sheaf of papers. He glanced at Javier and Sophia and offered them a grin. "If you want to save me some of Margo's gingersnaps, though, I wouldn't be upset about that."

Javier's lips quirked. "You drive a hard bargain."

Tuck's phone beeped, and he glanced down at the time. He needed to get going. "I'll contact you when we've got an update," he said, pushing up from the seat.

"But you've only just arrived," Sophia said, chewing on her lower lip.

"He's doing us a favor," Javier scolded her, even though his gaze glowed with warm affection for his daughter. Tuck's chest twisted tight. He missed the radiance of his presence, reminding him of the way his own father had been before he passed. Javier met his gaze. "You'll join the troupe for dinner soon, yes?"

"Wouldn't miss it," Tuck said, already striding toward the door of the caravan. Before he stepped out, he glanced up to see that Javier had followed close behind.

"You know I'd always hoped the two of you would end up together," Javier murmured low enough so Sophia couldn't hear.

Tuck swallowed hard, guilt throbbing through him again. The idea of ending up with Sophia brought a vision of those shackles looming overhead, the ones he'd run from the moment he left. He flashed Javier a lopsided smile instead. "You only say that because you want me back in the circus."

Javier's eyes crinkled. "We haven't had a tightrope walker as good as you were, Ace."

"I'll see you both soon," Tuck said as he hopped out the door, which Javier clicked shut behind him moments later.

He strode away from the line of caravans, kicking

up memories and dust with every step. Time to investigate Reynauld Industries.

"You know, I don't think black is my color," Leo said, his leg brushing against Tuck's in the back seat of the Prius they were crammed into.

Tuck's lips quirked. The man had been talking from the moment he arrived, making it clear this was a nervous habit of his. Still, Tuck hadn't been this amused on a job in a long while. Leo doled out pithy comments every step of the way, but even though he might be brimming with nerves at the idea of fieldwork, he put on a damn brave face that Tuck couldn't help but admire.

"Thankfully, no one's asking you to model your outfit on the runway," Dan said as he zipped down the busy streets toward North LaSalle. This time of night, the city was filled with enough bright lights to drown out the stars, which made the murky alleys even darker. The shadows in Chicago were hungry, seething things, and innocents didn't stand a chance.

"If you wanted to take a spin on the runway, I wouldn't mind watching," John commented, the man flirting as easily as he breathed.

"Thanks, handsome," Leo responded smoothly.

Tuck couldn't help how his skin prickled at John's comment, a bit of possessiveness curling inside him. Not that Leo was his. Leo hadn't avoided him ever since their night together, but he also hadn't hinted at wanting more.

However, Tuck would be working nice and close on this job with Leo Kennedy, and he planned to take ruthless advantage of their time together. If there was a chance, he would damn well steal it.

He nudged his thigh against Leo's again, enjoying the subtle shiver that rolled through the man. The electricity between them couldn't be denied even if he tried.

In the distance, 300 North LaSalle stood out, the skyscraper cutting its mark into the nighttime sky. Unlike their last big job which involved infiltrating the Aon Center, they wouldn't be breaking into a behemoth. Instead, Reynauld Industries resided in one of the nearby buildings that weren't nearly as large—yet they took up the entire place. That meant centralized security and less of a risk factor. Dan had already printed out blueprints of the building, Scar tapped into their wireless to hack into their cameras, and Tuck and Alanna had done a perimeter check the other night.

All in all, a walk in the park.

At least, in theory.

"Nervous, Kennedy?" Tuck asked, keeping his voice low.

Leo glanced over at him, those blue eyes softening for a brief moment before they grew distant again. If Tuck hadn't been paying attention, he would've missed it, but he'd been devouring every glance from the man for a while now. "With a big, bad Outlaw protecting me? Please. I'll just hide behind you and all those muscles."

Tuck smirked. "Right, so I'm just a slab of meat to you."

Leo's pupils dilated as he skimmed Tuck's body, and his tongue darted out to glide over his upper lip. "If you're offering."

"Thought you didn't do more than one night," Tuck responded, the words coming out teasing even though the question was genuine. If Leo was offering another night, he'd snatch him up faster than a jewel from a display case.

Leo opened his mouth, but before he could answer, the Prius jerked to a halt.

"It's go time, lovebirds," Dan said, tapping his fingers along the steering wheel. "Leo, be careful."

Tuck rapped the back of Dan's seat. "I see how it is."

Dan passed him a look. "You've been doing this for years. Leo's never been in the field before."

"No time to start like the present," Leo said. He reached up behind his ear, flicking on the comm, and Tuck did the same. The familiar crackle and pop of their communicators helped clear his headspace. He might've been flirting with Leo a second before, but now they were heading into a job, and any distractions could get them killed.

Didn't matter if it was a routine stroll in the fucking park.

Early on, he'd learned that every single job came

with unexpected risks, and if he wasn't vigilant, he'd end up a splatter on the pavement.

"Let's go," Tuck said, slipping out of the car. His door shut with a thump, the sound of Leo's door following suit a moment later. The slender man stepped onto the sidewalk, his shoulders hunched as he shot a glance at Dan's car.

"They're going to be circling," Tuck said, placing a hand on his shoulder as he guided him down the sidewalk in the direction of Reynauld's main building. "Drop the hunch, or folks are going to think you're up to no good."

Leo's Adam's apple bobbed as he swallowed, but he forced his shoulders down, his body relaxing as much as possible with the live-wire energy flowing through the air between them.

Reynauld Industries turned into a void at night with only a few lights left on, but nothing compared to the high beams that 300 North LaSalle cast. All the better for them. Shadows were the best places to operate within.

"We're in sight," Tuck said over the comms.

"I'm rerouting the camera feed," Scar said—she'd be placing it on loop for a half hour, giving them the time to dive in and dive out. Once Leo worked his hacking magic to attach a keylogger on the main systems, they'd be able to get the key piece of information they needed.

"You already fucked me, no need to take me on extravagant outings to impress," Leo flirted, though Tuck didn't miss the tension in his muscles.

"You're worth it, baby," Tuck responded even as his pulse quickened the closer they got to the back entrance.

The sight of the caravans was emblazoned on his memories. These monsters had sent killers to their homes.

At the reminder, Tuck's adrenaline careened like the control steering had broken. They needed to fuck Reynauld Industries hard—because if those assholes from the Stockyard paid another visit, next on the chopping block could be Sophia or Javier.

CHAPTER 8

Leo had worked in offices ever since he graduated from Loyola, but he could check off breaking into one after-hours as a new experience. One he found creepy as fuck.

Almost as jarring was the fact that he had a Glock 19 strapped to him and a knife tucked into the band around his left leg. Why Grif and crew had trusted him with a weapon was a fathomless mystery. He could scrap in a fistfight if necessary, but he'd avoided guns on principle from his first foster home onward.

Tuck stepped up to the back entrance they'd mapped out, and within seconds he was slinking inside. A beep, beep, beep sounded, but Tuck swept up to the glowing number pad by the door before whipping a jammer out of his sling bag. With a few deft motions, the guy disabled the security alarm, all fluid grace and sexiness that Leo couldn't help but appreciate. If he wasn't buzzing with a stupid amount of nerves right now, he'd be ogling Tuck through half of this—competence was a turn-on, and this guy had it in spades.

The beeping was silenced.

"Come on," Tuck whispered, his voice barely audible amidst the deafening quiet.

Leo swallowed and followed him in. Behind his computer, he could commit unspeakable crimes if he so chose, but he'd never left the comfort of a console to do them. However, if he wanted to get to the Stockyard, he needed to get his hands a little dirtier. He'd help the Outlaws break into Reynauld Industries and then find a plausible reason to divert them to the Stockyard warehouse. Tonight was the perfect opportunity—from the camera feeds he'd studied and all the intel he'd gathered, this was the best night to strike. The place should be clear.

Tuck wove through the maze of cubicles, and Leo slunk close behind—this was obviously an employee exit for smoke breaks if the crumpled butts by the door had been any indicator. However, they were looking for the server room so he could play some Mozart on his version of a keyboard. The hiss of the air conditioning kicking on almost sent Leo jumping out of his skin, but he felt the chill before he could fully freak out. Somewhere in the building, possibly on this floor, a security crew was surveying the place—only a few guys, but still.

He'd hacked into a thousand different forbidden spaces through the years, but this felt more illicit than any of them.

"Grif, your boyfriend drives like my Uncle Marty," John said over the comm. "Except Uncle Marty's love taps every two point five seconds were due to worry over blowing a BAC test. Don't know what Danny's excuse is."

Leo tried to resist the smirk that rose to his lips. He'd driven with Dan plenty before and could verify. Based on the air of gravity that had descended once they'd exited the car, Leo had thought this part of the job would be grim and serious. He shouldn't be surprised these fuckers kept on running their mouths.

"They never shut up," Tuck whispered close enough that his breath hit Leo's ear. "You learn to ignore them."

"So that's how you've remained relatively sane," Leo whispered back as they took careful steps down the hallway. For a moment, their brief banter had suppressed the nerves, but as they crept deeper into the building, the tension returned like a trail of flame.

Even with the security cams rerouted, they couldn't afford to make any extra noise or draw attention. The shadows slithered over him, and the only light source available was the dim emergency lighting, sallow and ineffective for seeing more than a few steps in front of him. The cool air crawled across any bare skin, and he suppressed a shudder.

Get in. Get out.

Find a way to the Stockyard's warehouse.

Another three incidents had occurred since the last one, and they'd continue to escalate the longer Craig Baldwin was active in this town.

He almost bumped into Tuck who moved smoothly in front of him, righting himself just in time. Fuck, he needed to keep his head in the game. Leo sucked in a shaky, slow breath, scanning each and every doorway they passed. His skin prickled. Tuck moved with the confidence of having memorized the blueprints, a surety to his steps that Leo envied. He'd grown so focused on trying to not make any extra sounds that he'd already lost track of their direction.

Tuck glanced back at him, his features stained in the shadows of the dimmed emergency lighting stationed along the corridor. He tilted his head to the side and mouthed, "In here." With that, Tuck cracked open the door to their left and slipped right in.

Leo followed, pushing the door shut behind him. They were plunged into darkness apart from the faint glow of the machines in the server room whirring and buzzing away. The velvet blackness around him should've been disquieting, but he could feel the hum of the infrastructure, a siren's lure he'd never been able to steer away from.

A flashlight flicked on, the sudden beam surprising him, and Tuck guided it around the room, revealing the typical setup—hardware, racks, UPS, and all that jazz. Leo's fingers itched the moment those rays illuminated the desk along the side wall that featured several display screens. The server administrator's desk —bingo.

Leo approached, his first solid footsteps of the night, and Tuck kept the flashlight beams trained in that direction, illuminating the way. Leo settled into the worn pleather desk chair and rested his fingers on the keys. Relief flooded him at the feeling of sitting behind a console, even in the middle of a building he was breaking into. Stealth, subterfuge, blending into the shadows—all of those things were way out of his depth, but this?

This he could do.

"This workable?" Tuck asked, leaning against the side of the desk.

Leo had already started booting up the computer and was watching the processes wake to life. "Installing a keylogger? In my sleep, lover boy," Leo responded with a smirk. "Finding a trail that proves Marcus Reynauld hired the Stockyard? Far less likely. A group like that doesn't seem the type to leave a paper trail."

"We just need to find a *money* trail," Tuck said, his voice low. "Some proof Reynauld paid off these guys. If we can nail him here, that's better than weeks spent poring over every company record, hoping they've been committing crimes."

"Not every company is the lush den of iniquity that mine was," Leo responded. Torres Industries had been as corrupt as they came before the Outlaws ravaged it. "Though, if they're dabbling in this, chances are there are other situations where they've gotten their hands dirty."

The computer screen blinked on, and like the pull of a starter's pistol, Leo's fingers raced across the keys. He breezed through hacking open the system administrator's user ID and password, diving straight into their security software, disabling the aspects he needed to in order to set this up. His vision tunneled in on the screen in front of him, the lines of code that appeared soothing his jumpy nerves. The other thing that didn't hurt was Tuck's steadiness by his side. He'd half expected the guy to be fidgeting or pacing while Leo got to work here, but instead, the man held the flashlight steady, his quiet presence settling Leo more than he would have believed possible.

Within minutes, Meterpreter was up and running, and he began to input the commands necessary to get the relay of information sent to the Outlaws' mainframe. They were in for a glut of intel, but he sifted through the company's network, targeting the connected computers involved in the aspects of the company they were concerned with—money, money, money.

"Getting this, Scar?" Leo asked on the comms.

"You've tapped into the motherlode," Scar said, her voice sounding distracted. Clearly, she'd already pored through the information. "However, the more recent accounting sheets seem to be traceable."

"Does that mean we're not finding any sign of the Stockyard?" Tuck asked, an edge to his voice suggesting impatience. Leo glanced up at him. Tuck's brows were drawn together, and even though his posture remained casual and he held the flashlight steadily, the sharpness in his gaze sliced.

This case was personal. Leo understood that, which

made the guilt sink in a little deeper. Tuck needed this wrapped up as fast as possible because his troupe was in danger. And Leo knew from his own experience just how dangerous the Stockyard could be when they had you in their sights.

"Chances are, we might not find anything on their systems," Scar reminded Tuck. "We're installing the keylogger to try and track future attempts."

"Which could end in another member of my old troupe dead," Tuck said, the bitterness clear in his voice. Leo resisted the urge to reach out and touch him, to offer some sort of comfort, even though his palm flexed at the ready.

The clomp of footsteps snared Leo's attention.

Someone was coming.

He shot a panicked look at Tuck who then flicked off the flashlight. Leo turned off the display screen of the computer monitor, leaving them in pitch darkness apart from the intermittent flashing lights from the server equipment. He sat frozen in the desk chair, the confidence draining from him with every footstep that boomed louder in their direction.

With boots that heavy, it was probably the security guard, but what if it wasn't? What if Reynauld had extra security measures in place and the Stockyard had been employed?

He chewed on his lower lip until he tasted the metallic tang of blood. If he couldn't even sneak into a fucking office building, then how the hell would he attempt to break into their warehouses?

A hand settled on his shoulder, the touch electric and familiar all at once. He glanced up, and even though he could barely see Tuck, he could feel the heat rolling off him, the faint scent of vetiver cutting through the stale, crisp server-room air.

Those footsteps sounded even louder now, and Leo had turned to ice in his seat. A drop of sweat rolled down the side of his face, the slow trickle tickling him as it wound to his neck. What if they got discovered? The Glock strapped to him felt heavier than ever.

The only thing he could focus on was the pressure of Tuck's hand and the heat between them as his nerves went into revolt. He sucked in breaths, slow and steady, the crackle of the comm in his ear breaking up the quiet.

Thump. Thump. Thump.

Right outside the door.

The footsteps stopped, and Leo's adrenaline spiked.

His hand inched toward the handle of the gun strapped onto him. He might know how to use it, but he hadn't fired on live targets. He glanced up at Tuck—the faint illumination from the blinking server lights reflected over his serious eyes which were trained on the door. Leo hated relying on anyone—however, if the guard threw the door open, he trusted Tuck would defend them—a novel concept for him.

A low voice sounded outside of the door, and another set of footsteps clomped along the hallway.

Leo held his breath.

A second later, the footsteps started heading back in the direction they came from.

Tuck's hand didn't move from his shoulder, and Leo focused on the touch as he cycled his steady breaths, listening to the footsteps grow fainter and fainter. After minutes had passed with no noise, Leo broke the quiet. "We need to go," he murmured, his mind whirring.

The comm crackled again. "You've got about fifteen minutes left," Scar reminded them.

Tuck let out a low curse as Leo switched the monitor on again, the glow of the computer screen making his features a little clearer.

"Is there some way we can trace someone from the Stockyard to here? Camera feeds? Anything?" Tuck asked over the comms even though he was staring at Leo as he said it.

Leo's heart wrenched in his chest. The man was clearly torn up about the prospect of the troupe members he cared about getting hurt. He deserved someone honest helping him, someone loyal like the rest of the Outlaws. Like Dan.

That'd never be Leo.

He'd learned early on that you were either useful or you got discarded.

Leo finished hiding the work he'd done, tweaking the malware and virus catchers so they'd bypass his keylogger. He then went through and erased any trail of what he'd done. Last thing he needed was another enemy.

His brain whirred faster than processor fans as Tuck paced back and forth beside him.

"Camera feeds will take time to go through too," Scar said, "and you're running out of time."

"We'll head there again as soon as possible," Grif interjected, hopping over the comms. "We've got access, so let's get to work."

Tuck's jaw clenched, but he didn't respond.

Leo licked his lower lip. This was his chance. He shut down the computer and turned to Tuck, making sure to speak into the comms. "What about setting up a trace at the Stockyard warehouse?"

Tuck's brows drew together.

"We haven't done any prep on their building yet," Dan said, jumping in. "That's way too dangerous, Leo."

Leo kept his cool even though he could see this chance disintegrating like firewalls in a computer he was hacking. They might not have done surveillance, but Leo had. This was the night to strike—minimal crews, and the warehouse should be empty. He kept his focus on Tuck. "If we put a trace on the Stockyard, we'll see the moment they get paid again from Reynauld Industries—and unlike the corporation, they don't need to hide their income source."

Tuck stopped pacing. "So, the next time they get hired for a hit against my troupe...."

"We'll be able to stop them," Leo said, his tone a hell of a lot more assured than he felt. He was spinning wool into silk at this point, but he needed to get to the Stockyard. The longer Craig Baldwin had to make trouble around town, the harder it'd be to get rid of them. And if they were going on another spree through Chicago, bodies would be stacking up left and right.

"Not bad, Kennedy," John said in the comms.

"I can check the feeds of the cameras in that area—see if anyone's around the warehouse right now," Scar said.

"I don't like this," Dan said, the worry clear in his tone. Leo's heart squeezed tight at the concern, all while he combatted the urge to deck his overprotective friend.

"If there's anyone in there, we're doing this another night," Grif warned.

Leo's heart thudded a little harder. They'd just gotten the green light.

Tuck offered him a lopsided grin so genuine it socked him in the gut. It was one he definitely didn't deserve.

If any of them knew what he was hiding, he'd be lucky if they were just upset.

The Outlaws might be a boisterous, snarky bunch, but they were also dangerous as hell.

If he wasn't careful, he might end up a casualty.

CHAPTER 9

THE MOMENT TUCK SLID INTO THE BACK SEAT OF THE
Prius, he knew he was in for an earful.

They'd managed to slip out of Reynauld's office buildings without another mishap, but that stealth mission been well planned. Organized in advance.

This? This was off the cuff and precarious. The sort of thing Tuck would normally never go for. Except after visiting Sophia and Javier earlier today, he understood what he was risking. He might have left the circus, but part of him was only able to do so with the knowledge that they'd be safe in their traveling band, that they'd be continuing to put on their shows every night. That if he ever chose to return, they'd all be there, doing the same thing they'd always done.

The idea that more of his old troupe could end up dead was a burrowing fear that crawled through him. He'd suffered enough loss—his father first. He might not have lost his mother in a physical sense after that, but... well, her current status could barely be considered existing.

"I don't like this," Dan announced once they settled into the back.

"I'd like to just state that I'm Switzerland," John declared, lifting a hand. "If Leo wants to attempt this, Tuck's not going to let him if the site is hot."

"I already hacked into one database for the night," Leo piped up, his tone as calm and cool as always. "If I add two more, I can get a hat trick." He paused for a moment and tapped his fingers against the back of Dan's seat. "Hey, a black hat trick, get it?"

John let out a groan. "That was fucking terrible."

Tuck couldn't help the wry twist of his lips. Not only had Leo offered a solution, but here he was, willing to dangle himself into danger to help even though this was riskier than what he'd originally signed on for. And Tuck hadn't missed the fear rolling off of him when they'd infiltrated Reynauld Industries—yet here he still sat, cracking jokes and attempting another break-in with him tonight. Tuck's heart pounded a little faster at the sight of him, all sharp angles and clever eyes, handsome as fucking ever.

"The warehouse is clear." Scar's voice sounded over the Bluetooth car system. "If you head there now, there don't seem to be any cars stationed nearby or anyone heading in and out."

"Still, keep your guards up," Grif followed on the comms, his tone like a blade, serrated and severe.

"You've got the comms hooked up to the car?" Tuck asked.

"I didn't want to miss anything," Dan said, smacking the gas pedal several times over absolutely nothing. John hadn't been lying about the way the guy drove.

"I've got earplugs," John said, casting a knowing glance at Tuck. Dan was still new, and his enthusiasm was adorable, but after years of listening to comms chatter—fuck, sometimes you just needed to shut it off or dial it down.

"What do we need to be worried about with the warehouse?" Leo asked, casting him a serious glance.

Tuck sucked in a sharp breath. "We're circling the place first—checking in the windows and making sure it's clear. Since we don't have it mapped out, we can't chance just diving in."

"Can't you guys hack them from a distance?" Dan asked, gripping harder on the steering wheel. Lit-up buildings with floor-to-ceiling windows and art deco flourishes whizzed by them, the streetlights and bustle of pedestrians on the sidewalk making the city buzz with energy even at the late hour.

Leo shrugged. "We might be able to, but I did a little digging about groups like theirs. Most of them wouldn't leave an electronic trail. Not like they're going to have paper invoices for hitman services, but they might have a name and amount listed at their desk. And if they do any electronic communications, the keylogger will give us the first look."

That was the advantage they needed. If they could at least find out when the assholes at the Stockyard planned on striking, he could alert his old troupe.

Tuck peered out the window, noticing the bricked warehouse rising into view, tucked deeper into the residential areas of the city. In the darkness, the reddish color looked more purple, and the shadows stretched out with serrated edges. Around neighborhoods like this, the buildings warned people away—barred-up windows, abandoned rowhomes, and graffiti marking up territory.

"That it?" he asked, soaking in the sight. The building was medium-sized and unremarkable enough to fade into the background. The floors stretched out with massive windows that gaped like voids, and while a few cars were parked along the street, there weren't any clustered in front of the entrance or back by the loading bay.

If they headed to the loading bay, they'd minimize their chance of detection.

"We'll drop you off here," John said, tapping Dan on the shoulder to signal him to stop.

Tuck cast a glance over at Leo. "You ready for this?"

Leo's lips formed a thin line, but his deep blue eyes had taken on a honed focus Tuck didn't think he'd ever seen on the man before. Nothing like the distant, avoidant guy he'd come to know or even the sexy, hot-as-sin one he'd taken to bed the other night. No, this version of Leo felt real in a way he hadn't seen yet, revealing a surprising dimension to the man.

"More ready than you think," he murmured, his tone grim.

Dan pulled to a stop along the sidewalk a few blocks away, and he turned around in the seat. His puppy-dog brown eyes flickered with concern as he glanced between them. "Don't do anything stupid. If you sense the slightest bit of danger there, leave."

"I'll keep him safe," Tuck promised. Dan's shoulders relaxed, and Tuck couldn't help the warmth that stirred in his chest. No wonder Dan Torres had cracked open an Ice King like Grif. That much genuine sweetness would melt anyone.

Too bad he wasn't in the market for sweetness—he wanted *interesting*.

And Leo Kennedy was as interesting as they came.

They exited from the back as silently as possible and slipped onto the sidewalk. With his long legs, Leo matched Tuck's stride, and they walked close enough that he could feel the man's body heat inches away.

While Leo had been all jitters when they'd approached Reynauld Industries, he possessed a determination now that Tuck found hot as fuck. He didn't know what had triggered the change, but it allowed him to focus on the job even more.

No movement stirred around the warehouse, and the windows glared vacantly down at him. Still, that didn't mean the inside was clear. It also didn't guarantee members of the Stockyard wouldn't roll up at any moment to return from whatever jobs they were running. His pulse quickened with the understanding that they were taking one hell of a risk.

However, he hadn't joined the Outlaws to stay safe.

"Let's head toward the loading bay," Tuck murmured. "If we can find a side door that way, it's a better spot to slip in and out than the front."

"Think anyone's inside?" Leo asked, caution edging his tone. Darkness sprawled out in front of them like someone had splattered ink on the pavement.

"That's what we'll be scouting for. If someone's in there, it isn't worth risking the Stockyard's attention to go inside tonight." Tuck's pulse thumped hard enough he could hear the boom, boom, boom in his ears. Any normal day he'd rarely register a job like this, but tonight all he could think about was rolling up to the circus caravans to find out they'd lost someone else.

He scoured the windows as they approached, both of them clinging to the sloping shadows along the sidewalks. No hint of light peeked from inside the warehouse, but that offered no guarantee. From Scar's surveillance and what he could see, they at least didn't have anyone stationed outside the warehouse. The place was registered to Craig Baldwin, the man most often associated with the Stockyard. From every-thing they'd pulled up about the organization, it was a group of pay-for-hire killers who'd started in Chicago.

They'd moved location a couple of times throughout the years, probably to lie low after the heat grew in Chicago—Scarlet hadn't encountered them in a long while. However, they'd returned and were already stirring up trouble.

Tuck and Leo neared the warehouse, and Tuck's senses whirred on overload as he soaked in every detail around him, from the scuff marks along the sidewalk to the scent of oily smoke emanating from this place. Leo strode behind him, the stiffness returning to his movements the closer they got to the warehouse.

Tuck placed a hand on his shoulder, feeling just how tense the man was. "Stick behind me."

Leo's lips quirked. "Didn't know you were vers."

Tuck bit back his laugh, the amusement crinkling his eyes. "You didn't ask." At that, he stepped in front of Leo, making sure to sway his hips a little bit more. He prowled forward and the shadows slid over him. He took comfort in the darkness, a liquid cover he could glide through like cutting strokes across a smooth lake. Tuck ducked down the side of the warehouse, casting a glance back to make sure Leo followed.

Silence ached inside the building, but he strained to catch any errant noises he might've missed. The loading dock appeared empty, but that wasn't any guarantee considering most warehouses operated in the pre-dawn hours. The accordion doors were locked up tight, and cracked asphalt stretched out of the back of the building, a large enough space for trucks to pull in.

Normal.

Everything looked too normal. Tuck's internal alarms were pinging, but he couldn't find any signs to justify the reaction.

"We heading up there?" Leo asked, brushing past him to slip toward the beat-up metal door next to the loading bay.

Tuck let out a mental curse and tried to get ahead of him. "What part of stay behind don't you understand?" he whispered as he moved past Leo.

There was a small square window in the door, so at least they'd be able to glimpse in. Tuck maneuvered his way over there, even though his shoulders prickled. He didn't like how exposed they were out in the back here. The moment someone pulled into the lot, they'd be spotted, and creeping around the loading bay wasn't the sort of thing he could explain away.

"You guys are being awfully quiet on the comms," Alanna blared in, almost causing him to jump in place. "Did you just sneak off to fuck?"

Tuck exchanged a glance with Leo, his lips quirking at the comment. Heat flared in Leo's blue eyes, and the way his gaze rolled over Tuck's body suggested the attraction hadn't died down for him either. Tuck sucked in a sharp breath.

Focus. He needed to focus.

"Maybe they're being quiet because they're actually doing their jobs," Grif piped in, his voice droll as ever.

Tuck crept closer to the door and peered into the window, not bothering to answer anyone on the comms. Those assholes knew better.

The space inside was dark, but the sparse moonlight coming in through the small window made it clear that this door led into a room, not a hallway. Probably an inventory office, if he had to guess. Leo stood beside him, his entire body humming with a tension that seeped over to Tuck too.

Diving into office buildings like Reynauld Industries didn't make him blink—he could waltz around security guards any day of the week. But the people in the Stockyard? They were bred from the underbelly of Chicago and wouldn't hesitate to kill.

Tuck's gloved hand landed on the doorknob, ready to turn it and peek inside. Couldn't hurt to take a look.

The screech of tires was the one warning he got.

Headlights whipped around the corner, straight toward the loading bay.

Fuck.

Tuck operated on instinct, yanking the door open and dragging Leo in behind him. He shoved Leo forward and brought the door closed with barely a snick. The sound of the car coming to a halt in the loading bay echoed through the quiet. Leo stared at him, wide eyed, and Tuck's heart stepped into double time. Blood and bones.

Well, they were inside now.

The stale smell of linoleum and concrete wafted his way. Tuck zeroed in on the room ahead of them. This was indeed an inventory office—a desk with an old Acer computer sat before them in sleep mode, and a metal door led deeper into the warehouse. To the right there lay a splintered wooden door—chances were, it led to a supply or water heater closet.

"Going to take the chance," Leo whispered before striding past him, heading straight for the desktop.

Tuck's adrenaline thump, thump, thumped in his ears as he strode back over to the door to check the window. Whoever had pulled up wouldn't just be sitting idle, and they'd either be entering this way or through the loading bay doors.

Their choices narrowed down to heading farther into the unknown of the warehouse, or…

This wasn't good.

"You need to get out of there," Scar said on the comms. "A crew just arrived in an old junker."

"Little too late for that," Tuck murmured. He stared out the window, watching four hulking guys hop out of the car he'd seen whipping toward them. These assholes were built for delivering beatdowns, and based on the slight bulges along their sides, packing heat as well.

"Goddamn it," Alanna cursed.

Yeah, Tuck felt that. They shouldn't have rolled the dice tonight. He'd leapt out of the window without a look just because his pulse was thumping over what might happen to his old troupe. He glanced over at Leo who'd already commandeered the computer. His fingers flew over the keyboard at a lightning pace, a light click-click-click sounding through the quiet. He was clearly setting about installing the keylogger on this computer as well. Tuck couldn't fathom how the guy wasn't freaking out right now. Maybe it was because Leo relied on him to protect them.

Tuck swallowed and swung his gaze to the window. No one stirred from farther inside the warehouse which was still painfully quiet, but at any moment, the guys outside could decide to march on in, and they'd be fucked.

Leo glanced up at him, their eyes meeting. "Just need a minute," he murmured low enough that his voice barely carried. The thump of car doors echoed through the lot.

Tuck looked back out the window. His pulse started thumping hard. The guys had ditched the car and were heading in their direction.

Of fucking course.

The only escape routes available were through the metal door to his left or the wooden one to the right.

"Time's up," Tuck hissed as he bolted forward, grabbing Leo by the shoulders. Leo's fingers didn't stop, landing a few more keystrokes before he clicked out of whatever he'd been up to and switched the computer back to power saving mode. Tuck almost dragged him out of the seat as he surged toward whatever the door to the right was. They couldn't risk entering the warehouse proper.

The doorknob rattled, and Tuck's heart leapt into his throat.

He opened the closet and slid inside without even looking, yanking Leo inside behind him.

CHAPTER 10

Leo had just managed to put the computer back the way he found it when Tuck dragged him away.

One second he was sitting at the desk, shoulders tensed and adrenaline going for a fucking sprint, and the next, he was getting shoved into a closet.

Oh, the irony.

The moment they'd arrived at the Stockyard's warehouse, the jitters from earlier had vanished, replaced by a grim determination that he might be hurtling toward oblivion. Except there was only one wrench—Tuck was here too.

The door closed, plunging them into total darkness.

Leo pressed up against Tuck, his back to the wall and a large metal structure at his side.

Pinned in place.

Stale air.

Nowhere to go.

Leo sucked in a shaky breath, one he barely felt. All

of a sudden, sweat prickled on his forehead as he leaned in a little closer to Tuck. He tried to draw in the scent of the man—something, anything to stave off the encroaching memories.

He'd been ready to face any number of murderers from the Stockyard, but a fucking closet was the thing that would do him in.

Sounds clamored from outside the door as whoever had entered stomped around inside. He and Tuck had hidden away just in time. The nerves from anticipating whatever the members of the Stockyard awaited them outside had nothing on the way his fingers were beginning to numb over in reaction to being stuck here.

He knew he couldn't leave.

He knew he shouldn't burst out of the door.

And yet, all he wanted to do was scream, run, bolt out into fresh air.

A shudder rocked through his body, and pressed up against Tuck like he was, the guy would definitely feel it. Tuck's hands rested on his shoulders, but Leo couldn't bring himself to look up at the man.

Outside the closet, the voices were muffled but clearly coming from inside the room. They couldn't afford to make a single noise.

Leo stayed still even though his mind began to scream and scream and scream.

The tinny odor seeped through his nose—metal? Blood? He couldn't be sure anymore.

Those wails had begun low and grew more pained as the

time passed, even though Leo had long lost track of whether it was minutes or hours.

They'd killed the man.

Tortured him until he was begging, until his screams were thready and barren. Until the sounds coming from him no longer belonged to a human.

And then they'd killed him.

Leo's limbs had locked up, but he couldn't move. Each time he tried to stretch, the walls were there, closing in on him, restricting anything but curling into this ball.

Confined.

Bile rose in his throat, even though he'd by now choked it back dozens of times until the acid soaked his throat.

The shakes traveled through his body again.

He was going to die here, locked inside a metal trunk.

His breathing quickened, and all too suddenly, he was ten years old again and trapped there.

His body full out shook, and the sounds of the guys outside the closet faded away in the wake of the sheer buzzing, buzzing, buzzing overtaking his mind.

Fuck.

Fuck, fuck, fuck.

He wasn't there. He wasn't in his parents' home.

He was in a goddamn water heater closet, and this time he wasn't alone. His heart beat faster like artillery fire as it tried to outpace his quickened breaths.

Leo's grip tightened on Tuck's shirt—when had he grabbed his shirt?—and he pressed against him as if he could somehow take some of the man's steadiness. Was the air getting lighter in here? His mind whirled, and his throat dried.

Goddamn it. Anything but confined spaces. *Anything.*

The rustling outside of the closet grew louder for a moment, and then a second later, those voices were trailing away, the heavy thud of footsteps heading deeper into the warehouse.

Frozen limbs.

The aluminum stench of blood.

Choking for each breath of air.

They'd left him in there the entire time. Mom, Dad, Craig Baldwin, and the rest of his fucking cronies. Couldn't have a kid running to squeal on them but too late to send him somewhere else.

So, the solution had been to lock him up while they tortured the person they'd been paid to kidnap and kill. Who cared how long they left a kid in there?

Leo's throat constricted again for what felt like the dozenth time. Silence pulsed around them in this tight space. The warmth of Tuck's chest and his steady breaths were the only tethers Leo could cling to in the moment.

He blinked, turning the world even darker for an instant.

Had he blacked out?

Tuck's lips brushed against his ear. "Take a deep breath in through the nose," he whispered, his voice steady. "Exhale through the mouth."

Leo's breath snagged at the sudden instruction, but

he forced himself to try, drawing in a breath and forcing it out.

"Good," Tuck said. "Now draw another one in through the nose, out through the mouth." He continued to use that steady, soothing tone, and his palms smoothed over Leo's shoulders, his back, and his arms in slow strokes.

Tuck repeated those words over and over, and Leo continued to try and breathe along with him, even though his pulse would jackrabbit and ruin it all, or those memories would spike in and set him off all over again. He reined them in and focused on his breaths, on the rhythmic feel of Tuck's hands on his body, on the solid warmth pressed against him, a surprising comfort despite the confined space.

Gone were the worries about the Stockyard guys who were going deeper into the warehouse.

Gone was the reality that they were trapped in the closet for who knew how long.

And finally… gone were the memories that threatened to send him careening over the edge.

Leo took in another shaky breath, some of the numbness in his extremities receding. Tuck's hands still smoothed over his shoulders and his back in comforting circles. The man had stopped murmuring directions somewhere along the way, but the susurrations still echoed in the air.

As Leo settled back into himself, he realized his fingers curled into Tuck's shirt, his body pressed against all the hard muscle that he'd felt up close and personal the other night. The man smelled like vetiver and musk, and Leo took in a deep, slow inhalation of it, a reminder that he wasn't mired in his memories. They might be in the Stockyard's warehouse and a breath away from discovery, but he had control here. He wasn't trapped.

His chest tightened as Tuck's hands continued to caress him.

No one had done something like that for him before.

He'd never gotten anything more than survival instincts and PTSD from his parents, but even his foster parents had stopped trying soon after he'd come to them near feral and detached. From then on, Leo had done everything in his power to prove he was worth keeping.

His eyes stung, and he sucked in another shaky breath, trying to dispel the intense and inconvenient emotion welling inside him.

He dropped his forehead against Tuck's chest. The man had witnessed his moment of weakness, but at least within the pervasive darkness, Tuck might not be able to see him.

"It's been quiet in the room for at least ten minutes now," Tuck murmured, his breath tickling Leo's skin. "We're going to need to make a break for it before anyone else arrives."

Relief thumped hard in Leo's chest over the fact that Tuck hadn't demanded answers or worse, asked if he was okay. The man just dove in to help and then took control, which was sexier than anything he'd experienced before. Everything about Tucker Hennings flipped his switch, but they'd already had their spin in the sheets together.

And Leo didn't do seconds.

He tested his voice for a moment, which sounded scratchy because of how dry his throat had become. "What do we do?"

"I'm going to crack the door open, and if the coast is clear, then things get simple," Tuck said, his movements slowing to a halt. Even standing still, his hands rested on Leo's shoulders, the warmth permeating through the fabric of his shirt.

"Simple? You keep saying that word. I do not think it means what you think it means," Leo teased, clinging to the slight bit of sanity he had left with all his might.

They were going to get out of this tight space. Even though he'd come down from the throes of the panic attack, his skin was still crawling, and the longer they stayed in here, the more he'd have to keep combating wave after wave of those old memories trying to encroach.

Tuck squeezed Leo's shoulders. "When I say the word, I need you to listen to me, understand?" he said, his tone quiet but sharp. "There's no room for error or we could get seriously hurt. We should've never come here in the first place."

Guilt thudded through Leo.

They'd decided to infiltrate the warehouse because he'd pushed. Tuck had been worrying over his friends at the circus, and Leo had offered a solution he couldn't resist. Sure, he hadn't lied—he'd done what he promised and set up a trace on their desktop. However, he was the reason they'd ended up here tonight.

And if something happened to Tuck, that was on him.

Bile rose in his throat, but he swallowed it back down. He needed to get his head in the game so they could open the damn door and escape.

"Understood," Leo murmured, finally pulling his forehead from Tuck's chest.

With that, Tuck released his grip on Leo's shoulders, and a moment later, the door had opened a slice—enough for the yellowed light to slip through.

Leo fought the desperate urge to lunge for it, and the sight almost launched him back into another spiral. As Tuck scanned for a sight of anyone out there, Leo returned to focusing on his breaths, fighting to make sure he didn't fuck them any further tonight.

Tuck glanced at him, his silhouette made visible by the crack of light through the opened door. "Get your Glock ready," he murmured and then pressed his comms. "Dan and John, we're coming out in a minute. Be there."

"Thought you came out a while ago," John cracked back, as cavalier as ever.

"Oh, thank fuck you're alive," Dan exploded over the comms, clearly distraught. More guilt layered on top of the rest.

"Ready?" Tuck whispered. Leo bobbed his head in a nod.

The opposite door lay a few yards away—their

salvation, their escape. All they needed to do was slip through it unnoticed.

His nerves bounced. One wrong move and they could get caught, and now this place teemed with members of the Stockyard.

"We're closing in on the street," Dan said over the comms.

Tuck cast him another glance. "Go time."

With that, he pushed the door open and lunged forward in one fluid motion. Tuck had already soared halfway across the room by the time Leo darted after him, scrambling to catch up. Somehow Tuck's footsteps barely made a clatter, and Leo fought to make his feet lighter all while trying to hustle after him so he didn't get left behind. Adrenaline crashed like thunder as his frantic footfalls made it seem like the destination shook in front of him.

Tuck reached the thick metal door leading out to the loading dock first and clamped his hand down on the knob. He glanced out the window and then shot a look at the door leading into the warehouse. Leo followed his gaze. The door wasn't flying open to reveal a horde of guys wielding loaded guns, but he didn't plan on waiting around for that eventuality.

Leo almost slammed into Tuck's back, but a second later, Tuck opened the door to outside and slipped through it. Leo's heart hammered, almost leaping out of his chest as he raced through the door. The night air bolstered him, fresh and intoxicating, filled with asphalt, diesel, and blessed fucking freedom.

Leo bolted after Tuck, the ground shaking in his vision and sweat beading on his forehead. The man melted into the shadows against the side of the loading bay, and Leo raced to join him.

Headlights swung around the bend as a car appeared on the asphalt, temporarily blinding him. Relief flooded through him—Dan and John had arrived.

He blinked for a moment, and Tuck's hand landed on his arm.

Not the Prius.

Not the Outlaws.

Oh, fuck.

CHAPTER 11

Tonight's plans had escalated from the disaster level of faulty spark plugs to that of a car fire in the blink of an eye.

Too bad the car heading their way was decidedly not on fire.

The Toyota pickup zoomed into view, its headlights cascading over them. Blending into the shadows got fucked when high beams like those eliminated them, and they were plastered against the wall next to the door they'd just exited.

Tuck pushed down the urge to panic that rose inside him.

One breath in. One breath out.

One step forward.

Tuck grabbed Leo by the arm and swung him around to his front. "Run," he commanded, hoping like hell Leo could keep his senses under duress.

The truck squealed to a halt, the scent of burnt

rubber filling the air. Tuck had already set his legs into motion. No other choice but to run as fast as they fucking could on the hope and prayer that Dan and John were zipping in their direction. Leo moved surprisingly fast for someone untrained, and he scrambled toward the side of the warehouse that emptied out onto the main road.

Tuck's calves flexed hard with the force of his steps as he launched himself away from the truck that'd be unloading in a matter of seconds. He dipped his hand down, and he grabbed his Sig Sauer and flicked the safety off. The edge of the building loomed into view, but they wouldn't be safe even after whipping around it. Those headlights illuminated every crack in the asphalt, and Tuck glanced back to watch their six.

Three guys hopped out of the Toyota with mean mugs, massive guns, and wearing enough black to hit up an industrial club. They'd clearly caught sight of them, which meant if he and Leo didn't get to the Prius in the next few minutes, they were fucked. Beyond fucked, if the folks inside the warehouse decided to join the party.

Tuck swung his pistol up, aimed at the closest guy, and fired.

Before any of those fuckers could unload a shot, he hunched down and barreled forward, following Leo around the corner of the building. Brisk breezes iced his cheeks. The bark of gunfire echoed in the air, the rat-a-tat-tat of live bullets, but they zipped past him.

Tuck's breath caught in his throat, and sweat pricked on his forehead. This was bad.

He looked at Leo. "Run for the main street and flag down Dan and John. I'll try to slow them."

Leo's brows drew together. Was he going to fight him on this? Every second cost here.

Except then Leo just nodded, turned, and bolted in that direction.

Tuck sucked in a sharp breath. After so much time spent doing recon for jobs, it had been a while since he'd entertained a gunfight. He guessed he was overdue.

He slipped his finger to the trigger as he peered around the side. Tuck dissected the sight in an instant—they'd closed the car doors, left the headlights on, and had broken out in a flat run toward where Tuck and Leo were concealed. Three hulking bruisers were coming their way. Tuck aimed for the middle guy's kneecap, fired, and ducked back.

Another round of bullets pierced the air, the uncanny sound reverberating through it, telling him the guns they packed were in the heavyweight class.

This night couldn't get better. Blood and bones.

Tuck raced after Leo.

His boots pounded against the asphalt, the force vibrating up his shins. At any moment the Stockyard bruisers would be zipping around the corner, and those bullets would find their marks. His heart lunged in his chest even as he kept his gaze steady on the street ahead of them. He tracked Leo as the man burst past the building and onto the sidewalk. His head whipped back and forth as he scanned for any sign of Dan and John.

Please be there.

The slight tone shift of footsteps midturn—the heavier lean—hit his ear. Tuck pivoted into a turn of his own to face the three hulking guys hurtling around the side of the building.

Leo needed to flag down Dan.

Tuck needed to get to Leo.

These men needed to hit the pavement—incapacitated or dead, he didn't care.

His finger found the trigger, his gaze landed on the first guy to lift his pistol, and Tuck fired.

The bullet zipped by with a whiz and was buried in the man's chest. A loud *"Oomph"* came from him, but Tuck didn't have time to sit idle. Not when the other two shiny fucking muzzles were aimed directly at him.

One shot was fired—Tuck caught the movement of the finger—and he ducked.

It whirred inches overhead, the small window of space between safety and a bullet through his skull.

Tuck's heart raced faster than ever, the adrenaline strangling him. Before he could fire his Sig Sauer again, the second bullet zipped his way.

Too fast to dodge.

He saw the trajectory before the bullet plunged through his shoulder.

Fire or run—he had the window of a single second to make the call.

Leo's voice cut through the din. "They're here."

Decision made.

Tuck turned on his heel and bolted toward the street, his calves straining as he all but flew across the pavement. The shock from the wound began to melt in pinpricks down his extremities just in time for the spot where he got shot to *scream*. His nerves rioted, and he clenched his jaw hard to bite back the pain that balled up his throat. Sweat beaded his temple, drops sliding down and sailing behind him as he pounded across the pavement. The shaky movements made the pain worse, but he couldn't stop.

He ran with his body tilted forward, zooming as fast as he could before more of their bullets could rip into him. Shouts came from inside the warehouse—the sound of gunfire must've alerted them.

Feet ahead, he saw Leo standing in front of the Prius, the back door open and him straddling the entrance. He stretched out his hand.

Vulnerability prickled along his back, but he couldn't afford to look behind him. The seconds would cost far too much. His shoulder screamed, and he clutched his limp arm as he ran to keep it from swinging around and making the wound that much worse. Dampness soaked his shirt, blood trickling down his arm.

The bark of gunfire sounded, and Tuck ducked. Leo dipped farther into the car. One of the bullets sailed to the side while the other pinged off the frame of the Prius. This was his opportunity.

Tuck's breaths came out sharp and staccato as he all but launched himself into the back seat. He slammed into Leo, who scrambled over top of him to try and grab for the door. Dan didn't wait, slamming his foot to the gas. The car lurched forward right as the rat-a-tat-tat of the pistols rang through the air again.

They were already sailing down the street, driving away from the warehouse at top speed.

Tuck lay somewhat tangled up with Leo, his skin sticky with sweat, each breath a little painful as he wheezed. The shock of going from full motion to a stop cascaded over him, followed by a motherlode of pain waiting in the wings as his shoulder throbbed.

"Fuck," he groaned, not wanting to move and jostle anything.

Leo peeled himself carefully away from Tuck, but even the slight shift had Tuck wincing. A fresh burst of hurt traveled through him, and he pressed harder against the bullet wound, trying to staunch the flow of blood which, guaranteed, would stain this car. All he could smell was the tinny scent surrounding him.

The Prius wasn't stopping as Dan continued to race down one narrow alley after another, far faster than Tuck would've believed possible based on his earlier driving. He let out a grunt and rolled onto his back, inching up against the opposite side of the car. Leo pushed up to his knees in the back seat within seconds to hover over him.

"Where did they get you?" Leo asked, a worry line creased between his brows.

"Shoulder," Tuck responded, his voice coming out thready from the pain. "Just another Tuesday."

"Well, that operation went tits up," John commented from the passenger's seat. "I thought you guys were just going to lurk around doing recon?"

"That was the plan," Leo filled in as he peeled his shirt off and passed it over. "Here. Try to staunch the blood flow with this."

Tuck accepted the shirt and jammed it over the wound in place of his hand. He attempted a once-over on Leo that he failed to perform without a grimace from the throb of pain, though he kept his tone light. "So, all I needed to do to get you stripped down again was take a bullet?"

Leo's eyes darkened with what looked like concern. "Please. You know I'm a hell of a lot easier than that," he joked.

Tuck's eyes fluttered, the adrenaline dropping at a drastic pace. Now that he wasn't under the dire threat of gunshots, the pain from the wound took over. He fought to keep his eyes open even as the lids grew heavier and heavier.

He blinked his eyes open.

The car had stopped, and Leo's hand rested over his, the man pressed up beside him. His jaw clenched as the pain slammed in with his awareness, making him want to drop back down into unconsciousness.

"Get him out first," Leo said, his voice tense. Tuck's heart pounded hard. He had a crew who'd become his family, and all of them cared, but he'd been wanting someone who was *his* for a long while now. The concern in Leo's voice, the warmth coming from him as he clutched Tuck's hand tight—it made his heart pound a little harder, even if he was just casting pennies into a fountain.

His vision focused as the back door creaked open and John appeared in view.

"I'm going to help you up, okay?" he forewarned.

Tuck let out a grunt, drawing a surprised jump from Leo who must not have realized he'd woken up.

"I'll push you up from behind," Leo said, letting go of his hand. Tuck hated the severance at once, especially when he began to try and lean forward, the bullet wound in his arm throbbing with wave after wave of agony, an ache so intense he thought his jaw would snap. Leo gave him the push, and he moved ahead so John could scoop an arm around him, his legs shaky as the tank of a guy helped him out of the car.

Tuck had earned his fair share of bullet wounds in the past—enough to know he hadn't escaped the critical window yet. He sucked in a trembling breath and stumbled toward the side entrance to On the Park.

His lids slid closed a few times, but he forced them open over and over, the adrenaline crash and the pain threatening to knock him out with a juggling club. John's solid weight guided him while Leo held him up on his other side and Dan led the way. The blaring lights of On the Park washed over him along with its too-clean scent. Before he knew it, they'd zipped up the elevator and were standing in front of the entrance to the penthouse.

Dan pressed their private buzzers, and the door yanked open a second later to reveal Grif standing in the center of the doorway, looking grim.

"Get him in," Grif commanded, sliding in beside him and taking John's place.

The ache in his shoulder had grown so unbearable that nausea rolled up his throat, but his limbs started to numb out in the process. Still, the moment Grif got him inside and lowered him to the floor, some thread of tension in him unwound. The man had treated his wounds for years now—not that he had professional medical experience, just enough experiences of getting torn the fuck up to figure out fixes for anything not life-threatening.

"Couldn't resist the game of tag, could you," Grif murmured as he set to work, the scent of antiseptic tingling Tuck's nostrils.

"They just made it so enticing, waving their guns all around," Leo responded dryly. Tuck didn't move his head to look, but he could feel the man's presence beside him.

"What happened to 'we're only doing a little recon'?" Alanna asked, crouching in front of him. "You look like shit."

Tuck couldn't help the smile twitching his lips. "Always count on you for the ego boost," he murmured.

Grif's hands moved steadily, tearing open Tuck's

shirt. "Looks like it went clear through." A second later, Grif splashed antiseptic on.

Tuck arched off the ground. The sheer agony that rolled through him in one fierce sweep scoured everything else from his mind apart from that searing scent. Fingers brushed over and over along his forehead in a soothing motion as he began to come down from the way Grif cleaned the area. He couldn't tell who was touching him, but the slight hint of sweat and rosewood cologne pointed to Leo. He focused on the feeling of those caresses, a gentleness he hadn't experienced in a long time.

His jaw might as well have glued itself shut, a cold sweat beading across his temples and his temperature slipping from too hot to too cold every minute or so. Grif knelt there beside him, working diligently, murmurs sounding from behind him as the rest of the crew discussed the situation. Alanna had already gotten bored and was talking to John and Scar—probably about what had happened tonight or about baking chocolate souffles, who the fuck knew.

Grif looked up past him. "Hold the bandage here, Kennedy."

Those fingertips stopped brushing along his head, and Leo kept the bandage in place while Grif taped it, his actions swift and sure. Tuck focused on breathing, his inhales and exhales shaky as the throbbing ache in his shoulder continued to dominate his focus. He'd been shot before, but this was higher up there on the "oh shit" scale.

Within minutes, though, Grif had bandaged him up and was helping tug him up into a seated position. He stared into Tuck's eyes, his own sharp and too intelligent. "You with me?"

Tuck forced a shaky grin. "Where else would I be, asshole?"

Grif smirked before pushing himself up off the floor. "You need to stop getting shot, Hennings. Thought you had those fancy circus reflexes."

"Clearly they're failing me in my old age," Tuck responded, deadpan.

"Let's move you to a couch or somewhere comfortable," Leo said, his voice deep with concern. "Then I'll get out of your hair. Enough excitement for the night and all that."

Tuck's chest sank at the idea of the man bolting again. Some of those men had spotted them, and he couldn't vouch for Leo's safety if he grabbed an Uber back to his place. Truth be told, he just wanted the man beside him. Whether it was watching Leo break down in the closet or the tender way he'd stayed by his side through all this, Tuck couldn't help the intense connection blooming inside. Being around him was like taking those first steps out at a show and seeing the crowd brimming with energy and anticipation.

"Stay," Tuck said, before he could help himself. His gaze locked on Leo's, but he couldn't read the expression in those somber blue eyes.

He didn't know what compelled him to ask—Leo

Kennedy was the King of Casual, avoider of anything past a single night.

And yet Tuck wanted to be the exception so damn badly.

Leo swallowed, his Adam's apple bobbing, and Tuck braced himself for the inevitable rejection.

"Okay," Leo responded, his voice quiet. "I'll stay."

CHAPTER 12

Why Leo had agreed to crash in the penthouse tonight was beyond him. Temporary insanity. Or maybe a pair of gorgeous dark eyes that had short-circuited his brain.

Here, he marinated in the guilt.

Leo turned onto his side on the plush couch, the moonlight spilling in through the balcony windows. He shouldn't have pushed to go to the Stockyard warehouse tonight. The need to find and excise Craig Baldwin had ridden him hard to the point that they'd entered into dangerous territory unprepared because of him.

Even though one fact continued to nag at him. No one should've been there. He'd been running surveillance on the place long enough to gauge activity.

As much as he'd flipped through scenarios, he kept circling back to one suspicion that grew by the minute. Someone must've tipped the Stockyard off.

He flung a forearm over his eyes as if that would distract from the overwhelming quietness aching through the place. Being in the penthouse at night was eerie.

During the day, the place was filled to the brim with noise—from the bickering and laughing of the six of them living here to the whir of machines, the hum of the computer, and the clink of exercise equipment. However, even Scar had slipped into his room tonight, and the living room was devoid of all the loud presences that usually paraded through here.

He should've headed home. Maybe he could still slip out. Enough time had passed that anyone trying to track them through the city would've calmed the search by now. Besides, he knew far more about evading the Stockyard than the Outlaws realized.

A creak sounded, drawing his attention. He pushed up from his slumped position on the couch to peer toward the hall.

Tuck approached, thin sweats slung low on his hips and sans shirt. That put all his sculpted muscles on display, including the tight V and the dark happy trail that led to one delicious cock. Leo couldn't help but wince when his gaze snagged on the thick gauze and tape on Tuck's right shoulder.

Tuck's eyes gleamed as they honed in on him. "It's not my first bullet wound and won't be my last."

Damn the man for seeing right through him. "Lucky for you, I find scars incredibly sexy," Leo purred, trying to lighten the charged air crackling between them.

"Couldn't sleep either?" Tuck asked, sauntering over to the couch. Leo cleared the blanket he'd barely been using, and Tuck took a seat beside him.

"Too amped still," Leo admitted even though he was tempted to give another glib, evasive response. After the near scrape earlier and the way Tuck had calmed him down inside the warehouse, he found the truth rising to his lips a little faster.

He stretched his legs out in front of him, trying to ignore how Tuck's proximity made his skin buzz, how he couldn't help but drink in the sleep-mussed state of his curls or the elegant curve of his lips. With him this near, it'd be so easy to close the distance between them and take a taste for himself.

"You can tell me to fuck off," Tuck started, and Leo's shoulders froze. Did he suspect something about the Stockyard? Tuck fixed his gaze on him. "What happened back in the closet?"

Relief flooded through him. His freeze-up felt like a lifetime ago even though it had been earlier tonight. Leo chewed on his lower lip, warring with himself over admitting what had happened. He could dodge out of this—and yet Tuck had already seen him at his weakest, a babbling fucking mess. Heat rose to his cheeks, and he stared down at his loose shorts, playing with the hem.

"Confined spaces," he admitted, unable to look at him even though he could feel the intensity of Tuck's gaze. "They've fucked me up since I was a kid. I didn't have the most... conventional childhood."

Leo glanced to the side to see Tuck dip his head in a nod. He knocked his knee against Leo's. "Understood."

One simple word. In the brief response, Tuck had offered the out yet again—that Leo could let the past lie, that the man truly did understand the pain digging up old, buried memories resurrected.

Maybe that was why his mouth continued to move.

"My folks were involved in some bad shit," Leo admitted, avoiding all mention of the Stockyard. "Most of the time, they got into trouble away from the house, but one night they brought it home. The guy in charge saw I was still there, and he…." Leo's tongue dried, but he managed to stumble through the words anyway. "He locked me in a trunk while they tortured and eventually killed a guy. I stayed in there for a day before they let me go."

The words pierced the air, as harsh and unforgiving as ever. When he looked at Tuck, the man's shoulders were locked. "Your own parents?"

Leo shrugged and let out a bitter laugh. "No love lost when I got put into a foster home."

Tuck's hand rested on his thigh, a solid weight he'd normally try to shake off. However, in the wake of the admission, he felt off-kilter, like he was one blow away from tumbling into bones. This touch soothed him— kept him together when little else did. He hadn't forgotten the way the man had calmed him in the closet, nor would he.

Leo hadn't come upon kindnesses often in his life,

and he'd go to drastic lengths to repay the few who'd offered them freely.

Which just made the stain of his sins that much darker.

The truth expanded in his mouth, begging to come out, but he swallowed it back down. What happened when he told them? They'd ice him out, and he'd lose the one chance for revenge on the organization that scarred him from an early age.

The one his parents had been a part of.

The one they'd eventually taken the fall for, landing themselves in jail while he ended up finding his freedom. At last.

"Yet, you're still here, joking, living, surviving," Tuck said, a wonder in his voice that crept right in through Leo's locked gates and opened them up. Should've expected as much from a thief.

Leo's throat squeezed tight. "What other choice is there?"

Tuck's gaze darkened. "Trust me—not everyone does." He reached forward and ran his thumb across Leo's lower lip, the tender movement sending a shudder through him, one that made his eyes sting. This man was going to unmake him.

Emotion clogged Leo's throat. He needed to get control over the situation and fast. Tuck's heat, his scent, his touch overwhelmed him—so close and intoxicating, he couldn't stand it. So, Leo did the only thing he could think of.

He leaned in to brush his lips against Tuck's.

Sparks tingled through him the moment they connected, and Tuck deepened the kiss with hungry strokes. The riot of butterflies exploding through his chest was trouble. Pure, unadulterated trouble. Yet Leo couldn't find it in him to stop—not after the whiplash of the night's events. He needed to sink into this—into the bliss of this man's mouth on his and the sinful feelings it summoned.

"Thought you didn't do repeats," Tuck murmured against his lips between claiming kisses that made his knees weak.

"Nngh," Leo responded, sliding his tongue against Tuck's in a scorching, wet kiss that sent aftershocks through his body. The chemistry between them was undeniable, and being up close with this man again had him ignoring all his self-imposed rules. Leo pulled back for a breath. "Is that a complaint?"

"Not in the slightest," Tuck growled before gripping his hip with one hand and drawing him closer.

A shiver rolled through him at the contact, and the rising hunger within grew insatiable, demanding more than just closeness. He needed this man inside him, wanted to feel owned, possessed, even if only for a moment. He straddled Tuck's lap, settling his legs on either side of him as he leaned deeper into the kiss, loving the brush of the man's rock-hard cock against his thigh.

Their kisses heated the air around them, and Leo's cock strained his shorts, precum printing on the fabric. The man's mouth moved with the same sensual grace he did, and Leo was addicted. He hadn't been able to forget the smooth, liquid way Tuck had thrust when he'd fucked into him, and the sex they'd had that night had been his masturbatory fodder ever since.

Leo ground his cock against Tuck's thigh, enjoying how the man shuddered against him. If they kept up like this, all the grinding and heat and feeling too damn good, he was liable to cum in his shorts. But tonight he needed more.

"I want you inside me," Leo murmured against Tuck's mouth.

"Just a warning—I'm one arm down right now," Tuck said, tilting his head toward the shoulder injury.

Leo's tongue drifted along his lower lip as he tried to suppress the flare of guilt in his chest. He flashed Tuck a seductive smile instead. "I can work with that. I've been told my bedside manner's parallel to none." He pushed off of Tuck's lap to grab his folded pants from the floor and slipped his hand into the pocket.

Tuck's lips quirked into a grin. "Do you carry an emergency stash with you everywhere?"

"Never know when you're going to get dicked down," Leo shot back, amusement welling in his chest. Not like his other flings weren't fun, but something about the way Tuck looked at him when he flirted felt more personal, as if he weren't just hitting on a random guy. It felt like he actually saw him.

Right, focus.

Leo dropped the packet of lube and the condom on

the couch beside Tuck. "Lean against the side of the couch and let me ride you tonight."

Tuck's dark eyes flashed with heat, and the air grew scorching. "Oh, fuck yeah."

Leo dipped forward and planted a kiss on Tuck's chest before trailing his tongue down the ridges of his abs, salty with sweat and pure deliciousness. His cock was tenting the fabric of his sweats, which left little to the imagination. Not like Leo could forget the thick length that had rammed into him over and over the last time they'd come together.

He hooked his fingers into the waistband of Tuck's sweats, and with a little coordination on both their ends, they ended up on the floor. Seconds later, Leo had shucked his shorts to the ground and pulled his ragged T-shirt overhead to join the pile. Before he settled back on the couch in front of Tuck, he cast a glance toward the darkened hallway. If anyone decided to take a midnight roam, they were about to get an eyeful.

"They're aware you're sleeping on the couch," Tuck said. "If they choose to wander through, that's on them."

"Oh, so this was a sure thing?" Leo teased, unable to help the sultry note sneaking into his voice.

Tuck offered a shrug of his good shoulder, looking up at him with those intense, consuming eyes. "I'd hoped."

The truth of those words speared right through Leo, touching a part of him he preferred to leave buried under six layers of sediment and stone.

"Lucky for you I'm weak for a man who knows how to use his cock," Leo responded, trying to keep things light. "And the curls don't hurt, gorgeous." He ran his fingers through Tuck's glossy hair, tugging a little bit. He enjoyed the low growl that emerged from the man, and he sank down to straddle him again. His cock was sandwiched between their bodies while Tuck's thick length nestled right against his hole.

The feeling of Tuck's velvet cock brushing along the sensitive bundle had his breath hitching as they ground together again, their lips meeting for another searing kiss. Leo's dick pulsed, threatening to end this party early, so he pulled back. In a quick motion, he lifted himself off of Tuck, grabbed the condom, and began to roll it down Tuck's delicious length, enjoying the way the man's head tilted back as he groaned with pleasure.

Leo's hole clenched in his anticipation to get filled by that thickness again, to feel him plunging deep inside. Saliva pooled in his mouth at the thought, and he quickly lubed Tuck's cock up next, swiping a little around his own pucker.

"Ready for me, sexy?" Leo asked as he faced Tuck.

As Tuck leaned back on the couch, there was a hot sort of effortlessness to the way he waited for Leo, like a predator ready to pounce—even though Leo was the one riding him tonight.

"More than ever," Tuck responded, his rich voice sending a shiver through Leo.

Leo soaked in the sight of him, the deep grooves and ridges of his abs, the light scruff peppering his jaw, and the muscled thighs straining as Tuck ran several strokes over his cock. Fuck, he needed this man tonight. Leo climbed over top of him, lining his hole up with that thick length.

Tuck quirked a brow. "What about prep?"

"I want to feel this tomorrow," he admitted, even though it sent a flutter of vulnerability through him. He wasn't lying. As much as he'd enjoyed his time with Tuck the other night, the reality that he left with only memories after every encounter had begun to sink in more and more.

"Fuck, that's hot," Tuck growled out, wrapping his hand around Leo's hip to stabilize him. "Sink down on my cock, beautiful."

Leo's dick throbbed at the heat in his voice, and he notched the head of Tuck's length against his hole, beginning to drop down onto it. An inch in, the pressure and burn was intense, so he just lowered himself onto Tuck's cock. The sensation arrested him, the combination of slight discomfort leading the way to the full stretch he adored. Tuck's long lashes fluttered as he filled Leo to the brim. He could feel Tuck's pubes scratch against him.

Leo rested a hand on Tuck's abs as he lifted himself up before sinking down again, the fast movement making the squelch of the lube audible. The tip of Tuck's cock slammed into his prostate, sending white-hot pleasure rolling through him. Tuck's grip tightened on his side, and Tuck began to roll his hips, the micromovements sinuous and fucking hot as hell, nudging against his prostate over and over again.

Leo ground against him as Tuck continued to shift his hips forward. He dug his fingernails into Tuck's abs as he gasped out, the sensations building quicker than normal. So damn full. His breaths came out ragged as he rode the waves of bliss that coursed through him every time they shifted. Even injured, Tuck moved with an enviable control and grace, one Leo could fast become addicted to.

Leo's forehead beaded with sweat, their staccato breaths and grunts weaving through the quiet of the penthouse. The moonlight streamed in through the balcony sliding door, casting the room in shades of deep blue. Tuck's eyes looked even more lust blown and debauched in this darkness, and the bite of his nails as he tightened his grip on Leo's hip had Leo riding him harder, desperate to feel that thick length slamming against his sweet spot over and over again.

The first time they'd fucked was wild and sexy, but the proximity here, how their eyes kept meeting again and again, felt intimate in a way Leo wasn't prepared for. He appreciated the shadows, hoping they softened and hid some of his expressions and some of the vulnerability bleeding from him tonight.

After the way Tuck had stroked his back during his panic attack and how the man had thrown himself in front of open fire to keep him safe, Leo's mind was wandering into dangerous, dangerous territory, and connected here with him, their bodies moving in graceful symmetry, he couldn't avoid them any longer.

His heart lurched. Tuck thrust into him hard, and Leo bit down on his lip as he moaned loud. The sound echoed in the quiet of the room, reminding him they were in a penthouse full of people. That only thrilled him more, the bubbling sensation creeping up inside him with each smack of their skin colliding, each desperate groan that escaped, each creak of the couch beneath them.

His balls drew up tight as Tuck continued to roll his hips, grinding against him each time in a way that pegged his prostate. The pleasure hit him hard, to the point that he could barely catch his breath.

"I'm close," Leo breathed out, moving in time with him, his palm plastered to Tuck's chest.

"Then come for me," Tuck responded in a low purr. "I need to feel you squeezing around my cock."

Fuck, this man's mouth.

Tuck thrust in deep again, and that did him in. His balls emptied out as bliss rushed through his entire body. His cock spurted, cum splashing over Tuck's cut abs, which made them look that much hotter. His legs felt boneless as he floated on wave after wave of the orgasm rolling through him. It spread all the way to his fingers and toes, the tingling aftermath leaving him with a comfortable buzz as Tuck continued to rock into him.

Tuck's grip on his hip tightened again, and a moment later, he felt the pulse of Tuck's own release inside him. The man's breath snagged in his throat, and he tilted his head back, the pleasure painting his features with a serenity that was fucking beautiful. Those long, fringed lashes lowered, his mouth slightly parted, and his entire body arching up into Leo like he needed to push himself in even deeper, somehow.

Leo's throat tightened as he swallowed, struck hard in the chest by the sight. Tuck slowly lowered himself, his body settling as he came back down from his orgasm, but he didn't try to push up or move.

Instead, they both remained still, their gazes locked as if something monumental had shifted between them tonight. As if the understanding had seeped beneath flesh and bone, deeper than Leo had ever allowed anyone.

He sat on top of Tuck, his cock buried inside him, and rested his palms on the man's chest that was sticky with Leo's fast-cooling cum. Only the moon and the stars had been witness to this lapse in his defenses, and still, a small part of Leo yearned for more with every ounce of his being.

As if it were possible to belong to someone. To have someone who was his.

Except—as he'd learned from an early age—that way lay madness.

Leo needed to distance himself before it was too late.

CHAPTER 13

Tuck woke up to excruciating pain in his shoulder and an empty couch.

He couldn't be too surprised Leo had bolted in the night, even though a pang of disappointment had him rubbing at his chest anyway. They'd crashed out on the couch together after that intense-as-hell fuck, and a secret part of him had hoped that meant he might be one step closer to drawing the untamable man in.

Clanging came from the kitchen which was guaranteed to be the noise that had woken him up in the first place. He'd at least tossed his sweats back on before he'd crashed out, but he'd need a shower sooner rather than later.

"Don't tell me the two of you had sex again?" Scar's voice came from the opposite end of the room.

Tuck pushed himself up on the couch with a wince, the movement jostling his bad arm. If he wanted to do anything to help protect his troupe, he'd need to heal up sooner rather than later. "Whatever gave you that impression?" he asked even though they hadn't exactly been subtle.

"The lack of a Leo Kennedy on our couch this morning, maybe?" Scar said, a gentle smile on his lips. He ran fingers through his dark ear-length strands that he'd artfully styled this morning. Scarlet always stayed up too late and got up too early, all of which meant Scar rarely slept.

Dan slipped in to lean against the side of the couch. "You and Leo hooked up again?"

Tuck sucked in a breath, the vulnerable part of him not wanting to admit anything. If it had just been a casual hookup for him, he wouldn't give a damn, but somewhere along the line, Leo had snagged his interest, and the more he got to know the guy, the more he longed to see those glimpses beneath the surface he rarely allowed.

"They definitely fucked," John said, stepping into the room, still in his pajama pants. "It smells like spunk in here."

Scar's nose wrinkled, their glasses moving with the motion. "Please tell me you didn't fuck on the couch."

Tuck couldn't help the slight grin that lifted his lips.

Grif slunk up behind Dan, wrapping an arm around him to draw him in close. "Like that couch hasn't seen action before." Based on the way Dan flushed at the comment, they'd done their time on it, surprising no one. Tuck's heart lunged in his chest at seeing the closeness between them, the yearning for something like that growing stronger than ever.

Dan fixed his gaze on Tuck. "But Leo doesn't do second rounds. At all."

Tuck's brows lifted. He hadn't expected that—thought it was just a loose rule. But Dan's brown eyes flashed with genuine surprise.

Alanna's loud, stompy footsteps announced her presence first. "If you fuckers are done talking about Tuck's magic dick, breakfast is ready."

John let out a snort, already striding over toward the kitchen. "You guys can keep discussing—I'm grabbing food."

Tuck pushed up to standing from the couch, trying to ignore the stabbing pain that came with the movement. Alanna was the best cook out of them, and her breakfast would disappear faster than leftovers in the fridge. He didn't miss how Grif's gaze landed on him, those ice blue eyes analyzing. Tuck swallowed hard. The injury might get him benched from this job, but he couldn't regret keeping Leo safe. He'd promised to protect him, and he took that seriously.

Grif murmured something low in Dan's ear, causing the man to flush again, and Tuck rolled his eyes, moving past them. The two were like goddamn newlyweds with the amount of mushy, sexy stuff they spewed, and if he were honest with himself, he was fucking jealous.

Tuck caught up with Scar on the way to the kitchen. He glanced over at Tuck, an apologetic look in his eyes.

"I'm sorry we weren't able to get more information from Reynauld's," he said, adjusting his glasses. "Maybe then we wouldn't have needed to go to the Stockyard."

Tuck shook his head. "No way are you taking the blame for that. My stubborn ass was determined to find answers last night. Seeing my old troupe did my head in a little."

Scarlet shrugged, sympathy in his dark eyes. "We've all got things that tangle us up." He left the statement there, but Tuck could see the shadows in Scar's expression hinting at the past he kept under more firewalls than his computers. Most of them didn't talk a lot about their time before the Outlaws, and for good reason.

They'd been drawn to each other because they were all a little bit broken from their pasts.

Tuck's damage remained a half hour south of them in an apartment she rarely came out of.

He stepped into the bright open kitchen where sunlight streamed through the windows. The modern-style kitchen was a draw to the penthouse, all the obsidian surfaces and the massive nickel-and-black table they all fit around in the adjoining room had become a comfort.

No matter where they snagged their meals or what they got up to the rest of the day, they all upheld the morning tradition of breakfast. Occasionally, they'd each miss one here or there, but for the most part, every morning started with all six of them around the table, and cooking rotated each day. He wouldn't give it up for anything.

He grabbed a plate and loaded it with the bacon, eggs, and pancakes Alanna had made, his stomach grumbling at the sight. After all of the chaos last night, he was hungrier than ever. He drenched his pancakes in syrup and took a seat right by John, who'd already started going to town on a full plate of food.

Grif plunked into the seat across from him, those eagle eyes still zeroing in on him.

"Don't you have a boyfriend to be staring at?" Tuck commented as he chewed on a bite of pancake, restraining a moan at the delicious burst of flavors. He wasn't sure what sorcery Alanna performed, but her pancakes were always the fluffiest.

"He stares at me plenty," Dan said, scooting next to Grif and biting into his bacon with an audible crunch.

"You can't do fieldwork until that heals up, Tuck," Grif said, cutting to the chase. "It's not just a graze."

Tuck's stomach dropped. He knew that one was coming. Except this job belonged to him. His old circus family was under threat—and now he couldn't be out there, taking point. Protecting them. He trusted the Outlaws with his life, but at the end of the day, he was the one who'd be walking up to Javier and Sophia's caravan to deliver the news if they fucked everything up.

"There's a new development on the job," Grif interjected.

"Let me guess," Alanna jumped in. "Reynauld just

up and died, and the Stockyard relocated to a new city?"

John snorted. "You know our luck's never going to be that good."

"I spent last night going through the files in the system Leo connected us to over at Reynauld's," Scar said. "There was a certain email chain between Marcus Reynauld and the owner of Plascourt, an energy company in the city. He's got a document for him that could be profitable for both of them. There's a fuckton of innuendo, but it sounds like our precious CEO is doing some insider dealing."

"And the in-person exchange is set for the end of the week," Grif finished for her.

"Which means if we get the folder from his place, we'll be able to nail him on those charges," Dan said, his eyes gleaming in excitement. Tuck bit back his amusement at seeing the enthusiasm from their newest member. Just a few months before, Dan was a terrified CEO stuck in a life he hated and surrounded by a bunch of corrupt old guys before they swept on in and torpedoed his company.

"What about those fuckers at the Stockyard?" Alanna piped in, asking the question that had been bubbling to the surface of Tuck's mind as well.

"If we can take down Reynauld Industries, they shouldn't be a problem anymore," Grif explained, jabbing the tines of his fork in the air for emphasis. "Without Reynauld Industries footing the bill, why are pay-for-hires going to do anything?"

Tuck chewed on a piece of bacon, focusing on the explosion of salt on his tongue rather than the uncomfortable flip of his stomach. What Grif was saying made sense. The Stockyard was filled with mercenary types who killed for cash.

Except he couldn't shake the feeling that the Stockyard was more intertwined with the company than it appeared to be. That even if they took Reynauld Industries down, the Twilight Circus troupe still wouldn't be safe.

Not like he could dictate their plan of attack on a hunch. Especially when a clear solution lay in front of them.

"That means we can take Leo off the job, right?" Dan said, chasing the eggs on his plate around with a fork. "If the Stockyard's not a factor...."

Tuck's chest squeezed tight. More logic.

More uncomfortable feelings he wasn't ready to face.

"No one from Reynauld Industries knows me, so they won't be an issue," Scar said. "But we did offer this job to Leo. It'd be kind of shit to just take it from under him."

"Except my best friend almost got shot," Dan grumbled. "Safe job, my ass."

"That's on me, sweetheart," Grif said, draping an arm around Dan's shoulders. "We shouldn't have gone into the Stockyard last night."

Guilt thudded hard through him. Tuck had been the one raring to go find some way to end this before his old family got hurt. However, rushing things could've gotten other people he cared about hurt.

"Hey, King of Martyrs," he said, catching Grif's eye. "We both know we wouldn't have gone if I hadn't pushed."

"You're both to blame," Alanna responded, her tone blunt even as her eyes twinkled.

"Not like it was a wasted trip," Scar reminded them, sipping on his coffee. "Leo installed a tracer on their system, so the second we see any suspicious pings, we can be on the alert to keep Tuck's old troupe safe."

Right. Leo's quick action had made the trip worthwhile. The man knew Tuck's secrets, acted well under pressure, and blended in with the Outlaws like he'd been with them for ages. Tuck's gaze drifted over to Dan and Grif casually pressed up against each other. His heart ached. He wanted what they had so badly, and Leo Kennedy was the first in a long time who had the secret, yearning part of him whispering *maybe....*

However, just because he saw a cozy future between the two of them didn't mean the vision was shared.

And all their close proximity due to the job right now?

It'd vanish the moment this ended.

CHAPTER 14

Leo blinked, the computer screen glaring at him. His eyes had grown bleary from staring at it for hours now since sleep had eluded him ever since he left Tuck still passed out on the couch.

The worst part was that he'd wanted to stay.

Plastered against the man, a security he'd been chasing for a long time had settled over Leo, the feeling of being wrapped up in a warm blanket at the end of a long day. He'd never found that from blood or foster family and definitely not from past hookups, but once in a while, he felt a flicker around certain friends, the human connection he'd been dancing around for years.

It was rare, tenuous, and truth be told, made him nervous as hell.

So, he'd left.

Leo pushed away from his computer and snagged his porcelain mug from the desk. Empty, of course. He'd lost track of the cups of coffee he'd drunk at this point, though his stomach had started to protest the volume of battery acid he kept dumping into it. He headed for his kitchen and poured himself more from the dwindling carafe anyway, nuking the coffee for a minute to get it hot again. He leaned against the counter as the microwave hummed behind him.

The information he'd connected to on the Stockyard's computer had begun pouring in, but apart from some nebulous emails, there wasn't a lot that was of interest. It appeared that either they did utilize the warehouse for goods during the day or they just coded their jobs that way. He kept tabs on them, but nothing was actionable at the moment, even though his skin crawled with the need to do something. Anything.

The microwave beeped above him, and he whipped around to grab his coffee, the heat from the mug permeating through some of the fog he was wading through today. He drifted back over to his computer and clutched the mug with one hand while he pulled up a document he'd already pored over a thousand and one times.

His parents' mugshots glared back at him.

Gerald and Carol Thatcher.

He'd legally changed his name the second the Kennedys adopted him because the more distance he could put between the fuckers who birthed him, the better. The day he'd been locked in the trunk had been the beginning of the end of his stay with them. When the cops threw heat on the Stockyard after Craig had used their house to off their victim, their almighty leader offered them up as the perfect scapegoats.

One night Leo had fallen asleep in his bed at the old rundown house on the outskirts of town, and the next morning he was stumbling through the halls of the DCFS building. His parents had been shoved behind bars while he'd gotten tossed into the system. And honestly? His life was a thousand times better there than it had ever been with the people who spawned him.

He rubbed at his chest, not sure if the pang there was from far too much caffeine or the old memories bubbling to the surface.

His phone began to buzz.

Leo glanced at the caller ID, surprised to find Tuck's name flashing there.

He answered the call, leaning back in his computer chair. "Couldn't get enough of me, Hennings?"

"What can I say, I'm insatiable," Tuck responded, his voice coming out in a sensual purr.

Leo bit his lower lip. His cock plumped at the tone of voice, and he reached down to adjust himself. He'd just gotten another hefty helping of the man's thick length last night, but already he wanted more. Leo shifted in his seat, the tender zing through his backside another reminder.

"You're something, all right," Leo responded, trying to keep things nebulous.

He'd broken his rules once for a repeat with Tuck. If he caved again, he'd be teetering into relationship territory. And he couldn't afford to get attached, not when he was keeping a major secret from the man. If any of the Outlaws found out about his connection to the Stockyard, all the camaraderie would vanish in an instant.

"Look, I need a favor," Tuck admitted.

"Oh?" Leo asked, his curiosity piqued. He clicked the tab with his parents' mugshots away, reopening the new information he'd been accumulating from his hack into the Stockyard's system.

"Last night I stopped by the caravans before our rendezvous to let Sophia know we were heading out," Tuck started.

Leo honed in on the phrase, dissecting it in the span of a second.

He'd been wondering if anyone else had known about their excursion to the Stockyard. His stomach dropped. Tuck's ex-girlfriend had been the one to recruit them in the first place—the idea of her selling him out to the Stockyard seemed ridiculous. However, if the Stockyard caught wind of her outsourcing and decided to put the pressure on? He'd heard and seen enough of their tactics to understand how quickly someone would cave.

"So, is that silence a yes?" Tuck asked.

Leo wrinkled his nose, grateful the guy wasn't in the room with him to see his mind whirring like a faulty laptop fan. "Sorry, I got distracted by the files I was scouring through from the Stockyard's computer. What did you say?"

"Find anything interesting?" he asked, a note of urgency in his voice.

"A lot of potential things, but if the average-looking warehouse orders they've got recorded are some sort of code, it'll take a while to parse that out," Leo said, skimming his fingertips over the keys of his laptop.

"Javier invited me to dinner with the rest of my old troupe tonight," Tuck said. "And I was wondering if you wanted to join me."

Leo's brows lifted. "Any reason you're propositioning me and not any of the five other people you live with?" His stupid heart quickened at the idea even though he needed to turn Tuck down. He wasn't relationship material, and leading Tuck into believing he might be wasn't fair.

"Because I'm pretty sure Javier's going to try to push me back together with my ex, and rather than faking chemistry with the people I view as siblings, it'd be easier to bring someone who gave me one of the best orgasms I've had in ages."

Leo snorted. The "no" rose to his lips despite the way his chest lurched at the thought of pretending to be with Tuck, even for a moment.

He paused.

If Sophia had somehow sold them out, Tuck wasn't the right person to get a gauge on her. This was his family, his ex-girlfriend who he remained on good terms with. And Leo wasn't sure if he should even bring up his suspicions to Tuck yet.

However, if he went to the troupe dinner with Tuck,

maybe he could find a hint to confirm or deny his concerns. Because at the end of the day, he couldn't believe it was a coincidence that the crews from the Stockyard had all returned to the warehouse around the same time when they should've been gone through the night.

"I'll go," he found himself saying even if the idea of showing up somewhere with Tuck like that had his heart going to war with his head.

"Really?" Tuck responded, his warm tone making him sound ridiculously pleased.

A flush burned Leo's cheeks, and he was grateful for the dozenth time since this conversation began that it was taking place over the phone. "Don't get ahead of yourself," Leo said. "I've just always been curious about what goes on behind the scenes at the circus."

"If a backstage pass is what you wanted, all you had to do was ask," Tuck responded, his voice dripping with insinuation.

A shiver rolled through Leo. Fuck, that was hot. Not like he topped often, but he appreciated knowing the option was on the table. "Duly noted," Leo responded.

"I'll pick you up at five," Tuck said. "It's a date."

Before Leo could argue that it wasn't, Tuck had already hung up. Leo chewed on his lower lip. He couldn't help but admire the man's determination even when fixed on a hopeless case like him. If that thought sent a silent thrill through him, well, he'd chalk the reaction up to lack of sleep.

He swiveled in his seat to face the computer again, his fingers poised over the keyboards.

Leo had one mission in all of this—to take out Craig Baldwin, which would dismantle the Stockyard from the top down. The man was the coldest creature Leo had ever met, and his parents might've committed some atrocities as peons, but Craig was the finger pulling the trigger.

He couldn't let these emotions emerging around Tuck cloud his vision—those were fleeting, while his goal had always been steadfast in a way little else in his life had been.

Still, he couldn't help the guilt that dripped through his veins like arsenic. Tuck possessed a warmth, a steadiness that Leo had only ever dreamed of, but he deserved someone far better than him.

Someone who hadn't been lying to him the entire time.

Only one thing to do about it. Leo pulled up a search and typed in Sophia's name.

Time to get to work.

CHAPTER 15

WHEN TUCK ARRIVED TO PICK UP LEO, HE'D HALF expected for the apartment to be empty.

The cramped studio didn't surprise him—they lived in Chicago—and Tuck fast got the sense that Leo didn't invite anyone in often. His belongings were all out on display, offering more details about him in one sweep of the place than anyone could manage to pull from months of conversation. Tuck soaked in the sight of the diploma on the wall, the picture of Leo amidst a bunch of people that looked like a family photo. Probably not biological. The computer setup with the multiple screens, too many cords, and stacked towers reminded Tuck of Scar's setup at home.

The guy had about a dozen Stephen King novels scattered around, a startling collection of Star Wars coasters, and an equal amount of abandoned coffee mugs. Tuck slipped a hand in his pocket as he waited for Leo to finish getting ready. Every hint of this guy made him thirst for more, a bunch of never-ending contrasts that kept his attention like no one else ever had.

The bathroom door creaked open, and Leo stepped out, looking stunning in a blue blazer with a fitted white shirt underneath and charcoal slacks that high-lighted those gorgeous, long legs. With his chestnut hair styled to the side with some product, he looked even more arresting than normal.

"Just a reminder," Leo said, his brows lifted, "this visit is purely for research purposes. Not a date."

"Sure," Tuck teased, the corners of his lips curling in amusement.

Leo pursed his lips, giving him a pointed look that Tuck ate up. He loved how easily he could just exist around Leo, how he didn't feel the need to compensate for his quietness or shorter answers.

"Ready to go?" Tuck tilted his head toward the door. Leo nodded, and they headed for the car.

Once they slipped inside his Audi and Tuck set out on the road, he cast Leo a sidelong glance. "You know you didn't need to dress fancy for a dinner at the cook-house, right?"

Leo snorted. "I'm flattered you consider this fancy. Sorry I didn't have more sweats and tactical turtlenecks to wear, Mr. Thieves Anonymous."

"Maybe I just don't want anyone else making eyes at you," Tuck teased, quickly gliding down one side road after another on the way to the outskirts of town.

"Please, have you met me? I'd like to see them try not to make eyes at me," Leo responded with the faux cockiness that had lured Tuck in from the start. He'd always seen the bravado for what it was, but something about the beat of silence afterwards or the occasional way the man's eyes softened after a statement had reeled him in until he was desperate for more.

The skyscrapers rose all around them, lit up at this time of night in a symphony of angles and glass. Shadows blanketed the city in an ink-stain quilt, the darkness here feeling more impenetrable, more absolute. Nights in Chicago served as a reminder of the duality of the city—filled with life and yet swarming with death, day in and day out.

Too quickly, the circus tents signaled the way in the distance, their silhouettes familiar. Spotlights marked out the open area that had been taken over by the Twilight Circus's traveling show. The troupe would all be cramming into the cookhouse for dinner, which made this a great opportunity to catch up and see everyone. Maybe he should've come by his lonesome, but he couldn't regret dragging Leo out with him. Any attempt to get to know the man a little better, to see him a little more, was worthwhile.

"Do you miss it?" Leo asked, his voice breaking through Tuck's thoughts.

Ah, the ever-loaded question.

"I miss the troupe sometimes. I miss the peace of the tightrope, the simplicity of the act," Tuck started as he headed for the beaten-earth parking lot. Familiar bitterness surged to his tongue as the memories loomed—that question, this place. "I don't miss the monotony and pressure of performances though. I don't miss everyone knowing every last detail about you because you grew up around them."

Even though on some nights, he missed those things too. Some nights, that tug to the circus called like the opening strains of music in the tent.

"Isn't it the same with the Outlaws? With you all living together?"

Tuck's lips twisted with his grin. "Not in the slightest. You think I know anything about those secretive fuckers' lives before we joined? The only one I know a little more about is Grif because his vendetta's been clear for a long while."

"Well, and Dan," Leo said with a wry smile. "Though I don't think he's got too many skeletons in his closet." A hint of wistfulness lingered in the way Leo said that, and Tuck couldn't help but question just what the man had been through. The bits he'd revealed had been beyond horrifying, and how Leo had turned out so... normal after a childhood like that was admirable.

Tuck passed him a glance. "You'll likely find out more about mine tonight."

Leo's gaze met his, a flare of curiosity in those blue eyes. "And you're okay with that?"

"As long as you're not planning some elaborate blackmail scheme," Tuck teased, needing to lighten the mood. Truth be told, he wanted Leo to know, which terrified him a little—but not nearly how much it'd scare Leo. And Tuck had already realized the man needed to be coaxed. Any overt moves would send him racing in the opposite direction, so he had to be careful.

"Damn, you got me," Leo responded, his tone cracker dry.

Tuck turned off the ignition and smoothed a sweaty palm down his gray tee. He'd considered wearing jeans but opted for traveler's pants instead, preferring the flexibility. His gauze had been taped down enough that most of the troupe wouldn't notice the injury, but he'd probably have to offer up an explanation or two.

"Let's head to the cookhouse," he said, cracking his car door open.

Leo followed suit, stretching when he exited. "Watch out, I'm going to write up an expose into circus life next."

Tuck snorted. "Right, with the whole journalism career you've got."

On the fringes of the city, the stars attempted to peek out from the navy canvas of the night sky, those crystalline points drawing his gaze. They walked comfortably together, close enough that their hands occasionally brushed. Each touch sent a shiver up Tuck's spine, and he resisted the urge to reach over and grab Leo's hand. He couldn't help but imagine that sort of ease between them.

His heart pounded hard, the yearning bubbling inside him to the point of pain.

The cookhouse tent lay off to the side, white with a

peak in the center, and he could see several of the troupe already milling about the entrance.

"Wait," Leo said. "I'm coming here to ward off your ex, so what is it you're introducing me as?"

"My boyfriend," Tuck responded, his lips curling with a satisfied grin.

"Ah, that," Leo said, sounding a little faint. "God, that's one terror-invoking word."

"Would you prefer lover? Paramour? Fucktoy?" Tuck teased as they got close enough to attract notice.

"The last one has merit," Leo responded, a little steadier. He sucked in a breath, and in an instant, his mask slipped into place, his face transforming into the smooth, charming expression he wore to the bars. "All right, boyfriend. Let's get this dinner over with."

At that, Leo reached down and slipped his palm against Tuck's, weaving their fingers together.

Giddiness flushed through Tuck at the intimate gesture.

Except this wasn't real. He tried to ground himself with that reminder, even though he badly wanted it to be real.

Not like he got much time to dwell. The moment Zeb and Linc spotted him, they began to jog over. The pair of them had been doing the trapeze together for years, to the point that they worked in tandem with every aspect of their lives—whether it was hanging out or attacking chores. Being with the troupe was like that. Tuck's role had permeated into his daily life until he'd sometimes entirely forgotten who he was.

While he had his designated role in the Outlaws, it shifted with every job. The freedom had allowed him to find himself over the years, to figure out the man he was beyond his talents. And yet, the pull of home here, the way threads of the circus life still wove through his fabric couldn't be denied. He'd missed this place—more than he wanted to admit.

"Javi told us you were coming, but I didn't believe him," Zeb said, the lithe man reaching them first. He was tall and muscular, all dark hair and tanned skin that drew the eye. Linc looked just as gorgeous with his shaved head and seductive grin. If Tuck hadn't been with Sophia back in the day, he might've considered hooking up with one of them, but loyalty meant everything to him.

"Who's this?" Linc asked, scanning Leo from head to toe with a hungry look.

"My boyfriend," Tuck asserted, nipping that shit in the bud. He didn't miss Leo's amused smirk over the flex, but to his surprise, Leo didn't comment.

"Pleased to meet you," Leo said, offering a hand to Linc, who took it and shook. A little too long.

"Man, Sophia's going to be so disappointed," Zeb said, shaking his head. "Pretty sure she was hoping to rekindle something."

"Too soon, if you ask me," Linc responded darkly. "We just buried Asher."

Zeb shrugged. "You know how they fought though. She had one foot out of there for a long time."

Tuck restrained his eye roll. Oh, circus gossip. They

all might rib each other in the Outlaws, but they were all adults there. To most of the people at Twilight Circus, he retained the same judgments and sins from his youth, like the time he stole Auntie Bella's makeup or when they'd all gotten into a water fight with the hoses and ended up soaking the inside of the Big Top.

"Well, lucky I snapped up Tuck when I did, then," Leo said, jumping in to seamlessly smooth things over. "Now, I was promised some food?"

"Where'd you meet this guy, Ace?" Zed asked, clearly charmed by Leo already.

Leo mouthed "Ace" at him, which Tuck ignored while responding, "On the job."

"You're in luck," Linc said, leading the way toward the tent entrance. "Margo made her goulash tonight."

Tuck's stomach rumbled at the thought of the meal he'd loved as a kid and had gotten excited for thousands of times in the past. "We better not wait or there won't be anything left."

He laced his fingers back through Leo's and followed Linc in through the tent flaps to the cookhouse. After all his time away, the sight drew him into the past at once, as if he were still one of the troupe, shoveling as much sustenance as possible into his face in preparation for the show tonight.

Indoor lanterns stationed along the perimeter lit the tent up, and a crowd of close to twenty people gathered inside, either plunked into the picnic-table-style booths or lingering by the stockpots filled with goulash and the stack of bowls and silverware. Tuck absorbed the scene —the scent of paprika and beef fragrant in the air, the yellowed lighting casting everyone in an off sheen, and the chatter as vivid and vibrant as ever.

Tuck headed for the pots of goulash, his palm still pressed against Leo's. He couldn't help the part of him that was imagining this was real—bringing Leo to meet his former family to show him where he'd grown up.

Margo stood by the food—their resident cook and chief bottle washer on the road, she was the real power-house behind this operation, for as much as Javier put on a damn good show. When Tuck approached, her gaze snagged on his, and a bright smile crinkled her features. She looked the same as ever—sweeping purple skirts, her hair a tangled bun of spun silver on top of her head, and a long pendant with a crystal at the end, this one tinged purple as well.

"Ace, it's been years," she said, slopping some of the goulash into a bowl for him. Her gaze traveled over to Leo, and she was preparing him a bowl as well before he could even speak. "Sophia said you'd be joining us, but I figured you were a figment of my imagination by now."

Tuck snorted. Margo always leaned toward the dramatic, but the woman had tutted over him from an early age—especially after his father passed. His father might've been the one who died, but he'd lost both parents that day. "Margo, this is Leo, my boyfriend," he introduced, the words rolling off his lips so easily.

Leo was already swallowing a spoonful of the goulash and almost choked on it.

Margo arched a brow. "Javi's going to be disappointed."

Clearly, everyone had designs on him he hadn't been aware of. As if Sophia's husband hadn't just died and been buried a few weeks before. Tuck shook off the discomfort that rippled across his skin at the thought. Asher might not have been popular, but he was still one of their own.

"I'm sure he'll manage," Tuck responded with a half smile that dropped as he regarded her. "Have there been any other incidents since the first one?" Tuck could feel Leo's presence buzzing to attention beside him at the mention of the job.

Margo heaved out a sigh, resting the ladle against the pot. "Outright? No," she murmured, leaning in closer to him. "But I swear they're lurking around here."

"Enough with the tall tales, Margo," Javi boomed as he stepped up beside them. He cast Tuck a knowing glance. "If you listen to her long enough, she'll have you convinced there are murderers lurking around the corner of every tent."

While Tuck understood what Javier was doing—keeping the troupe from dissolving into panic—he couldn't discount Margo's suspicions so easily. An ugly group like the Stockyard didn't seem the sort to fade away, and they were still on the payroll of Reynauld Industries. Truth be told, who knew how long Marcus

Reynauld had been using them to handle his dirty work?

"I'm glad you joined us, Tuck," Sophia said, approaching from his side. She already wore her performance attire—a red silk top and loose harem pants that clung to her curves. Where had she even appeared from? He'd been operating in a small group like the Outlaws for so long that he forgot the larger chaos he'd grown up in.

Leo tensed beside him, and a moment later, the man placed a hand on his arm. "Who's this?" he asked, his tone too sweet.

Tuck bit back his grin at the move, even if the possessiveness was fabricated. Something about it felt right—enough so that he could be patient if it meant winning this man over. "This is Sophia, my best friend growing up."

Sophia's dark eyes scoured Leo, a quick scrutinizing sweep, and the question flickered into her gaze as she looked back at Tuck.

"Sophia, this is my boyfriend, Leo," he said, sliding an arm around Leo's waist and drawing him in close. This close, he could smell the rich rosewood of his cologne, which reminded him of the way Leo had climbed onto him and rode him into oblivion last night.

Sophia offered a dainty hand. "Pleased to meet you," she said, her smile strained at the edges. "If you want any stories about Tuck, I've got them all—not just as his best friend but as his first love too."

Irritation flickered through him. While this was a

farce, if he'd actually been introducing a significant other, that sort of move might scare them away. Had Sophia reached out to him for protection or just as a misguided attempt to drag him back into the troupe? While the threat was real—he'd found the obits for Mugs and Asher—everyone seemed more concerned with tying him to the Twilight Circus again in some manner.

Leo pulled away from him to shake Sophia's hand, resting his overtop of hers. "If you've got a solution for the snoring, I'll take it, because the man is louder than a chainsaw."

Tuck couldn't help the warmth in his chest at the effortless way Leo navigated a potential minefield. If he hadn't already been impressed with the man, he would be now. Before he could say anything, Leo swept Sophia off in the direction of the tables, clearly insistent on befriending her now. He shook his head, a rueful smile rising to his face.

A hand clapped onto his shoulder. He glanced back to see Hernando, their resident strongman, looming behind him.

"Heard you were here to visit," the guy said, his deep, scratchy voice so familiar.

Tuck turned to face him. He'd agreed to visit the troupe for dinner not just to catch up with old friends but also to get a pulse on what was going on. Despite the chaos rippling through the tent, he hadn't missed the way they were buzzing with tension, how the absence of Asher and Mugs grew louder despite the noise, and how often many of them peeked out past the tents as if keeping guard. He wasn't sure if the Stockyard had tried anything more.

Or if, like Margo suspected, they were watching and waiting for word to strike again.

CHAPTER 16

The moment Leo had been introduced as Tuck's boyfriend, getting Sophia's attention had been easy.

He leaned against the table, perched on the bench as he ate another spoonful of goulash. The flavors exploded on his tongue, and he took a moment to savor them. The food had been so good, he'd gone back for seconds—home-cooked meals were a rarity for him. He found listening to Sophia's old stories of growing up with Tuck more engaging than he wanted to admit. She was clearly trying to make Leo jealous—plenty of comments on how well she knew him and furtive looks in Tuck's direction—but even if Leo hadn't been pretending, he wasn't the jealous type.

Tuck hadn't been wrong about her interest, but he wrestled with figuring out her motivation for involving the Stockyard. If she wanted Tuck so badly, why draw him into this mess in the first place and then tip off the Stockyard?

His only working theory was that she'd gotten involved with either them or Reynauld Industries. Something wasn't stacking up with the way the woman had lost her husband and seemed less than concerned about it. In fact, her sole focus was locked onto the man he'd ridden like a goddamn stallion last night.

"Does he still give that subtle look when he wants you to say something?" Sophia asked. The enthusiasm in her voice couldn't be faked, nor the feverish adoration as her gaze drifted over to Tuck again. However, the guy she rambled on about seemed nothing like the man Leo had come to know. So, either he didn't know Tuck at all, or he had done a lot of changing since he left the circus.

"I wouldn't know," Leo responded, keeping things superficial. "I'd have to stop talking long enough to see."

The man he'd met earlier, Zed, strolled over, placing a hand on Sophia's shoulder. "Hey, was the guy who you were talking to this morning here for me? I'm seeing this chick, Amelia, while we're in town, and she was supposed to drop something off." He waggled his brows.

Leo's internal alarms pinged.

"Ew, I don't want to know what nastiness your hookup is sending over," Sophia proclaimed.

"You know you're at least a little bit curious," Zed responded, casting her a lascivious glance.

"Never have been, never will be," Sophia said, those pert lips pursed as she delivered an arch look.

Curious how she never answered his question. If their cook had seen members of the Stockyard lurking around and Sophia was talking to strangers, that strengthened his suspicions. Were the Outlaws getting baited into a trap?

Leo glanced at Tuck, only for their gazes to catch. The man's dark eyes heated with a tenderness that should've made him queasy. Yet instead, his heart beat a little faster, and the fluttering in his chest threatened to have him floating away. Tucker Hennings was the sort of steadfast man who still had his ex pining for him years after they'd broken up, yet he focused all of his attention Leo's way.

He should be dissuading him. Hell, he should've never come here in the first place.

Instead, he winked and blew him a kiss.

Tuck shook his head, the earnest grin doing something stupid to Leo's insides. Clearly, he was catching the flu.

"Finish up your dinner," Javier advised everyone. He'd been easy to pick out as the ringleader in a second, with his oiled beard and mustache, booming voice, and stage presence in spades. "Then report over to the main tent—it'll be showtime before you know it."

"You have no idea how good it feels not to have to report over there," Tuck murmured from beside him. One moment he'd been across the room, and now the man stood right next to him, his lips close enough to brush against the shell of Leo's ear. Not like he should've been surprised. Tuck and Alanna were the main stealth operators for the Outlaws.

"Rub it in, why don't you," Zed said, lobbing a lazy punch at Tuck's shoulder as he ambled by. "Don't be a stranger, Ace."

Leo arched a brow. "Are you going to explain the Ace thing? It sounds like a mutant variant of Superdog."

Tuck snorted. "Just my performer name. Mutant Superdog sounds way more fun."

Sophia stepped in front of Tuck, running her fingers along his forearm. "I feel like I barely got to talk to you. Come visit again?" she said, a slight note of flirtation in her voice. No wonder Tuck had brought him as a buffer.

"We'll gladly stop by for another dinner," Tuck said, taking the opportunity to slide his arm around Leo's shoulders and draw him in tight. The sad part was, Leo barely had to pretend to enjoy slinking all up against the man's solid warmth. Sophia's dark eyes flicked to Leo and an imperceptible flinch flashed there. That wasn't the answer she'd been fishing for.

However, was it just garden-variety jealousy or something more sinister?

Tuck leaned in and pressed his lips against Leo's neck, which caused a shiver to run down his spine as the sensual gesture had his cock waking up. He preened a little under all the attention Tuck doled out to him. He didn't wonder for a second what Tuck Hennings would be like to date—he was the sort of guy whose focus eclipsed anything else in the room.

Basking in his warmth would be like reentering sunlight after being locked away—an experience Leo knew intimately.

But after undergoing the extreme, the loss of that focus would be devastating. And he didn't have enough of a heart to risk pieces of it.

"Thanks for entertaining me," Leo said, giving Sophia a wink before Tuck ushered him onto the next people to whom they were making their round of good-byes. He bobbed his head and smiled at person after person, his focus lingering on Sophia in his peripheral. She'd already started striding away, a frown on her lips as she headed toward the tent's exit.

Before she left, one of the women stopped her, a serious look on her face. The two started an intense discussion that piqued Leo's interest. However, before he could start attempting to lip read, Tuck drew his attention.

"Ready to head out?" he asked, reaching down to thread his fingers through Leo's like they'd done heading in. Sure, they were just playing a part here, but Tuck probably didn't understand how monumental this was.

Leo had never held anyone's hand. Ever.

Definitely not either of his parents'.

He'd barely had any friends, so no dice there either.

And he'd never had a relationship.

He swallowed hard at the sense of intimacy slamming into his chest hard. There was far more of it in this simple touch than he'd ever experienced during any sex he'd ever had.

Leo managed to unlock his jaw to respond. "Yeah, let's go," he said. They ambled over toward Tuck's Audi in a surprisingly comfortable silence despite the awareness buzzing through Leo at the way their fingers remained intertwined even after they'd left the tent behind.

"What's on the agenda tonight?" he broke the silence to ask, needing to ignore the electricity sparking through his veins right now. "Another dramatic break-in? How about chasing down one of the Stockyard crews?"

Tuck let out a long exhale. "Grif benched me—I'm running point for the rest of this job since my shoulder's busted up. Figured visiting here as often as possible will help me make sure the troupe's safe."

Guilt twisted him up in knots. Tuck would've never been in that compromising spot if he hadn't pushed them toward going to the Stockyard warehouse last night. "Should I be helping out, then?"

"That's up to you," he said as they stopped in front of his car. "They're targeting Reynauld's apartment next, so Scar can jump in if needed. Last night was a lot more than you're used to—no one blames you if you want to step away now."

"Please," Leo said, forcing his voice to remain light. "You'll have to work a lot harder to scare me away, Hennings." He'd come closer than ever before to the

Stockyard and getting to Craig Baldwin. Leo couldn't let that go now, even if he wanted to.

He suddenly realized that they were standing in front of Tuck's car with their hands still pressed together. Tuck was inches away from him, close enough to kiss, and Leo licked his lips, wanting to taste him, to memorize the feel of him, a desire that was completely foreign.

He should be running in the opposite direction, and yet no part of him wanted to.

Leo leaned forward and brushed his lips against Tuck's.

Tuck let out a low groan against his mouth, the noise rippling through Leo as the man deepened the kiss.

During one moment, it was the tentative caress of lips, and in the next, the kiss turned into tongues, teeth, and gasping breaths. Leo sank into the taste of him as rich and heady as the heat that combusted between them. He gripped the front of Tuck's shirt to stabilize himself, his knees growing weak seconds into this kiss. He didn't bother to restrain his moans, loving the way Tuck slipped into command and devoured him like he'd been doing this for years.

He'd kissed a thousand times before, but they'd all been for one purpose—for a spin in the sheets, some fireworks that'd be gone before the sun rose.

However, this—he couldn't pretend this was for anything but sheer want.

This man had intrigued him in a way no one else

had ever managed, and to make it worse, he didn't push.

If he'd tried, Leo could've just shut him down and run away.

But instead, Tuck had to be all patient and sexy, luring him in with those small smirks and giving him the space he needed.

Tuck's hand returned to what felt like his favorite spot along Leo's hip as he gripped him tightly there, drawing their groins together. Leo surrendered to the bliss rolling through him in waves that tangled with the newfound warmth in his chest that he sure as hell didn't know what to do with. This kiss was scorching but as languid as a summer day—unhurried, without agenda, simply a way to enjoy each other's taste and feel.

Leo's mind dizzied with the power of their connection. These were sparks he'd never experienced in his life before. No one innocent could understand his upbringing, but he didn't want anything to do with people as terrible as the Stockyard either. Yet Tuck and the Outlaws bridged the two extremes on either end of the grey territory he waded, and all too fast, he'd felt an understanding amongst them he'd struggled to find anywhere else.

Tuck took one step forward, then another, guiding Leo so his back pressed against the car as he continued to kiss him like they were sailing along the highway with no exits in sight—all open asphalt and a horizon full of promise. A slight chill in the air nipped at his ears, the contrast making the heat of their kisses even more incendiary. Tuck's stubble brushed against his skin, and his lips grew tender as they lost themselves in the motion, breaking for breath that was fast coming in ragged pants.

Tuck finally pulled back to look into Leo's eyes, his feverish and full of the same longing and want thudding through Leo at a rampant pace. "Should we take this to your place?"

Leo's brows drew together on reflex, his mind moving a pace slower, drunk on lust. To his place—to fuck. He didn't invite the guys he fucked to his apartment, but apparently, he was breaking all sorts of rules with Tucker Hennings.

"Yeah, let's go," was all he said, his voice husky.

A second later, Tuck was pulling away from him, and Leo already regretted the separation from that glorious heat and muscle.

"What are we waiting for, then?" Tuck asked, looping around to the driver's side of the car. He flashed a handsome-as-hell smile and slipped inside.

Leo tugged the door open and joined him, settling against the comfortable cushion. The car smelled herbal, like sage and rosemary, the same scent that lingered around Tuck's room as well. Within seconds, the car started up, and Tuck peeled out of the circus grounds like a man on a mission.

Tension buzzed between them, growing headier with each inhale Leo took, and the idea of bringing this man home, of tasting him again—fuck, he couldn't get enough. All of the desire tangled with the guilt inside him over pushing the visit to the Stockyard, over the secret he was keeping. If Sophia was plotting anything sinister, he needed to protect Tuck because the guy clearly had blinders on when it came to her.

"Did you find out anything more about what's going on?" Leo asked. He'd been paying attention when Tuck started asking Margo questions, even as he'd stuffed his face. While Tuck claimed it was just a visit to his old family, he'd clearly been sleuthing as much as Leo had been, even if both of them had different concerns.

Tuck slipped onto the highway and picked up speed, the surroundings hurtling by. "The Stockyard's definitely keeping an eye on them," he admitted, his tone terse. "Which means we need to be careful. Any wrong moves could end in the troupe getting hurt again."

"Why does Reynauld want to keep them under his thumb so badly?" Leo asked. The question had been plaguing him for a while. While the circus troupe was probably a valuable commodity, hiring the Stockyard cost some serious cash. There had to be something else going on behind the scenes, but so far, the only person pinging his radar was Sophia.

Tuck let out a ragged sigh. "That's what I'd like to know too. Twilight Circus has been a solid fixture for a long while, but we're not the most profitable venture on his roster. Does Reynauld just want ironclad control over all his enterprises?"

Leo licked his lips. "And there couldn't be someone in the troupe involved?" He braced himself the moment the question hit the air, expecting the resistance.

Tuck's shoulders tightened. "I don't want to believe any of them would be involved," he admitted, thrusting a little harder on the gas pedal. The Audi zipped forward even faster across the highway. "But I haven't been a part of the troupe in years. I don't know everyone there anymore, and even the people I grew up with have probably changed."

Like Sophia. Leo didn't voice his thoughts aloud, though, even if he wanted to. Out of everyone in the troupe Tuck still trusted, Sophia was clearly high on his list. After all, he was risking himself to help her in the first place. A slight stirring of jealousy crept through his veins. Even after breaking up and all of their years apart, Tuck still gave his loyalty to this woman.

Leo couldn't even imagine that sort of devotion from anyone.

And yet, when Tuck looked at him with those intense eyes, a warmth in them Leo was unfamiliar with, he couldn't help but yearn.

The surroundings grew familiar, the beat-up corner store signs, the lines of rowhomes, and the gutted stone church a block away. Tuck found a spot along the street and pulled in.

Leo's heart beat a little harder. Was he actually going through with this?

He'd always fucked guys and left. Always. Yet not only had he given Tuck another chance, but now they were contemplating a third… at his place. His tongue dried, and the invitation to come up got stuck in his mouth.

Tuck turned in his seat to face him, the shadows sharpening his elegant nose, the dip of his cupid's bow, the black hair curling across his forehead and licking around his ears. The lust percolating through Leo's veins was nothing new, but the sharp feeling expanding in his chest was.

Before Leo could open his mouth, Tuck's phone rang.

Tuck glanced down, his brows furrowed, and he answered the call.

Leo watched as Tuck's expression morphed from concern to shock. His stomach dropped.

"I'll be right there," Tuck said, his tone strained. He jammed his phone back into his pocket with enough force that he almost ripped the pocket. "Fuck!"

The raw curse resonated through the car. Leo didn't dare breach the silence.

Tuck looked up at him, his dark eyes helpless. "Sophia and Javier's caravan…."

"What's going on?" Leo asked, giving him the nudge.

"Someone set it on fire."

CHAPTER 17

FOR THE SECOND TIME TONIGHT, TUCK PULLED UP AT THE circus grounds.

Except this time, the fire trucks and flashing lights were a clear indicator that all wasn't right. The show wouldn't be going on this evening. Not after this.

He white-knuckled the steering wheel, staring at the clouds of smoke that billowed around the caravans. His stomach lurched, the memories threatening to pull him under at the familiar acrid scent.

Tuck had dropped Leo off at his apartment, all thoughts of their evening plans forgotten as he'd alerted the Outlaws and looped back around from the way he'd come. Had a member of the Stockyard been lurking around the circus grounds while he'd been there? Had they recognized him and Leo from their recon job at the warehouse? Too many questions muddled his mind, but he wouldn't get any answers in here.

This time when he stepped out of his car, the warm

feelings from before didn't trickle on in. No, instead the panic gripped him by the throat, stealing his breath.

Sophia and Javi hadn't been inside the caravan when it had gotten torched. That was the one solace he clung to, even as the violation of the act crawled under his skin. Javier's caravan had been a haven for everyone in the troupe, whether they needed a friendly ear and some advice or simply someone to sit with them through their struggles. The plush velvet cushions, the ornate glass ornaments dangling from the ceiling, the countless paintings and notes he'd kept from everyone as they grew up—all gone.

They hadn't just lost a caravan, a home. They'd lost the Twilight Circus's refuge.

Tuck approached, his throat growing thick as he struggled to ignore the burn behind his eyes that had nothing to do with the smoke.

The troupe had congregated a bit away from the caravans, and the loud sobs carried through the laden air, even from here. Tuck stopped still at the sight. The spot where Javier's old caravan had been was now a mess of creaking, charred beams and thick, oily smoke. The smell was noxious, nauseating, and brought him back to *that* day. And Javier's caravan hadn't been the only one—others had been collateral damage, half burnt, sections of their wooden frames gaping and open.

His former family had gathered together en masse, Margo collapsing against Frederick's shoulder, Hernando helping carry furniture out of one of the partially damaged caravans along with several other people he didn't know. Javier stood in the middle of the fray with the firemen, conducting the scene with the assuredness he'd always possessed, even in the wake of this tragedy. Sophia crouched on the ground, tears streaking her face. Zed leaned over her, and Amelia had joined them, resting a hand on Sophia's back. Linc moved from one member to the next, checking in to see who needed help.

Tuck's fingers numbed as he approached his former family.

Sophia looked up, her expressive eyes glossed with tears. Something snapped within him at seeing his childhood best friend so devastated.

"Hey, I'm here," he murmured, sinking to the ground beside her. "Tell me what I can do to help."

"Thanks, man," Zed murmured, his voice gruff, and Amelia shifted back to give them some space. Tuck slipped an arm around Sophia, who devolved into a fresh round of sobs. He glanced up to meet Zed's gaze and saw a somber respect in the man's eyes.

Tuck swallowed hard, trying to suppress the way his skin was crawling at the clouds of charred smoke, the scent thick enough to choke on. He focused on Sophia, squeezing her tight. This loss wasn't going to just affect her, though—the entire troupe would feel this.

They might wander from city to city, but those caravans were their homes—the tethers they clung to.

And they'd already lost so much.

Tuck wouldn't allow them to lose any more.

Tuck had barely slept overnight. He'd spent most of the midnight hours at the circus, helping his old troupe sort through the wreckage of their caravans. They'd figured out temporary sleeping arrangements until they'd be able to start rebuilding, but anything in Javi and Sophia's caravan was lost.

Scar tapped him on the shoulder, concern in his eyes. "You sure you're okay?"

Tuck bobbed his head, tugging on the messenger bag at his side as he paused steps away from the door. While the rest of the Outlaws scoped out Reynauld's apartment in preparation for the heist, Tuck had a stop of his own to make. He'd filled them all in over breakfast and then texted Leo the information. The amount of consideration from Leo surprised him with the way the man seemed to know when to push and when to let things go.

He'd realized from the moment he met Leo, though, that he was something special, a truth he'd come to see more and more of as they got to know each other better. If only he'd be able to hold onto whatever was blooming between them.

"I'll be fine," Tuck said, his voice still a little raspy. After the events of last night, he needed to stop Reynauld Industries. Stop the Stockyard. It had gone on long enough. Scar nodded in understanding, and at that, Tuck exited the penthouse. He descended by the elevator to where he'd parked last night, and minutes later, he hit the road and headed for the apartment in the South Side he only visited once in a long while.

After seeing the flames and the wreckage last night, he needed the reassurance that she was still alive.

Even if her existence could barely be considered as much more than just that.

Tuck pulled up in front of what was supposed to be a park, the metal fencing half rolled and patchy, the spot of green mixed with asphalt and mostly dead. The apartment building was a weary gray, and the windows had bars along them, even on the upper floors. He grabbed the bag he'd brought and approached the entrance. Tuck didn't bother trying the buzzer, just pushed the rusted door in. The scent of mildew and rotting wood barraged his senses.

He'd offered to get her out of here, but she fit with this decrepit place in a way he didn't want to understand. The steps creaked as Tuck ascended, his fingertips numbed like they'd been last night. Visiting always made him feel like his skin was being flayed, yet he couldn't seem to sever those threadbare ties.

And after last night, he needed the reminder of his past. Though whether he was soothing or aggravating the raw pain in his chest, he wasn't sure. He just couldn't shake the impulse to come here today.

When he reached the second door on the second floor, he didn't bother knocking. Chances were, she was home and wouldn't answer. Tuck pushed the door open, unlocked like everything else in this building seemed to be, and the odor of cheap vodka assaulted his senses. The studio apartment was dim to the point that she almost sat in darkness, but he made out the skin and bones figure pressed into the recliner.

Tuck swallowed hard, pushing the door shut behind him. "Hey, Mom."

She barely startled at his words, but the faint movement from her told him she was awake. Awake, asleep, drunk, sober—he couldn't tell the difference anymore.

Ever since Dad died and she'd started drinking.

Ever since the accident that cost her everything she had left….

He turned on a lamp as he stepped closer, which cast the place in a sallow yellow light. His mother flinched, her dark black waves clinging to her oily skin. The burn marks were always visible, ropy scars along the right side of her face that trailed down across her entire torso. Her posture had contorted over time from her attempts to hide the scars or keep them in shadows, and the shift from the bright, vivacious woman who starred in his childhood memories to the husk who hunched before him made his heart hurt.

The drinking had spirited her away the moment dad died.

"Tuck," she slurred, her voice thick—most likely from a combination of sleep and booze.

He swallowed hard as he stepped in closer, bringing over the bag of groceries he'd bought. All non-perishables, which had been a good decision because based on the foul stench coming from her kitchen, she'd let things begin to rot in there. Food wasn't the only thing rotting in this house. He winced as he reached his mother's side, the wet Band-Aid smell of unwashed skin mingling with the heavy lidocaine cream she used for the burns.

Once upon a time, Felicity Hennings had been the best fire juggler in the Twilight Circus. Except two things never mixed well—inebriation and fire play. After Dad died and Mom started arriving to shows drunk, the inevitable had happened.

Javier and the others had offered to help with her care, with the deep depression she'd sunk into, but Felicity's performing days were over. Tuck had started feeling trapped by the circus life at that point, and the losses combined with the intense med bills pushed him out the door.

The charred scent of the caravan still haunted him as if he hadn't washed and changed before coming over. All he could think of when he'd been helping pull belongings from the wreckage, though, was the woman who sat before him now with her lower lip quivering and her eyes unfocused.

This close, he could see an infection brewing on her arms, the rotting scent strong enough to gag and the red inflammation bright. Tuck swallowed the lump in his throat. He didn't visit as often as he should, but every time he showed up to see the woman who'd loved him, who'd raised him, like this—it broke something inside him.

"You haven't been cleaning yourself," he

murmured, not as a question because the signs were all evident.

"Mmm fine," his mother slurred, the words hard for her to get out.

Tuck's chest ached. Why he'd thought coming here might help was beyond him. It was as if he wanted to inflict as much emotional pain on himself as possible. Just... after seeing the way the fire had destroyed the caravan, the reminder had been too strong of the night Felicity had burned herself with the flash paper she planned on using for her next trick.

And part of him wanted the reminder that she was still here. That even though she'd faded away over time, she wasn't six feet under like his father.

"All right, Ma," he said, reaching down to scoop her out of the wrinkled recliner she was glued to. The fragile woman barely weighed anything at this point, just bones and skin, and Tuck tried to ignore the tightness in his chest at the realization of how much she'd wasted away. "Let's get you clean."

He hoisted her up and carried her over to the bathroom that might as well have been a closet. The tub had once been white but turned a dingy grey from disuse and not getting cleaned. Nothing in this apartment had been cleaned for a long time, but he couldn't force his mother to rouse herself from the hold this sickness claimed on her mind. He'd tried to get her placed in care, offered to hire help, to get her put in a different home.

Those fights had gotten ugly, and each time, Tuck had ended up dropping the subject.

The woman seemed determined to drink herself to death, a grim reality he still wrestled with.

He helped her shrug out of the stained dress that looked more like an oversized T-shirt and started the water before lowering her in. The woman needed a nurse for care at this point with the amount her burn scars got infected, but she'd fought him tooth and nail on the idea. On a normal day, she resisted this sort of assistance, but with how unfocused her eyes were, she was barely there.

The water pooled around her, already turning a shade darker from the filth coming off her. Tuck swallowed back the gag that rose in his throat at seeing her decline. He reached in his pocket for his phone, about to place it on the sink behind him.

A text from Leo lit up the screen.

Hope you're doing okay.

His phone was filled with texts from the other Outlaws asking what had happened, if he needed anything, and gratitude choked him. However, tonight, there was only one place he wanted to be.

Can I come over later? Tuck texted out to Leo.

A moment later his phone buzzed with the reply. *Only if we're resuming where we left off.*

His lips twitched. He could imagine the insinuation dripping from those words. The heat in his chest at the promise in Leo's words bolstered him. He put his phone down on the sink and lowered himself next to the tub.

"Come on," he murmured as he began to clean out the rash on her arm. "We'll make this better."

The visits made him die a little each time, a reminder that he was applying salve to a bleeding wound, one that would eventually take her in the end.

CHAPTER 18

Ever since Leo got home from work, tension simmered through him.

The hours had moved at an achingly slow pace from the moment he'd invited Tuck over.

Stupid. The whole thing was fucking stupid. He should be distancing himself from Tuck, forcing space between them, and what was he doing instead? Inviting the guy over to fuck. Again.

To make matters worse, a lot of activity buzzed over the Stockyard's systems today. He'd been tracking them ever since he'd hacked into their main server the other night. He hadn't seen any alerts or obvious code indicating they'd been behind the burning of Sophia and Javier's caravan, but with the way the troupe members mentioned seeing guys lurking around, it was guaranteed the Stockyard was the culprit.

Leo stared at his computer screen. He'd hunched

down at his desk once he got home, desperate for distraction.

Well, the Stockyard provided.

His gaze snagged on an email that just went through—this one between Baldwin and the same anonymous sender that had appeared multiple times over the past month.

Mark Twain Park—Twilight.

Twilight Circus.

Convenient that they'd be meeting then. Leo worried his lower lip between his teeth. He needed to let the Outlaws know. His fingers flew over the keyboard as he copied the file, sending it to Scar. She'd know what to do with it. He fired off a quick text to Dan too, warning him that there was activity on the Stockyard's computer.

As for Tuck, he'd tell him in person.

A shiver ran through him at the idea of the man coming over here. Any hope of keeping his distance evaporated the moment he invited Tuck to his apartment. The place had been his sanctum for a long, long while—even Dan hadn't been there before, something he'd always been grateful his best friend didn't push. However, he hadn't hesitated to give Tuck his address the other night.

Leo didn't know what the hell to make of that. The incendiary chemistry between them was the sort of electric that drew his curiosity over and over. The same allure he felt when sitting behind a computer and deep diving into systems as Polonius, a sense of infinite opportunity within his grasp.

A knock sounded at his door, snapping him to attention.

Leo hopped out of his seat, regretting the fast movement after sitting hunched over like that for so long. His back twinged as he strode to the door while brushing down his shirt to smooth out the wrinkles.

When he swung the door open, the sight of Tucker Hennings had saliva pooling in his mouth.

Tuck had freshly showered, which was made clear by the way his simple black tee clung to his defined abs, and the tight traveler's pants he wore left little to the imagination. His defined ringlets were still damp, and the scent of vetiver wafted his way, all man and fucking delicious. When Tuck's warm gaze settled on him and his lips crooked into a half smile, Leo couldn't help how his heart lurched like an out-of-control car.

He lifted a bag before entering. "I come bearing gifts."

Leo stepped aside and snapped his mouth shut after realizing it was just hanging open. He didn't miss the detail that Tuck had a backpack slung over his shoulder. Clearly, someone was making presumptions about an overnight visit.

Yet another thing he didn't do.

The delicious smell coming from the bag hit him as Tuck strode by and walked over to the kitchen counter on the other side of his studio like he'd been here a thousand times before.

"You brought dinner?" Leo asked, his brows drawing together.

Tuck's eyes crinkled with his smile. "I figured you'd be hungry."

His traitorous stomach rumbled on cue. Still—he'd assumed Tuck would be over for a quick fuck. Adding in dinner somehow felt more intimate, which should send him screaming in the other direction. His shoulders froze, and he realized Tuck was watching him, his gaze observant.

"I can't have you fainting on me with what I have planned for later," Tuck added, his voice dripping with heat. Leo knew what he was doing, but he grabbed the lifeline anyway.

"Planning on riding me hard, Hennings?" Leo flirted, giving Tuck a scorching once-over.

Tuck's grin spread as he leaned against the counter. "Among other things."

The twinkle in Tuck's eye had him intrigued, but the fact that Leo hadn't eaten since lunch drew him over to the paper bag. He pulled out the two Styrofoam containers and cracked one open.

"Burgers from Iron Grill?" His heart stuttered. He ordered from the restaurant as often as possible—and only one person knew about that. However, the effort Tuck had gone to…. Goddamn. He swallowed the tightness in his throat, needing to lighten the mood. "I see Dan doesn't last under interrogation."

Tuck smirked. "What do you think?" He slunk over with effortless grace and snagged the other container.

"Though I shouldn't be surprised at what a fan of meat you are."

Leo arched a brow. "You calling me a slut, gorgeous? Because you're not wrong."

Tuck barked out a laugh before taking a bite of his burger. Leo hurried to do the same, as if his meal might evaporate if he didn't dive in. The juices dripped down his chin, and the salty flavors of cheddar and bacon exploded on his tongue. He wiped his mouth with the back of his hand. When he glanced up, Tuck's scorching gaze was locked onto him. Amusement danced in his chest, and he ran the tip of his tongue along his bottom lip nice and slow.

"How do you make eating a goddamn burger pornographic?" Tuck asked before chewing on a few fries. He dropped the bag from his shoulder to the floor, getting comfortable. And by some miracle, it wasn't freaking Leo out.

"It's a talent," he said. All too quickly, he polished off the burger, taking the time to lick each of his fingers afterwards.

Tuck let out a low groan while Leo gave his pointer finger an extra suck.

Leo's phone buzzed with a text from Dan, the reminder a splash of ice water on his libido. As much as he'd loved the sexy direction this night had been heading, Tuck deserved to hear what he'd learned up front.

"I already sent the info to Scar, but there's an update," Leo prefaced, his tone coming out serious. Tuck switched gears at once, his shoulders tensing on alert. Clearly, the guy had been having a less-than-thrilling experience with the bad-times brigade rolling in. Something Leo had only contributed to through all of this with his external agenda. "An email came through that makes it look like the Stockyard is meeting with Reynauld regarding your former troupe. Whether it's to change the parameters of the job, pay for another hit—whatever—they're going to meet up, and it can't spell good news for Twilight Circus."

Tuck tapped his finger along the counter, still leaning against it as he let out a slow breath. "I want to be there."

So did Leo—only not for the same reasons.

This was his chance at Craig Baldwin.

Except unlike last time, he wouldn't put Tuck at risk. Not for his agenda. As much as he wanted to deny it, the man had worked his way under Leo's skin and into his thoughts—and even worse, his hopes.

"Remind me to never complain about my life being too boring," Leo commented, needing to lighten the mood somehow. He leaned backward against his kitchen island, his legs almost bumping against Tuck's, who was facing him.

"Is this life so bad though?" Tuck asked. Despite the casual way he asked, the hint of gravity to the words had him wondering.

"My alt identity as Polonius should be enough of an indicator," Leo said dryly. "Clearly, I've got the same leaping-into-danger instinct as the rest of you crazies."

"When did that start for you?" Tuck asked, his dark eyes zeroing in on him.

Right, care and shares. This was where he made a comment about being raised by a pack of wolves or abducted by Skynet. A few laughs and he'd deflect by poking at something personal or better yet, stripping down to offer his mouth or his ass up.

"High school," Leo found himself saying instead. "I'd moved in with the foster family, and I couldn't reconcile myself to these people. So normal—family dinners, actually talking to each other, and a steadiness I'd never experienced. Like... the good sort of folks who'd show up to help if your car broke down."

"You can't just flip a switch and ignore the past." Tuck's gaze was serious, reflective. "When I left the troupe, I wouldn't have been able to leap into working a nine-to-five as a call operator."

"So, you ended up in another type of troupe—of thieves," Leo said, his heart thumping a little harder in his chest. He'd never expected to voice these thoughts out loud and for someone to understand him. Ever. "I didn't want to commit crimes like my folks did, but I couldn't seem to fit in along the straight and narrow either. I took to computers and thrived there."

"I had the feeling there was more to you," Tuck murmured, his voice filled with something deep that terrified Leo even as he longed for it all the same. "We're not as different as you think."

Leo swallowed hard. God, he wished. Except Tuck was a kind, loyal person raised by a loving, albeit unconventional, family. Leo was the fucked-up byproduct of two for-hire killers who inconveniently squirted out a spawn. Tuck was made for love, for commitment—Leo, for isolation.

"What pushed you to leave the circus?" Leo asked. For once, he wasn't deflecting. Part of him wanted to know what had marred the perfect family he'd witnessed back at the troupe dinner.

Tuck heaved a sigh. "That's a two-beer conversation."

"How about bourbon?" Leo responded. He stepped over to the counter where Tuck leaned and brushed by him, making sure their skin touched in the process. A sinful zing zipped right through him. He grabbed a bottle of Bulleit, unscrewed the cap, and passed it over to Tuck.

Tuck's defined lips quirked, and he took a swig before passing the bottle back over to him. Leo accepted, finding a spot along the counter next to him. Leo trailed his tongue along the rim and offered Tuck a wink to encourage him.

"My parents raised me in the circus, and I honestly loved growing up there," Tuck started. Leo swallowed a sip of bourbon, the smooth liquid burning down his throat while Tuck continued his story. "However, Dad died when I was a teenager—embolism. And after that, Mom may as well have died too. I was over there earlier today," he said, gesturing for the bottle again.

"Hence the need for a distraction tonight," Leo responded, putting two and two together. His heart pulsed hard in his chest at the thought that out of all the close connections the man had in his life, Tuck had reached out for him.

"Mom started drinking hard, which is something you can't fuck around with during a show. She was a fire juggler—you do the math. Between her early 'retirement' and the drinking problem that's never abated, I couldn't stay. Too many bad memories, and even a traveling circus can feel confining after a while. The same thing day after day surrounded by the same people. I needed out, so after Mom's accident, I left."

Even though the way Tuck outlined the words was cut and dry, his tone steady, Leo could see the pain flickering in his deep brown eyes. Leo's chest tightened. He might've lost his parents to jail, but that had been a fucking blessing—a way to start over and live the life he'd never gotten growing up with them.

However, had he really been living? Or just continuing the same game of survival he'd been drowning in his entire life?

Tuck's loss had been the sort to grieve, and yet the man wasn't shutting himself away from the world. No, he'd forged friendships and allowed people in again, even if they caused him more pain.

"So, the caravan fire...." Leo prompted, needing to slice through the quiet somehow. Anything to silence these surfacing thoughts.

"Reminded me far too much of another fire." Tuck attempted a smile that fell into a grimace far too fast.

The depth of the emotions churning in his eyes had Leo moving toward him before he could stop himself.

Leo slid a hand against Tuck's cheek, letting his thumb brush across his lower lip. "So, let's get to distracting then. Anything you want."

His heart thumped hard in his chest in reaction to the intimacy of the comforting gesture he was giving, the space between them buzzing with more than just lust.

"Anything?" Tuck lifted a brow, some of the despondency in his eyes filtering away, only to be replaced by scorching heat.

Leo's lips curled with his grin. "Am I going to regret offering that?" His cock started to grow a little harder in response to the proximity of this man, curiosity brimming inside him at the single word.

"Dinner wasn't the only thing I brought over," Tuck said, brushing past him to grab his backpack from where he'd dropped it on the floor. "After we fucked around with my aerial rig, I thought you might want to give something else a try."

Leo bit his lower lip, trying to ignore how his cock perked up at the memory of those silks wrapped around his hands and how he'd gripped them hard as he got rocked forward. Tuck unzipped the bag and tugged out a few cords of black rope.

Well, damn, his cock grew stiff as a fucking bat at the sight.

Tuck's gaze traveled down the length of Leo's body, stopping right at the erection tenting his goddamn pants. He smirked. "Well, that answers the question of whether you're interested."

"Depends," he said, his voice coming out low and husky. "You offering to tie me up and fuck me?"

"That's the hope," Tuck responded, standing close enough that his breath puffed against Leo's skin. Leo couldn't help but notice the way he wound the rope around his hands, testing the constraints. Fuck, that was hot.

Leo cocked a brow at him. "Then what are we waiting for?"

CHAPTER 19

The feel of the hemp rope in Tuck's hands loosened something inside him, a tension that'd been stretching tighter all day.

From the moment he'd first hooked up with Leo, he'd gotten the feeling the guy would be receptive to this—shibari wasn't something he played around with often. He wasn't about to start busting out ropes with a one-night stand, but he'd come to trust Leo in a way that surprised him. He'd only ever brought them out with long-term partners, but if he were honest, he'd been hoping for that outcome with Leo from the moment he realized what insane chemistry they had.

Leo might swear he was anti-commitment, but Tuck hadn't missed Dan's surprise when he'd mentioned a repeat. The man had already bent rules for him, softening in unexpected ways, and Tuck was willing to be patient. If what he suspected was correct, Leo avoided intimacy because he'd never known it—and that reality broke Tuck a little. Made him want to wrap the man up in his arms and never let go.

Leo led the way to his rumpled bed, and Tuck followed close behind.

By the time they'd crossed the room, Leo had stripped his shirt off and flung it to the ground. Tuck couldn't help but devour the sight as Leo's hands headed straight for his sweats, ready to drop those too. He was slender in the way that drew Tuck's attention—the exact sort of long limbs he loved to work with in trying different binds. The dusky rose nipples and the light brown happy trail leading to his waistband had Tuck salivating, and he couldn't wait any longer. He needed to feel this man under his hands.

Leo had just gotten his sweatpants hiked down to his thighs when Tuck closed the distance between them, crushing their mouths together.

Tuck swept his tongue inside, devouring the man in a hungry, feral kiss. Leo melted against his touch. There was a desperate need to Leo's movements, as if he was experiencing the headiness of these powerful feelings for the first time. As if he'd only skated on lust before now without the added dimensions to anchor all of those intense sensations. Leo stopped struggling with his sweatpants, clutching tight to Tuck's shirt instead, his erection nudging against Tuck's hip.

Tuck skimmed his fingers through Leo's thick hair, tugging a bit on the ends as he got a solid hold. Leo let out a thready moan. The sight of the caravans last night and the visit with his mother today had been twisting him up inside like tangled rope—confusing, conflicting emotions that had no proper place. Whenever he got like that, shibari offered the perfect outlet. A way to physically set those ropes in place with a beautiful symmetry he hoped to emulate.

He continued to ravage Leo's mouth, enjoying the smooth glide of their tongues, the sweet taste of him, like coffee and cream. Leo shimmied, and a moment later, he was kicking off his sweats—completely bare. A thrill rose inside Tuck at the realization.

As much as he wanted to feel the press of his skin against Leo's, he wanted to watch the hemp rope bite into his skin even more. He wanted to sink into Leo while he was restrained, his lithe body trembling for release.

Tuck drew back to steal a breath, and their noses brushed together, sending a tender warmth rushing through him. He was well past the point of no return when it came to the way he felt for this man. The promise there was undeniable, and if Leo was willing to take the risk, Tuck longed to give him everything he'd been missing out on.

"You keep kissing me like that, and I'm liable to come before you ever bind me up," Leo murmured against his mouth.

"We can't have that, can we?" Tuck responded, taking a step back. He didn't miss Leo's slow perusal and the way his gaze snagged on the rope in his hand. "Have you ever played with restraints before?"

Leo shrugged, leaning in to nip at Tuck's lower lip. "Just casually."

"You'll need a safeword, or at least the color system —green for all good, yellow for caution, and red for stop," Tuck said, running his palm down the front of Leo's torso, pausing to wrap his hand around that long cock and give it a tug. Precum smeared against his palm in the process, and he couldn't help but give him two more lazy strokes. "And I'll need to do check-ins. You'll need to snap your fingers. Have to make sure you're not losing sensation in the limbs."

Leo's tongue traced his lower lip as he bobbed his head in an eager nod. "Let's do color system. Where do you want me?"

"On your knees, beautiful," Tuck said. Heat scorched through him as Leo followed the command, dropping to the floor in one fluid movement. Fuck, it had been so long since he'd gotten to play with anyone.

And this wasn't just anyone. Leo's surrender was the sort of gift Tuck wouldn't be able to forget about. This was a man who had been given no reason to trust anyone, and who had walls a thousand feet tall, and yet here he kneeled, placing himself in Tuck's care. His chest squeezed tight at the thought.

"How flexible are you?" Tuck asked, feeding the rope across his palms until he clutched the bight, the tails falling down on either side.

Leo glanced back, his blue eyes smoldering. "As flexible as you need me to be."

"Bring your hands behind your back and reach for

your opposite elbows," Tuck commanded, already sinking into the familiar headspace he'd been longing for, a heady focus that silenced everything else. In this moment, all of the worries of the threat to his troupe, the Stockyard, and his mother faded into the background. Here and now, it was just him and Leo.

Here and now, he was in control.

Tuck crouched behind Leo, pressing a kiss into the dip between his shoulder and neck. He drew in a deep inhale of the man's scent, the rosewood cologne that lingered around him and seemed to travel straight to Tuck's cock. Lifting the rope up, he teased the length across Leo's skin, watching his entire body shiver at the sensation. His hands were behind his back, and his pretty cock hung heavy between his legs, the tip an angry red and dripping with precum. Tuck nearly salivated at the sight.

"You look stunning," Tuck whispered, his lips brushing against Leo's ear as he began to wind the first set of ropes around his forearms in a single column tie. The feel of the ropes beneath his fingers, the process of setting them in place had already cast a spell over him. A heady buzz settled across his skin, making it more sensitized, more aware. His cock ached from the confines of his pants, and the rhythm of the rope gliding across his fingers reminded him of the tranquility he'd only found while walking the tightrope.

All too quickly, he was wrapping the black rope around Leo's chest, loving the way it stood out against his smooth, light skin. Tuck brushed his thumb over one of Leo's nipples, enjoying the full-body shudder that rolled through him.

"Fuck," Leo moaned.

Tuck licked along the side of his neck, adoring how he twitched, even though his forearms were firmly behind him. "Check-in," he murmured.

Leo twitched his fingers behind his back. "Green."

When Tuck brought the column tie to wrap around the rope along his torso, Leo had begun shifting, trying to get friction on his cock. Fuck, he couldn't blame him. Tuck continued with the meditative motions of wrapping the rope around Leo, the stress melting away from him and transmuting into pure, unadulterated desire. He was beyond turned on, aware of every hitch of Leo's breath, the delicious way he smelled, the decadent way he tasted.

Tuck needed to sink into him more than he needed his next breath.

He wound the black ropes around the middle again, completing the box tie. A sense of completion stirred inside him, even as his cock ached hard.

Tuck pushed up from the ground to soak in the whole picture.

Leo kneeled on the ground, the black ropes wrapped twice around his front, his shoulders pulled back with the tie around his forearms. From behind, the thick bindings were fucking gorgeous. The man looked like sin all tied up, and the effects of the restraints were clear in his expression. His cheeks were flushed, and his blue eyes had taken on the dreamy hue that signaled he was letting go—something he could guarantee the guy never did on his own.

"How do you feel, beautiful?" Tuck murmured as he crouched in front of him.

"Like I'm high as fuck," Leo responded, a lazy smile rising to his lips.

"Ready to feel even better?" Tuck asked, running a palm over his erection.

Leo's expression sharpened with lust. "Hell yes."

Tuck wrapped his hands around Leo's hips. "Let's get you up."

"Shouldn't need help with that," Leo joked even as he rose to his feet. Tuck scanned the room, his gaze snagging on the microfiber couch a few feet away. With careful steps, he guided Leo toward the back of the couch. Once Leo's knees bumped against it, Tuck directed him down, bending him over.

"Fuck, I need to get inside you," Tuck said, his voice hoarse with lust. He burned for this man in a way he wasn't used to, with the sort of sparks that could either create something beautiful or end in utter destruction.

Leo's chest was pressed against the top of the couch, his ass thrust out behind him and those long legs on display. The miles of creamy skin tempted Tuck, especially with the black ropes binding his arms back, making Leo ready for the taking.

"Please." Leo's voice came out strained. He glanced back, his lashes looking even darker in contrast with the intensity in his bright blues. Strands of his hair stuck up from where Tuck had plunged his fingers through it, and the flush along his cheeks made him look debauched.

Tuck swallowed, his throat suddenly dry. He tugged down on his zipper, the *shiick* echoing through the room. His pants rustled as he ditched them, and a second later, his tee was joining the pile. He reached down to snag a condom and lube from his pocket before settling himself behind Leo.

"God, the way you look," Tuck breathed out. He brought his thumb between those plump ass cheeks and swiped the tip against Leo's hole. A loud moan came from Leo as he tilted his hips toward the couch as if trying to get friction anywhere he could. Not like it was possible with the way his front side pressed against the couch, the man helpless to touch himself or do anything but ride Tuck's cock.

Tuck squeezed the base of his dick, trying to keep himself from coming at the thought.

He rolled the condom on and slicked his length with lube, the rising need a steady thump inside him. Leo looked gorgeous bent over the couch like this, but Tuck's focus zeroed in on the ropes binding him up, the trust the man placed in him—the gift he'd never expected from Leo Kennedy.

Tuck traced around Leo's tight pucker with two fingers one, two times before sliding them inside.

"Oh God," Leo moaned, trying to thrust back even though he could barely move. Tuck pumped his fingers in and out, brushing against the spot that caused Leo's whole body to tense with pure euphoria. He continued to tease him, checking in on his hands as he prepped him. Precum dripped down Tuck's cock, several drops splattering on the floor. Fuck, he wasn't going to last long once he got inside this man.

"Can't wait any longer," Tuck grunted out, barely able to form sentences with the desire flooding through him. He withdrew his fingers and a moment later was lining up his cock and slowly sinking into that tight heat. Inch by inch, he filled Leo deeper, and the man's noises grew loud enough to shake the walls.

Tuck gripped Leo's hips tightly to brace himself, summoning flashbacks of their first time together.

At last, he entered him completely, fully seated inside the man. The scorching heat, the tightness—it was enough to drive him to delirium. Tuck sucked in a shaky breath as he ran his palms across Leo's arms and then his hips in soothing strokes. Leo let out a whimper in response, the sound reaching inside Tuck's chest and gripping tight.

"Please," Leo begged, his voice thready with emotion. "Fuck me."

Tuck stroked along his arms again, running his fingertips along the beautiful bindings keeping Leo in place. He could feel Leo trembling beneath him—clearly, something was surfacing, which wasn't uncommon with rope. However, he'd never gotten this response from a bottom before, and he couldn't help but feel the connection between them tightening like the tie he'd placed around Leo.

"I've got you, sweetheart," he murmured before resting his palms on Leo's hips.

Tuck gripped him tight and pulled back, only to sink in deep again. Leo let out a gasping breath as he drove home, and Tuck began to move more, finding his rhythm. That felt so damn good—too good. He could feel his balls tightening already, the need for release imminent after the hell of a day he'd had, the heightened levels of arousal from playing with rope, and the way he'd begun to fall for Leo. The scent of sweat mingled with Leo's rosewood cologne, and Tuck basked in it as he fucked into him harder.

The couch creaked under their movements, but Tuck held tightly onto Leo since the man was bound up for his pleasure. Breaths rasped out of Leo, desperate noises and long, undulating moans that echoed through the studio apartment. The man was as loud and vivacious in bed as in his daily life, and Tuck wanted to savor every precious drop of that energy, that spark.

Tuck thrust inside Leo over and over again, sweat prickling across his temple. The slap of their skin echoed through the room, and Leo's body grew flush beneath him, making the stark black of the ropes stand out even more. Tuck checked in again, reassured by the twitch of his fingers before he continued to fuck into him hard, the pressure beginning to build to unbearable levels.

The way they connected here—this wasn't just a casual screw.

As he sank into Leo, Tuck felt a serenity he rarely

reached, an understanding from a kindred soul. He'd grown up in a close family and continued to surround himself with one in the Outlaws, but he was the quieter one, the reserved one. Yet Leo seemed to unlock a deeper part of him with little to no effort, and that was beyond rare.

His breaths came out stuttered as he picked up his pace, needing to feel the sting as their bodies slammed together.

"Fuck, fuck, fuck," Leo gasped out. "I'm going to come."

A second later, Leo's hole pulsed around his cock as his cum splattered against the back of the couch.

The tight squeeze was enough to tug Tuck over the edge. His balls drew up, and the release swept over him with a blinding force. His load shot out of him as he surged forward, buried deep inside Leo, their sweaty skin glued together. Bliss radiated through him, one wave after another that snared his breath. Tuck's cock pulsed with another tiny aftershock of orgasm, pumping any remaining fluid into the condom.

For a moment, he just stayed still there, his softening dick buried deep in Leo's ass as he rediscovered his equilibrium after the way the experience had knocked him off-kilter. He'd needed a distraction tonight, but Leo had become so much more than that. The man had somehow become a safe place, a solace at the end of a long, shitty day. His heart stuttered in his chest, a warmth spreading from deep inside out to his fingers, his toes.

"Let me get you out of the ropes," Tuck murmured, slowly pulling out and beginning to undo the tie. Leo rose to standing even though his legs had started shaking hard and his arms trembled. Tuck made quick work of unwinding the ropes from him, his motions deft and practiced even as his mind remained fuzzy and his body pleasantly buzzed in the wake of the explosive orgasm.

The moment the black ropes pooled onto the ground, Tuck got his hands around Leo who was still shaking, and he held him upright. He couldn't help but trace the marks the ropes had left on his skin, as if their time together remained branded on his body. Leo had a hazed look in his eyes, the crash after playing like that probably more intense than he was used to.

"Come on," Tuck said as he guided Leo to the opposite side of the couch and helped him curl up there. Tuck stepped into the kitchen to wet a towel and grab a glass of water before returning to Leo's side. He cleaned up their cum before grabbing one of the throw blankets from the side of the couch.

Tuck slipped in behind Leo and brought the blanket over both of them. He pressed a kiss to the top of Leo's head.

"What are you doing?" Leo asked, his voice a little slurred still. Genuine confusion wrinkled his features of the sort that made Tuck's heart ache.

Tuck reached over for the water he'd placed on the coffee table and brought it to Leo's lips. Leo took a few sips before settling down with his back pressed against

Tuck's chest. Tuck skimmed his fingers through Leo's hair over and over again, watching as the man's lashes fluttered and a contented sigh slipped from his lips.

"I'm taking care of you," Tuck murmured, resting his chin on the top of Leo's head as he wrapped his arms around the man a little tighter, as if worried he'd vanish.

With the track record they had, Leo very well might.

"I'm staying with you tonight," Tuck said, his tone firm. After playing like that, he wasn't willing to let Leo rush off somewhere—not like he'd be able to dart off as easily as he usually did now that they were in his own house.

"Mmm," Leo responded, his lashes fluttering as his eyes closed. A moment later, Leo's breaths evened out with sleep and his body stilled.

Tuck leaned back against the couch, holding tight to the man in his arms.

Tomorrow might bring an empty spot on the couch beside him, more threats to his old troupe, or a confrontation with the Stockyard, but tonight, he'd just bask in the comfort Leo had offered, enjoying the warm man plastered against him who'd given him his most precious gift. His trust.

Tuck swallowed hard. The more he got to know this man, the harder and harder it was to imagine letting go.

CHAPTER 20

Leo paced around the penthouse, tugging on the cuff of his long-sleeved black shirt.

Craig Baldwin was supposed to meet with Marcus Reynauld tonight.

The target he'd been looking to eliminate for years, the specter in his nightmares, would be out in the open.

Except he didn't know if he'd be able to accomplish what he needed to after last night. The way he'd collided with Tuck, how he'd let the man sleep over—and Leo himself hadn't tried to bolt—it was all new terrain, but one thing had become abundantly clear.

He was in over his head with Tucker Hennings.

"Are you sure you want to go tonight?" Dan asked for the thousandth time. He glanced at Grif who was tugging on his shitkickers. "Wouldn't it be better if Leo stayed home? What if someone recognizes him?"

Leo clenched his jaw. Dan just wanted to look out

for him, but if he got his way, he'd thwart the one shot Leo had at Baldwin.

"I started this job, and I want to see it through," Leo said firmly before Grif could speak up.

Grif shrugged. "We're all just doing rounds through the park. The guy heading there tonight wasn't at the warehouse when Leo and Tuck went—we already confirmed that."

Dan heaved a sigh and shot a worried glance at Leo whose heart twisted at the sight. Leo reached over and placed a hand on Dan's shoulder, trying to ignore the sweatiness of his own palm. "Hey, I go through the same thing whenever you're on a job," Leo reassured him.

Dan worried his lower lip. "Fine. Just stay close to Tuck and don't get shot."

Leo couldn't help his grin. "Like I need a reason to get close to Tuck." Even as he talked about the man like he normally would, he couldn't help the thrum in his chest at the idea of how many layers they'd each peeled back in such a short time.

"What's that?" Tuck's voice carried from the other room as he approached without a creak to his footsteps. The man could be damn near invisible when he wanted.

Leo arched a brow and cast him a scorching look. Damn Tucker Hennings for looking so hot in the stretchy black pants and form-fitting black shirt he wore. Leo remembered the feel of every one of those ridged muscles under his fingertips. His body buzzed with awareness at Tuck's proximity, the memories of last night surging to the fore in a dizzying rush.

Leo had never experienced a high like that during sex before, and between the overwhelming sensations and the tender way Tuck had stroked him, tears had leaked down his face unbidden. He thought he'd be crippled by overwhelming shame in the morning after breaking down, but something about curling up with Tuck had soothed the rawness he'd been left with in the aftermath.

And waking up in his arms had been a revelation.

"Dan's just telling me I need to plaster myself all over your body," Leo drawled, his voice dripping with insinuation. Dan rolled his eyes, and Grif smirked.

"Sounds like the right plan to me," Tuck responded in a serious tone even though his eyes twinkled.

"All right, but who's actually going to be doing their jobs out there?" Alanna said. If he hadn't already gotten to know her, he might be offended by the blunt, caustic way she'd dropped the comment, but he'd realized in a short span of time that was just part of her internal coding.

"We're obviously relying on you do to all of the work." Grif dripped sarcasm as he slipped a pistol into the band around his calf.

"With great power comes great responsibility," Scar intoned, even though her eyes danced. She sat behind her desktop at the ready, her dark, chin-length hair styled today and pink gloss on her lips even though she still wore the same oversized hoodie as usual.

"Because Uncle Ben was clearly referring to mouthy criminals when he stated that gem," John added. He lay sprawled out on the sofa with his hands behind his head.

For all intents and purposes, Tuck and Leo should've been the ones staying behind—not John, Dan, and Scarlet. However, after the caravan fire, Grif had caved, allowing Tuck and Leo to patrol the far perimeter while he and Alanna took the park itself. As long as they skulked around in the background, they wouldn't be pinging alarms or getting themselves into further trouble.

Except if Leo got a shot on Craig Baldwin, he was going to damn well take it.

"You ready?" Tuck asked him, skimming his fingers across Leo's lower back.

A shiver rolled through him, this time having nothing to do with the sinful way that felt. Even though his life's goal for as long as he could remember had been to take down Craig Baldwin to be truly free from his past, he couldn't risk Tuck again. If anything happened to him…. Leo swallowed hard and offered a fake smile. "As ready as I'll ever be."

THE SUN WAS CLOSE TO SETTING BY THE TIME THEY HEADED out, and the ride toward the park buzzed with tension.

The Outlaws had planned on the proper avenues for their heist to nab the proof of insider trading that would topple Reynauld, but after the caravan burned down the other night, Grif had made the call to monitor this meeting. They'd already missed one attack on Tuck's troupe and couldn't afford to miss another. Leo's knee bounced with nerves as they zipped closer. Grif drove with the smooth confidence of someone who knew these streets by heart.

Something wasn't adding up.

He'd suspected Sophia, but after her father's caravan burned down, he couldn't make sense of why she'd torch the place where she was living, especially after the Stockyard had killed her husband. Maybe he'd gotten it all wrong.

In the distance, the business centers and condos surrounding the park rose into view. The approach of night offered plenty of shadow to disappear into, the inky stain splattered across the buildings, creeping along the sidewalks and slithering through the tree trunks and branches. Sunlight clung on with last desperate rays that gilded the clouds across the sky. In the center of the big buildings lay the park fringed by trees with a section of playground spaced out. Leo's mouth grew dry as bone as Grif slid the car into park along a side street.

He'd been after Craig Baldwin for so long, he didn't know what he'd do if they took him out tonight. Except, for the first time in his life, he wanted something more than he wanted revenge: Tuck.

The man could never know his past though. The truth sank heavy in Leo's gut—not that he'd compromised their mission from the start. Not that he'd grown up with parents in the Stockyard. Not that he was a little too broken to ever truly be loved, no matter the tender way Tuck looked at him.

Fuck. The realization was one he couldn't escape.

Maybe they were doomed from the moment they'd met.

Grif leaned back to look at Leo and Tuck. "Keep to the perimeter of the park. Alanna and I will stealth through and try to get close enough to pick up their conversation on the UZI."

"Yes, sir," Leo responded, firing off a lazy salute.

Tuck rolled his eyes and cracked the door open. "We'll signal on the comms if we spot anything and head straight for the cars."

"Don't want to tip Reynauld off before the infiltration," Grif said, his lips a firm line. That would take place in a few days, and then this would all be over. Job finished, even if the Stockyard wasn't. Leo's gut churned with a brew of emotions. Could he ever really be free if Craig Baldwin was roaming out there unencumbered?

Focus on the present.

"Catch you crazy kids later," Leo said before slipping out behind Tuck. The man was already sliding toward the sidewalk, almost blending in with the jagged shadows. A second after Leo departed the vehicle, the sound of car doors shutting echoed behind him. He didn't cast a glance backwards, but he knew Grif and Alanna were advancing into the park interior. The crackle of the comms should've been a comfort, but all it served to remind him of was how this team had welcomed him in, how easily he'd melded in to working with them.

Even though he'd been lying to them the entire time.

Leo felt the chill of the asphalt beneath his feet, the steel and stone buildings surrounding them and the shadows that had permanently stained him. Tuck had transformed from his normal flirty, warm self into professional mode. Quieter, sharper, like the honed edge of a blade.

Trees lined the perimeter of the park with their cragged branches and threadbare leaves, but Leo's focus remained trained between the trunks on every subtle movement he caught sight of. At any point, the members of the Stockyard would show, and vigilance pressed into each vertebra of his spine tonight. Tuck meandered next to him as if he didn't have a care in the world, but Leo had known the man long enough to understand that every ounce of him was poised and aware.

Leo resisted the temptation to brush his fingers across the pistol tucked into the holster strapped to his torso. Every shifting shadow made him want to reach for it, but most of the time, they were just branches or leaves trembling in the errant breezes. The streets around them buzzed with people, the evening hours flooding the city with folks escaping from their nine-to-five jobs, which was where Leo would be if he hadn't called in today.

Firing a gun at this hour was risky, but he couldn't pass up the opportunity if it arose. He'd made sure to choose the pistol with the silencer.

Grif came on over the comms. "Park's currently empty." Leo had to skim the area a few times before he caught sight of where Grif leaned against one of the trees closest to the playground containing a few slides, monkey bars, and platforms painted tan and deep green.

Alanna was harder to spot in the waning light. In the all-black she wore, she almost blended in with the chain-link fence separating the park from the denser section of trees. They'd each found opposite sides of Mark Twain Park to linger around close enough that they'd be able to pick up whatever was being said with the listening devices they'd brought.

Leo tugged at the hood of his sweatshirt, the thick fabric doing little to keep away the burgeoning cool air and nerves. His mind had turned into a war zone he wanted to evacuate, but with the heavy silence between him and Tuck while they strolled along the opposite side of the street closest to the business plaza, he couldn't avoid those intrusive thoughts.

Were these hopes of something more with Tuck idiotic? He'd never tried it before, but he'd also never met anyone more patient who understood what life was like in the morally grey area where he existed. Most of the guys he'd slept with were too normal, and even Dan, before he'd met Grif, had been a sweet little cinnamon roll unaware of how cruel the world could be.

Red and gold streaked across the sky with urgency. Twilight had arrived, which meant the meetup should be happening any moment now. His veins prickled with adrenaline even as he and Tuck paced evenly along the sidewalk, strolling from one length to the other as if they were ambling toward a casual destination instead of patrolling.

Every time he caught sight of someone new walking around the bend, he tried to avoid eye contact, observing details in his peripheral. Mostly, it was women running by in their neon jogging gear, younger guys walking fluffy retrievers, and the occasional suited professional exiting their car to head toward the condos stacked on the corner of the block.

A pristine slice of normalcy that made his skin crawl.

Nothing he could ever exist in.

Tuck slowed his pace as he veered off the path and headed to the red-bricked building closest to them. He found a spot to lean and settled in, tilting his head at Leo to do the same. The vantage point of the park from here was great. Leo supposed they could only stroll so many times without starting to look suspicious.

"A guy's entering the park," Alanna said over the comms. "Businessman, probably from Reynauld's."

Leo rested his back against the cool red brick, scanning the park for the target. He caught the long, loping strides of a man with a briefcase who kept his gaze down as he headed past the playground and toward the tree line.

That was about as suspicious as their crew was being. Leo had long known how to spot criminal activity though. Growing up in the thick of it helped hone those instincts immeasurably.

"What about the Stockyard?" Leo murmured, casting a glance at Tuck.

"Haven't caught sight of anyone who fits the bill yet," Tuck responded, his rich, low voice giving Leo a tether to cling to.

Leo wasn't looking for some asshole in black though. No, he searched for the stocky, pit-bull-faced motherfucker who ran the Stockyard. He'd be able to recognize those features blindfolded and underwater.

Which, if Craig got ahold of him, was where he might end up.

"Incoming," Grif warned over the comms. "From my end of the park."

Leo glanced over to spot a figure approach that was heading in the same direction where the businessman waited.

The moment he got a better look at the silhouette, his stomach sank. Tall and built, this guy had to be someone working for the Stockyard. It wasn't Baldwin himself.

Maybe that was for the best. Leo tried to gulp down his disappointment. If Baldwin had arrived, the chance of danger for the Outlaws increased exponentially.

"I'm getting the device recording," Alanna said. "If

they're going to target the troupe, we'll get the details and cut them off at the pass."

Tuck swallowed hard, the sound an audible *click* beside him. Guilt trickled through Leo. Here he was attempting to get revenge against Baldwin, whereas Tuck just wanted to protect the people he cared about. He didn't deserve the man's attention in the slightest.

Leo couldn't shake the adrenaline that rushed through him like he'd tripped a wire somewhere along the way. He stared at the opposite end of the park where the two men met.

"We should move," Tuck murmured, nudging him in the side.

Leo pushed up from his slouch against the wall and followed Tuck who began those casual strides toward the opposite end of the business center, heading toward the end of the block. They were close enough for firing distance, in case Grif or Alanna got themselves into any trouble.

They'd almost reached the end of the block when three men rounded the corner.

Leo's blood ran cold.

The thick nose, the pockmarked face, and those thin lips and dark, cruel eyes were recognizable on sight. The stocky man was bookended by two hulking guys, but only an idiot would discount the real threat of the guy in the middle.

Craig Baldwin.

Craig stopped midstride, his gaze piercing right through him.

"Well, now, if it isn't Leo Thatcher," he drawled, his hand resting at his hip—most likely on his gun. "When Darren told me he'd seen you, I could barely believe it. At least until I realized someone had hacked into our systems. You'd always been a clever little fuck."

Leo could feel Tuck's stare boring into him, but he froze under the scrutiny of the man he'd seen in nightmares for years and had never been able to escape from even after he'd started over with a new life and a new name.

"Thought we'd draw you out for a conversation," Craig said, his grin stretching a little wider.

Oh, fuck.

This was a trap.

CHAPTER 21

Tuck stared at the man beside him, a complete stranger.

Shock had ripped into him like a .50 BMG the moment Craig Baldwin started talking. He'd recognized the fucker from the pictures he'd seen of the leader of the Stockyard—except Tuck had been expecting him in the middle of Mark Twain Park as a part of the meeting.

Not walking straight up to them like he'd been waiting all along.

Waiting for Leo.

Too many things collided in his brain at once. Leo's shitty past. His insistence on going to the warehouse. That out of all the jobs they'd tried to drag him in on in the past, the man had taken this one.

Each truth burrowed deep like mines waiting for him to step on them so they could obliterate everything he'd believed to be true.

Everything he'd hoped that was growing between them.

Shattered.

Except there were three guys from the Stockyard walking their way, armed and wielding the advantage of surprise. Which meant Tuck would need to shelve this shock into the processing later category. Right now, he needed to focus on getting out alive.

Leo whipped out his pistol as if he'd been bracing himself for this the entire time.

The moment he did, the click of fingers to safeties sounded.

Tuck had a split second to react.

Run, and he could leave Leo to face off against Craig and his cronies.

However, there was no question—Leo would die.

Tuck didn't think and just moved. One second, he was upright, and the next he'd flung himself on top of Leo hard enough to send them both crashing to the pavement. The crack of a bullet burying into concrete echoed through the air, but whether it'd been Leo taking the shot or one of the guys from the Stockyard, well, only time would tell.

Time he'd spend getting the hell out of here.

They slammed against the ground, but Tuck had already launched into a roll, yanking Leo by the forearm to drag him along with. He righted himself, not letting go of Leo's arm. The man wasn't resisting, but panic blared in his eyes.

One glance to his side revealed the muzzles of pistols aiming directly at them.

"Run," Tuck commanded before releasing Leo's arm —otherwise, they'd slow down, and they couldn't afford to. His legs were already pumping as he raced down the sidewalk as fast as he could manage, flying in the direction of the condos at the end of the block. The business center here might be abandoned, but right up that street were folks walking their dogs or taking a casual post-work stroll because the sun had just set, and the night sky was still gray.

Shooting into a crowd of civilians would be messy. Tuck only hoped the Stockyard had lasted as long as they had by avoiding heat like that.

Otherwise, he and Leo were fucked.

Leo clutched the pistol tight and glanced back, his breaths coming out as hard and furious as the way they pounded pavement. "Duck," he spat out, this time bumping Tuck in the side.

Tuck moved on instinct, but a sharp grunt came from Leo a second later. Not like the man stopped his stride as they raced away from Baldwin and his men.

"Grif, it's a trap." Tuck forced the words out over the comms. "Both of you, get out of there now."

"Are you taking fire?" he asked, his voice sharp.

"I'll try to lose them," Tuck gasped out, almost lunging for the front door of the complex of condos. He spared a single look at Leo. "If you want to stay alive, follow me."

He couldn't think about everything he'd just learned about the man—not now.

Tuck glanced at the men from the Stockyard behind him. Pistols pointed his way, fingers on the triggers—oh yeah, they were about to make him dance. Fuck. The cream door to the condo building swung open, and Tuck didn't wait for the guy to walk through it before he was swinging around and barreling inside. Leo crashed in behind him, and the man spat out a curse as they hurried past.

Window. Back exit. He needed another way out, somewhere he could dive through to lose himself amidst the early evening rush of the city. To blend in with the shadows where he belonged.

His soles slapped the linoleum as he cut across the fancy foyer of the complex, all black rails, marbled flooring, and pale white walls. Leo's footsteps pounded a pace or two behind him, but Tuck couldn't afford the second to check in on him. Not like he wanted to see the man's face right now. His insides had begun numbing over, reverting to just survive, survive, survive.

"We're heading for the car," Alanna barked into the comms. A shout sounded in the background of the transmission, and Tuck's heart lunged in his chest.

A narrow corridor stretched deeper into the building at the end of the main foyer. To the right lay an elevator, and to the left was a set of doors that looked like they led to the stairwell. Corridor it was. Tuck's calves flexed with his powerful strides as he vaulted headlong in that direction. There was no room for hesitation. Not when the assholes from the Stockyard would be bursting in behind them at any minute.

Tuck's heart pounded hard, the thump-thump-thump reverberating in his ears, and he soared down the corridor, leading past what appeared to be a laundry room, a place with an ice machine, and a whole other load of closed doors he didn't give a damn about. His gaze zeroed in on the end of the hall. Where it emptied out was unclear, but he saw the glint of glass, and that was all he needed.

Leo's breaths huffed out from behind him, a reminder of who was racing along with him. The man he'd believed just last night he'd be able to trust. With his life. With his heart. His chest tightened—whether from the sharp breaths he was sucking in as he pushed his body to move faster, faster, faster or the betrayal waiting to unload, he wasn't too damn sure.

The slam of the door they'd entered through echoed like the ricochet of a bullet.

Craig and his cronies would be after them in seconds.

Sweat pricked on his forehead, and his breaths came out sharper as he pushed himself hard, moving so fast, he flew over the linoleum in bounding leaps. The end of the hallway careened into view, a stretch of glossy windows surrounding a back exit.

Fucking salvation.

"Head to the door," he panted out, offering direction to Leo who lagged a few paces behind. The thought of the man drove shards into his heart, but he wasn't cruel enough to abandon him to the guy who would strip the skin from his body before gutting him.

Grif came in over the comms. "We're at the car. It's too hot to get in though."

Tuck and Leo wouldn't last long on foot with Craig and his men chasing after them. Blood and bones.

He had to try anyway.

The glass door loomed in front of him, mere feet away at this point. The rising clatter of footsteps behind him alerted him to the pursuit about to begin again. If he lagged in the slightest, gunfire would be coming, and he doubted he'd be lucky twice. His shoulder still seared with the souvenir he'd gotten from his last encounter with the Stockyard, which was only exacerbated by all this running.

Tuck slid to the side right as he reached the exit, his hand slapping against the handle hard enough to sting. He yanked the door open, catching a fresh mouthful of the crisp night air. Without pausing, he burst through and continued racing across the pavement, digesting his surroundings as he went.

A narrow alleyway stretched in either direction, chain-link fence decorating it in spotty sections. A fairly empty parking lot and another building lay across the street, and to the left, the end of the block dumped out onto a bustling main road, the view of skyscrapers clear from the stacks of neon light stretching up into the horizon.

Not even a question. Tuck bolted to the left.

Leo's heavy breaths sounded behind him, breaking

through the vacuum of silence in the alley, so different from the rest of the sounds of the city. His mind rioted at the thought of the man by his side, the doubts and fears threatening to take over, but instinct had seized the wheel and wouldn't let go. They needed to get out. He would deal with the fallout afterwards.

"We're heading to 18th Street," Tuck announced over the comms, the words coming out choppy between staggered breaths. He inwardly thanked everything for the prep they'd done beforehand to study the area.

Not like they'd been able to plan for the fact that the Stockyard had baited them in the first place.

No response came over the comms, and Tuck gritted his teeth. Grif and Alanna had to get to the car. No other option was acceptable.

Any second now, the assholes from the Stockyard would be busting through the back door in pursuit, and here, there wasn't any buffer for the bullets. He and Leo would be easy pickings.

His soles slapped hard on the asphalt as he raced forward, silently willing an answer to come through on his comms. Sweat beaded on his forehead, the drops threatening to trickle down his face. This job had been filled with problems from the start.

And now he knew why.

His vision shook with his heavy footfalls as he kept his eyes on the prize: the end of the alley where it dumped into 18th Street. Sure, Craig and his men could follow them out there, but if they tried to open fire, they'd cause mass panic.

Except all it would take was to lag in front of the wrong alley. He'd never make it out alive.

Tuck tried to swallow another aching breath down his dry-as-fuck throat as he ignored the throb of his muscles and the pulse of the still-healing gunshot wound on his shoulder. Based on the wetness he could feel trickling from it, all this movement had tugged the gash open again.

Didn't matter. He could deal with it later.

Tuck clenched his jaw, squared his shoulders, and threw himself headlong toward the street that was growing rapidly closer with every step.

"Locksley, did you make it to the car?" Tuck asked, using Grif's codename. Only silence responded back to him. Fuck, fuck, fuck.

He'd reach the end of the alley at any second, but if they didn't have a ride, he'd need to pick a direction and hope Craig and his cronies didn't catch up.

"Where are we going?" Leo huffed out next to him, the first words he'd said before Craig showed up and shattered every belief Tuck had held about the man.

Tuck all but leapt onto the sidewalk of 18th Street, which was buzzing with cars and tire squeals at this early point in the night. The streetlights had flickered on, but the ambient gray of the faded light lingered. A guy in a starched suit spat out a curse as he swerved past Tuck on the sidewalk. Leo slammed into his side at their abrupt stop.

"We're on 18th," he repeated, his worries mounting with every second he went unanswered.

Leo turned to look behind him, reaching for his pistol. "They're coming." He didn't bother to disguise the urgency in his voice, and a moment later, he was pulling the pistol out, his finger slipping to the trigger.

This day had gone to hell in a matter of seconds.

They were out here in the middle of a sidewalk swarming with people and traffic zipping by in either direction. Duck into a random business, and they would essentially trap themselves. Head down a less populated side street, and if the Stockyard guys caught up, they were fucked. Tuck's adrenaline pumped as his gaze narrowed down the diminishing options.

And if they didn't move, Craig and his men wouldn't hesitate to take a shot.

His stomach bottomed out.

Alanna's voice came over the comms. "18th and Indiana."

Tuck started moving before she finished speaking. He darted to the right, his legs protesting the continued running when he severely needed to catch a breath. Leo raced alongside him, lagging behind a pace or two. Tuck didn't miss the man's wince or the way his left leg dragged.

"Hold on a little longer," Tuck said, his voice gruff. Leo might've lied to them, but Tuck couldn't sentence him to certain death, even if his heart had already started to fragment. Didn't matter. He'd still get him to safety.

And then cut him loose.

Tuck swallowed hard as he swerved past a couple of

college kids ambling along, weaving through a throng of arm-in-arm couples clearly out for a night on the town. All he could smell was sweat, diesel, and metal, the gritty scents swarming him on every inhale. His gaze was glued on the end of the street, watching each car that whipped around the bend.

He glanced at the alley they'd bolted from, stark angles of shadow and steel. It wasn't hard to catch sight of Craig Baldwin. The guy might not be a hulking mass, but his bulldog features made him stand out. Same as the hand reaching for his side.

Tuck's blood froze. Was he going to shoot right into the middle of the crowd?

Tires squealed, drawing his attention at once.

Blue Prius.

The cavalry had arrived.

"Follow me," he said, meeting Leo's gaze. His heart pounded harder. The man's lips were pressed thin, but he offered a grim nod.

Tuck didn't stop running as the car slowed down far too fast, grinding against the curb like it owed them money. A second later, the back door flung open. Tuck hurled himself inside, not bothering with any finesse. He crashed against Alanna and then bounced against the back of the driver's seat. Leo launched himself inside after him. Before he'd begun pulling the door shut, Grif had already surged forward, engine revving.

"We've got a tail," Grif muttered through clenched teeth, glancing in the rearview. The car picked up speed as Grif began to swerve through traffic, the motions fast and jarring even as he kept his transitions smooth.

"What the fuck happened back there?" Alanna exploded, her gaze flashing angrily.

Tuck's throat tightened. What happened was that Leo should've never been a part of this operation in the first place. Scar would've been a liability for a reason—because there was bad blood between her and the Stockyard.

Leo had been a liability too, and they'd never even known it.

Tuck had hoped…. Fuck. His heart cracked in two, an ache in his chest growing like he'd sustained another bullet wound. This was the sort of pain he hadn't experienced in years because he'd been bobbing along on the surface, not letting himself get attached. And then came Leo Kennedy bounding into his life with his blinding chemistry and sharp sense of humor, showing Tuck a vulnerable side that had reeled him in.

At least, back when he thought he knew him.

Tuck glanced at Leo who leaned against the inside of the car, clutching his thigh with a grimace, and his stomach clenched tight.

"Lan, see if you can get a shot out the window," Grif said, his brows knitted in concentration. Even though the man emitted pristine cool, the slight clench of his jaw gave him away. In classic Outlaws fashion, a simple job had turned into an on-fire garbage can.

Alanna rolled the window down and grabbed her pistol. Tuck didn't move from his spot in the middle, but a glance into the rearview mirror showed a cherry red pickup truck tailing them. It swerved through traffic just as fast, cutting off folks who honked and cursed in the process. Alanna chewed on her lower lip, strands of her dark hair whipping all around from the icy breeze pouring in through the window. Her dark eyes narrowed, and she waited with her finger on the trigger, muzzle pointed out into traffic.

The headlights flashed behind them.

"Thanks, asshole," Alanna called out before aiming downward and firing, one, two shots in rapid succession.

The car made a hard jerk to the right, the squealing sound echoing through the air. Folks blared their horns all around, and a loud crunch followed. Tuck peered behind him in time to see a white sedan smashed into the side of the red pickup which was growing smaller and smaller as they sped away.

Minutes passed in aching silence as Grif continued to glide down the Chicago streets with the finesse of someone who'd lived here his entire life. Alanna was scanning out the window on the off chance they got any more tails, Leo was clinging to his side of the car like he might leap out at any moment, and Tuck sat in the middle, his heart pumping like he was still racing through these streets.

"They knew we were coming," Grif said, his voice echoing through the car.

"They did," Leo responded, his voice surprisingly steady even though a visible tremor rippled through his body. The anger bubbling in Tuck's chest warred with the instinct to reach out and comfort him.

Grif's jaw twitched. "When we get back to the penthouse, you owe us an explanation."

The ominous silence that followed filled in the blanks.

The trust had been broken, and in a life like theirs, that meant everything.

CHAPTER 22

If Leo had to pick the worst from the menagerie of shitty fucking memories that constituted his life, he'd be overwhelmed by choices.

This one, though—this one threatened to be up there in the top five. Not because he was tortured, dying, or left to fend for himself, terrified.

No, in this case it was because for the first time in his adult life, he'd hoped. He'd come to genuinely care for Tuck, and he valued his friendship with Dan more than any other. Hell, he even appreciated the rest of the motley crew who'd welcomed him in with a barrage of noise, sarcastic comments, and bickering.

And he'd lied to them. Put them in danger. All to chase his vendetta against the man who ran the Stockyard.

Each step up to the penthouse felt like the tolling of a bell as he headed toward his sentencing. His left leg burned from the pain and exertion—the bullet had grazed him back there when they'd been escaping, but if he'd stopped to take care of it, they wouldn't have made it out alive.

Stupid. He'd been so stupid.

Thinking that just because Craig Baldwin hadn't pursued him over the years, he'd forgotten. Thinking he could hide behind his changed name, as if he'd somehow cleansed himself of the sin of his upbringing. Thinking he could lie to Tuck and the others without the whole thing blowing up in his face.

He cast a glance at Tuck when they entered the elevator but wished he hadn't.

The grim set of Tuck's lips and the hollow expression in those long-lashed, dark eyes was a far cry from the wry, warm man he'd come to know. Tuck hadn't said more than a few words to him since the truth had come out, but he hadn't needed to. Leo could feel the waves of disapproval from here, and worse, the hurt of betrayal, which made him the biggest monster on the planet. He'd always known Tuck deserved better than someone like him.

And even after Tuck had discovered Leo's disloyalty, he'd still saved his life.

If Leo had stayed and tried to fire at Craig and his two men, he would've become another dead body in their trail of too many.

Or worse.

Leo shrank in on himself as the elevator reached their floor, and one by one, they all stepped off. Alanna delivered death looks his way, but her silence stung far worse than any acid that normally spewed from her lips.

He'd been convincing himself he was doing a public service in taking the Stockyard down. In trying to end Craig Baldwin's life.

However, when the man had appeared around the street corner, the truth slammed into him like a Mack Truck.

Leo had been trying to banish his bogeyman for years.

If Craig Baldwin was dead, maybe those nightmares wouldn't haunt him anymore. Maybe he wouldn't freeze up in cramped closets or live this fucked-up half life, never letting anyone in.

He swallowed hard, trying to ignore the sting in his eyes. When they stepped inside the penthouse, Dan, Scarlet, and John were all waiting by the door.

"What happened out there?" Dan asked, his eyes wide with worry and his skin a shade paler.

"That's what we'd all like to know," Grif said, stalking past them to wrap his arms around his boyfriend and press a kiss to his lips. He stepped behind Dan and rested his hands on his shoulders before swinging his Arctic gaze on Leo.

Leo swallowed, nerves rushing through him in a fierce sweep. As comfortable as he'd gotten with the Outlaws, with all of their stares boring in on him, the reminder slammed home that this was a crew of highly trained criminals... and killers. Some might have taken more lives than others—he didn't want to know Grif's body count—but all of them were deadly when need be.

"Baldwin showed up for me," he said, the words dry against his desert throat. "My parents used to be a part of the Stockyard."

The silence continued, apart from a sharp breath from Dan whose brows drew together as the realization began to settle in. Fuck.

"When they were sent to jail, I was sent to a foster family," Leo continued, his voice toneless but surprisingly steady. "However, I've been keeping tabs on them through the years, doing what I could to thwart them in the small ways I could."

"Until you saw this shiny opportunity," John said, his tone mirthless. The man was always casual, easy smiles, laugh lines, and constant teasing—at least, until now. Now his eyes were devoid of all that, leaving a terrifying calm.

Leo swallowed back the lump in his throat and stared at the floor, unable to look up and see the betrayal in Dan's eyes. To witness the heartbreak in Tuck's. "I thought if I could just kill Craig Baldwin, maybe it would all stop," he admitted, his voice barely audible.

Grif stepped in again, demanding, "What do they know?"

"That I hacked into their system," Leo murmured. "He hadn't brought up the rest of you. He might have pieced it together or he might not have. I'm not sure."

"You know the whole reason I stayed behind was

because they'd recognize my face," Scar said, a hopeless note in her words and an edge to her tone. "Fuck, of course you did. You just didn't care what it might cost us."

Leo swallowed hard, his eyes burning with the emotion he forced back. Not like he had any counter for that. He'd been so determined to take down the Stockyard that he'd dragged the Outlaws into his mess.

"How could you?" Dan's voice trembled. Leo forced himself to look up, and the sight socked him in the gut. The accusation in Dan's eyes, the hurt blazing there sliced straight to the core of him. "I thought...," Dan continued, but he stopped, choking on the words.

Leo's heart felt like it was being clawed out of his chest. Dan had been his friend for years, the sole person he'd become close to for a long time—his ride or die.

"Why didn't you ever tell me?" The words came out soft, but the betrayal Dan felt rang clear.

Leo tore his gaze away. "I've been trying to escape that past for a long time."

"It goes without saying, we're cutting you loose from this," Grif cut in, stepping between him and Dan. The man loomed, all broad shoulders and a killer's expression, those eyes cold enough to freeze. "We let you in—we don't often do that."

Leo forced a tired smile. "This where you tell me you need to kill me?"

"Don't," Dan said, grabbing Grif's forearm.

"That's on you, Leo," Grif said.

"If you start running now, it might even give us a bit

of a challenge," Alanna drawled, looking at him with dead, dark eyes.

"Knock it off, Lan," Tuck growled, slicing a hand through the air. "He made his point, and we made ours." Even now, Tuck still defended him. The pain trickled through him like cyanide, killing him slowly.

"As long as you don't interfere in our business and keep your distance, we won't pursue anything," Grif continued. "But if you cross a line with us again, we won't hesitate to act."

Leo's throat tightened. This was better than the eventuality he'd expected, and yet the idea of getting cut out of this group, of never speaking again to Dan or Tuck—he didn't know how he'd be able to stay in the city.

"Understood." Leo pushed the word out, though what he wanted was to sink into the grains of the hardwood and disappear. He was used to being disappointed in others, again and again and again. Except this time, he was the disappointment. Shame coated him like a slimy film he wanted to scrub off.

He looked again at Dan who stared at him with a lost expression. Fuck, he felt the same way. His life had been so compartmentalized—work, friendships, and his past—yet they'd all become muddled during this job. If he'd hated the shift, this would be easy. However, the more time he'd spent working with the Outlaws and the more he'd shared with Tuck, he'd found himself longing for a future like the one he'd begun to imagine.

His hollowed heart was all he'd ever known, so he

hadn't recognized it when the empty space had started to fill. At least, not until it was too late.

"I'll escort him out," Tuck said, his voice gruff.

Right. Out. He was leaving.

Grif gave him an up nod, and Alanna crossed her arms, glaring at him with extra menace. Everyone's stares zeroed in on him, and regret thudded with the same tempo as his heartbeat.

Tuck swept past him, and Leo took that as his cue. He followed behind Tuck, anxious to get out from under the judge and jury of their stares, yet not wanting to go all the same. Once he left, that was it—he wouldn't be allowed back in.

The walk to the elevator was as silent as the ride up had been, the sort of quiet that crawled under his skin and lived there. He focused on the metal doors, waiting for them to open. The tension weighed thick in the air, and not the thrilling kind. Away from the scrutiny of the rest of the Outlaws, he leaned heavier on his good side since his left leg ached something fierce. He needed to clean out the graze.

"Shot?" Tuck asked, his dark eyes unreadable.

"Clipped," Leo said. "I'll be fine."

The elevator doors opened up, and they both stepped in.

Leo leaned against the side, running a hand over his forearm as he scrutinized the polished gray tile on the floor. "I'm sorry, Tuck."

He wanted to say more—how the man had changed him. How he'd regretted putting them in danger from the second he made the choice to do so. How getting to know Tuck made him want to leave those goals of revenge behind.

Yet he remained silent.

"You know," Tuck said, finally speaking up. Leo couldn't look away if he wanted to—and he did. "I thought we had something. I haven't felt chemistry like that in years, and hell, the pieces of yourself you gave? I thought they were damned special." He sucked in a shaky breath, one Leo could feel from where he stood feet away. "I don't give my trust easily. And you? I trusted you, Leo."

Leo was all too aware of the past tense.

The ping, ping, ping of the elevator echoed through the tense space between them. What arguments could he even make? In the end, he'd screwed Tuck over when his circus family was on the line. He couldn't walk back from this.

He loathed the silence that was between them now, when before the air had been light, the current fluid.

Leo looked up at the ceiling, unable to bear the weight of Tuck's stare any longer. "I'll send the rest of the info on the Stockyard over to Scar," he murmured. "Maybe it'll give an advantage."

Tuck grunted in response, and then the quiet returned.

The elevator settled on the bottom floor, and the doors opened. They stepped off in unison, heading the short distance to the entrance. Each footstep dragged with the weight of the knowledge that this was the last time he'd be heading into this building. The last time he'd be swinging over to plan some crime, visit his best friend, or see the guy he'd found himself falling for. His stomach churned like he'd chugged acid—but no, the crippling guilt had only just arrived.

His leg had begun to ache something fierce, and he knew he'd need to take care of it sooner rather than later, but the idea of patching himself up in his apartment, alone, soured his stomach. If he hadn't fucked everything up between him and the Outlaws, he would've been spending tonight around the crew, planning the rest of the job together. They'd be sharing a meal, laughing together, giving each other shit.

He'd once found the idea of those breakfasts terrifying, but as of late, longing squeezed his chest tight at the idea.

He wanted that.

He wanted Tuck.

And in pursuing his stupid revenge against the Stockyard, he'd lost it all. The guy, the gig, and he hadn't even taken Craig fucking Baldwin down. Leo tried to ignore how his eyes stung.

They both came to a stop at the entrance, and a heaviness descended with the weight of everything he wanted to say. He'd realized too late the ways he'd begun to change, and he hated the way he'd hurt Tuck. For a moment, neither of them moved. They just stood here in front of the door. Once Leo stepped outside, this was over.

Leo forced himself to look up and meet Tuck's gaze.

The sight squeezed his heart tight. Fringed by heartbreaker lashes, those gorgeous brown eyes were filled with the same sort of anguish that welled inside him. Shadows sloped along Tuck's face, deepening his serious expression, and Leo soaked him in, memorizing each minute detail, from the scar on his upper cheek to the evenness of his posture resulting from not only his years in the circus but those as a thief.

Leo grabbed the handle, holding his stare. "I regret not telling you," he murmured, the words falling from his lips. "If I could do it all over… I would've chosen you."

Leo turned to face the door. He struggled to swallow the lump in his throat as he tugged it open and exited the building. Icy tendrils blasted him at once, wisps that curled around him like chains, threatening to drag him down.

The Chicago wind was bitter tonight.

CHAPTER 23

As always, their plans had sailed down shit creek in a flaming boat.

After the surprise visit from the Stockyard, the reveal that Leo used to be associated with them, and the attack on Twilight Circus's caravans, the heist to break into Reynauld's condo had to get bumped up.

To tonight.

More than ever, Tuck wished he was going to be on the job. After everything that had gone down, he needed to pour himself into a distraction. However, they were already at a disadvantage due to Leo's past with the Stockyard, and his troupe was under more danger than ever. Going out into the field would be a mistake.

And he'd made enough of them from the moment he'd agreed to help Sophia.

Tuck rolled up off his bed. He'd been staring at the wall for way too long, and it wasn't providing any answers. The ache in his chest grew by the hour, and he couldn't erase the look in Leo's eyes as he'd left.

I would've chosen you.

If only he could believe it.

A knock sounded on his door. Tuck slunk over and opened it—only one person would bother with the courtesy.

Dan stood in the frame, a frown creasing his brow. "Mind if I come in?"

Tuck tapped his fingertips on the side of his leg. It didn't take a genius to figure out what Dan would want to talk to him about. As much as he itched to avoid this conversation, to save himself from the heartbreak, he wasn't about to shut Dan out. "Sure thing," he said, stepping away to let him inside.

Tuck sauntered over to his bed and plunked back down, hunching forward. Dan didn't sit beside him but leaned against the wall instead, crossing his arms and nearly clutching them.

"How are you doing?" he asked, those concerned eyes flicking Tuck's way. "With… you know—all of it?"

Tuck rifled his fingers through his curls, not even knowing where to start. His mind had been rioting from the second Craig Baldwin dumped Leo's secret on them. His initial response was to cut him out—the betrayal had carved into him with a jagged knife. And yet, his instincts still had him protecting the man, making sure he was okay, and his mind had wandered to Leo about a thousand different times today.

"Unexpected, right?" He opened the door to the

conversation, recognizing that Dan needed to unload as much as he did.

"I've known him for years," Dan murmured, tugging on the hem of his shirt. His gaze zeroed in on the floor. "Sure, he'd always been dodgy about his past, but I just thought he didn't like sharing or maybe had a tough time in the foster system."

"More than a tough time," Tuck responded. Had Leo told him more than he had his own best friend? The idea that the man might've confided in him despite the past clearly haunting him tangled Tuck up on the inside. "Some of the things he experienced in… well, I guess while he was growing up with his parents, were pretty horrific."

Dan passed him a sharp stare. "Did he really open up to you?"

Tuck gave a one-shoulder shrug. "Not about the Stockyard thing, but yeah… he did." The realization twisted him up even tighter. Part of him hated Leo for those beautiful glimpses of vulnerability because they'd reeled him in hook, line, and sinker. It made him want to protect the man, to show him the care he'd never experienced.

However, he couldn't reconcile that version of Leo with the man who'd been hiding his identity the whole time. Knowingly placing them in danger.

The night they'd gone to the Stockyard warehouse— Leo had pushed for it, even if he hadn't been obvious about the attempt. The manipulation had been purposeful. Tuck swallowed hard, trying to ignore the acid churning in his stomach.

"Fuck, I wish this was cut and dry," Dan muttered. "He lied and placed us in danger, so he's done, right? But if I went by that principle, I would've never joined with you guys in the first place."

Tuck hunched forward, staring at the floor. Dan wasn't wrong. Grif had met and fallen for him on a job trying to take down Dan's company—and had lied about everything beyond the way he felt in the process. Except this was different, wasn't it? A headache threatened to steal him away at the mere thought of parsing all these conflicting feelings.

All he knew was that he was hurting with a bone-deep pain, and he didn't know how to fix it.

"That's something we can revisit after the job's done," Tuck said, getting up from the bed. He cast a glance at his clock, the neon numbers signaling just how close they were to go time. "Let's get ready for this job."

Dan nodded and pushed up from the wall. "Not for nothing, but I've known Leo for a long time. And maybe he didn't tell me about his past, but I'm not blind. I recognized the way he compartmentalizes a long time ago. I've never seen him rewrite his rules like he did for you." With that, he led the way out of the room, leaving Tuck in a dizzying tailspin.

Tuck's heart pounded harder in his chest as all those worries and regrets tangled around in his head. He followed Dan out and headed into the living room where the rest of the gang was already gathered. The problem of Leo Kennedy wouldn't be resolved tonight.

No, tonight, they would take down Reynauld Industries and protect Tuck's troupe.

Grif had been right—if the Stockyard couldn't get paid, they wouldn't keep attacking the Twilight Circus.

Alanna was dressed in all black and doing her stretches on the floor. She'd be the stealth tonight, so she needed to stay limber. Her long ponytail hung down her back, and a determined look settled in her sharp eyes. Grif and John had also suited up, donning all black clothes with enough stretch to run and climb. Both of those guys were built like brick shithouses, better for taking a punch than fast movement, but the balance would be good tonight, especially if Reynauld had enhanced his personal security.

After last night, who knew. They couldn't afford to wait, on the off chance the Stockyard got wind of what they attempted or had figured out who they were. Baldwin had been focused on targeting Leo, but the man wasn't an idiot. He would've taken notes on who'd accompanied him and, guaranteed, he'd already attempted to trace their details. Because they clearly needed another dangerous enemy.

Scar had even dressed up for the occasion even though she was staying behind. She wore her ear length chestnut hair slicked back in a pompadour, and her crimson lipstick was sharp. She leaned back in her cozy computer chair behind the main rig, at the ready.

The sight of all those computers just made Tuck think of Leo—another stab to the heart.

A steady buzz settled over the room like an oncoming storm, the readiness that arrived before they embarked on any heist, whether it was a massive job or a smaller scale infiltration like this.

Dan stepped up to Grif and planted a kiss on his lips. Grif grabbed Dan by the hips and brought him flush against his body, the two making out like they were the only ones in the room. Jealousy painted a streak through Tuck at the sight. At what he'd thought he was on the precipice of having—someone to hold, someone to kiss before a job, someone waiting for him at the end of one.

"God, you're gross," Alanna called over to them.

Grif lifted his middle finger, giving Dan one more long, lusty kiss before pulling away.

"Stay safe," Dan said, looking up at him with a serious gaze. Dan was manning comms tonight while Scar handled disabling security systems and guarding the perimeter.

"It's not fun if there isn't a little danger," Grif teased, his eyes sparkling.

"So says the man who keeps accumulating enemies like trading cards," John drawled, sliding another knife into his boot. "I, for one, wouldn't mind a nice, simple job without any danger. Fuck fun."

"No one likes you anyway, John," Alanna shot back.

"I'm pretty sure you do," he responded, showing

teeth with his grin. Alanna rolled her eyes and hopped up to her feet.

Grif fixed his gaze on Tuck. "When you get to the caravan, keep your eyes peeled. The Stockyard already struck once, and if they're on the move, there's a high chance you'll be recognized. Keep active on the comms."

Tuck snorted. "Please, you'll be having the joyride tonight. I'm just hanging around the tents with Javi and maybe Margo." Even still, his adrenaline filtered in, steady pinpricks of worry at the thought of another attack on the caravans. This time, those might not be the only things targeted. The Twilight Circus couldn't afford to lose anything else…. They'd lost enough throughout the years.

The reminder of visiting his mother was fresh in his mind today, mixing with all the complicated memories of the time he'd spent with Leo after, the comfort he'd taken with the man, and the trust he'd believed had been fluid between them.

Tuck grabbed one of the comms from the coffee table and slipped the earbud in. Even though he was sitting out this round, being connected to the team helped. He'd been working with these guys for years, and the family he'd found in them… well, damn, it was unparalleled.

Unlike Leo, who'd be sitting in his apartment, alone. Guilt filtered through Tuck that he tried to shake off. The man had made his bed—drawing them into the mess with the Stockyard under false pretenses.

Tuck needed to focus on anything but him.

"Running through the drill one more time," Grif said as he finished strapping a pack around his torso. "John enters the building as distraction and the main guard."

"I'm disabling the alarms," Scar volunteered, "and checking the security cams."

"I'll relay everything," Dan added, his eagerness at the simplest of tasks infectious.

"While I'll be making sure the Twilight Circus doesn't end up crispy fried," Tuck commented, his tone paper dry.

"Right," Grif said with a nod. "And Alanna and I will sneak in and steal the documents. It's a quick snatch and grab."

"Don't you dare say it's a simple job," Scar warned. "Because we have the worst luck in the city—potentially on the planet."

"More likely, we'll arrive, find the place swarmed by members of the Stockyard, and have to run screaming while we fail at the easiest task," John responded, already walking toward the door with an easy stride.

"Can you order food for when we get back, Scar?" Alanna asked, batting her eyelashes menacingly. "Pretty please?"

Scar arched a delicate brow. "Should I get extra egg rolls this time so mine don't get stolen?"

Alanna snorted. "Probably a good idea."

Despite the turmoil coursing through him, Tuck soaked in the conversation, the flow of his crew around him, and the sheer comfort they brought. He might be sitting out on this job, but that didn't mean he could kick back with a drink and fuck off. His former troupe needed protection, and he'd keep them safe.

"Get an extra container of fried rice, too, because someone's a thief," Grif called out. He gave Dan one more kiss before sauntering toward the door to where John waited.

"Cough, Alanna, cough," John said with a twinkle in his eyes.

Alanna marched over, stomping the whole way as she headed out behind the other two. "See you fuckers later. John's a maybe because he might get sacrificed along the way." With that, they disappeared out through the corridor to head toward the main door.

Dan grabbed a seat on the couch and set his laptop up on the coffee table while Scar didn't budge from her seat behind the rig. Everyone was assembled and in place, which meant Tuck's departure time had arrived.

"I'll comm in if anything comes up," he said, hooking a thumb in his pocket and striding toward the door. In his gray traveler's pants and loose olive tee, he didn't feel in the slightest like he was headed into a job —just a visit to his former troupe. On his way down, he shot a quick text to Javier, letting him know he was en route. He'd already clued Sophia in that by tomorrow, their problems should be over.

He skimmed over the texts from Leo that had accumulated ever since they hooked up—stupid shit like memes or random comments, flirty jokes that lit up his day, and the occasional check-in that warmed him to the marrow. Fuck.

Job first.

Then he'd figure out what to do about Leo Kennedy.

He exited On the Park, stepping out under a night sky threatened by all the smog and city lights crowding Chicago. Every inch of this city had become familiar through the years, no matter how many places he'd traveled through. Somehow, this one had made a mark, from the looming buildings with their unique architecture to the broad stretch of Lake Michigan, inky black, fathomless, and mesmerizing at night. His home was filled with diametric opposites—the wealthy and the poor, innocent folks trying to live their lives and assholes trying to ruin them, a blend of black and white that always turned to gray, gray, gray.

He never felt that more than he did today.

Tuck strode over to the Prius they'd been using as of late that was parked in the lot next door. Blood probably still stained the back seat from the events of the past few weeks, and they'd have to do a thorough scrub before switching the car out for a different one. Even though he had a steadfast home now in their penthouse, the amount of change and newness in his life kept him engaged like nothing else. He might miss the circus sometimes, but he couldn't find it in him to regret the move he'd made.

He never regretted joining the Outlaws.

Tuck slipped into the driver's seat and started the ignition, the engine thrumming.

"Someone save me from Alanna and John," Grif muttered over the comms, starting the normal conversation that infused every heist. It'd be nonstop chatter until the stealth work began, and Tuck embraced it, if only to quiet the chaos in his brain tonight.

Tuck zipped through the back alleys of Chicago, the main streets glutted with traffic and noise, until he was hopping on the highway with the windows down. The breeze streamed in, whipping his curls around until they stung his face, and he welcomed the brisk, bracing air.

Tonight, he was heading to the circus.

Tomorrow, the job would be done.

CHAPTER 24

Leo had spent the entire day in his dim apartment, which seemed apropos with the way his heart had gone offline after the events of yesterday.

After his best friend and the guy he'd been falling for had rightfully cut him out.

Six showers hadn't helped scrub the guilt away.

His screen glowed back at him, the longest friendship he'd had. He scoured through file after file. He wanted to be Polonius tonight—anyone but Leo Kennedy.

He needed to dig into the Stockyard hard, find some way to bury them. Because they had his number. If he didn't find an avenue to disassemble them, there was nowhere in Chicago he could hide. After all, changing his name and starting a new life clearly hadn't done shit.

And yet he found himself scouring the files he'd brought up about the Twilight Circus—background checks, etc. Something still unsettled him there, even though the situation had been put to bed. Christ, come tomorrow, they wouldn't even be a problem for the Outlaws anymore. Truly, they weren't his issue.

Except he couldn't sit idle with the thought of anything happening to Tuck. He'd already brought enough unwanted trouble to the man's door.

He took a sip of the cooled mug of coffee by his desktop rig, nothing near as pretty as the one Scar worked with. His phone had remained silent all day, and he couldn't shake the disappointment. While he'd fucked up things with Tuck for good, a part of him had hoped Dan might reach out. That he hadn't irrevocably fucked the one solid friendship in his life.

Being on the Stockyard's radar, out of the Outlaw's good graces, and losing his best friend… Chicago might need to be in his rearview.

Instead of looking into the background of the members of the Twilight Circus, he should be looking into new jobs in new cities.

His eyes glossed over a little as he continued to click through document after document on the lot of them— Margo, Hernando, Sophia, Javier….

His heart ached something fierce, but he couldn't begin to heal. Not here, at least. Maybe not ever. This was why he hadn't bothered getting close to people all these years. Inevitably, you disappointed them. With his parents, his existence had been the main issue, and with his foster family, it was his lack of kumbayaing with the rest of the family. He was the casual friend, the guy to fuck but not to keep, and he'd preferred it that way for so long.

It beat feeling like this.

Leo grabbed his mug and took a sip of the ice-cold liquid. It added to the acid in his stomach, a fitting brew at this point. Maybe he should switch to gin. At least he'd be able to numb out his mind. His old route of trolling Thirst for a hookup wasn't holding the same appeal. All it would do was remind him of the chemistry he'd felt with Tuck and how, for the first time, he'd begun to open up to someone.

To let him in.

And he didn't *do* that.

Leo clicked open a more recent file from the tracker he'd set on the names.

The insurance claim for the caravan that got torched. Right, of course they'd get on that since they'd be picking up their tents and moving to another city in no time. He skimmed over the information, and then paused on the payout.

His eyes widened, and he almost dropped the mug in his other hand.

The payout was triple the amount a caravan should cost—at least.

Numbers and patterns had always been easy for Leo —hence why he'd started hacking years ago. They were far easier than people, steadfast when little else was. And all too fast, the pattern began to extrapolate in his mind, painting a deadly picture.

He'd had the wrong target in mind this entire time.

Only one person fit all the parameters—proximity, information. He hadn't figured out motive yet, but this payout tipped the scale.

Before he could get in his head or question himself, he called Scarlet.

"Leo?" Scarlet said, her voice ringed with caution.

"Where's Tuck?" he asked.

"I shouldn't give out that information," Scarlet responded.

"At the risk of sounding cliché, this is a matter of life or death," Leo said.

A pause sounded over the phone, one that extended for an eternity as his pulse leapt out of his skin.

"He's over with the troupe," Scarlet said, clearly not thrilled with sharing the fact.

"Fuck," Leo cursed. "He's in trouble."

Because if Tuck was with the troupe, that meant he was dangling himself in front of the person who'd tipped off the Stockyard on the night of the warehouse infiltration. The one who'd been working alongside them this whole time.

Javier.

CHAPTER 25

Tuck stepped into the Big Top for the first time in years.

He hadn't avoided it purposefully, but a part of him had steered clear, worried that once he stepped inside, he'd feel that lure again. As if that life could tug him back. The scent of popcorn and sweat still drifted in the air even after the place cleared out. Everyone had already either retired to their caravans or had escaped to unwind, but he'd promised to patrol the grounds tonight to keep an eye on the troupe. If the Stockyard planned on launching another attack, it'd be here.

His gaze lingered on the empty metal stands, remembering the thrill of seeing them filled with excited faces and the frisson of excitement in the air the moment the stage lights flicked on and the performances began. The red-and-white stripes of the tent welcomed him in, beckoning him up to the heights he used to soar, reminding him of the intoxicating adrenaline rush every time he stepped up to the tightrope.

A familiar figure strolled across center stage, the man who'd always belonged there.

Javier approached with a steady, familiar stride and a broad smile that had always felt singular even as he blasted it at everyone. "So, you've come to watch over us tonight?"

"That's the plan," Tuck said, hooking his thumbs into his pockets as he strode over to meet him. He could almost feel the tremors in the air from the noise, the energy that pulsed through this place during each show. "Where's Sophia at?"

Javier's grin tilted at the side. "After all of the chaos of the past few days, she decided to call it an early night after her performance."

Tuck shook his head. "I don't blame her. Better she stay somewhere safe anyway. There's been too much chaos surrounding her in all this. I don't think the girl can take any more heartbreak." Truth be told, the way Sophia had been dragged into this, not only losing her husband but the caravan she'd grown up in, nagged at him. However, he hadn't been able to figure out why the hell the Stockyard or Reynauld would be targeting her specifically.

Javier strode his way, even though he always looked more at home in the middle of center stage. "Come on. Take a seat and we can catch up."

Tuck nodded and followed him over to the stands. He settled onto one close to Javi and hunched forward.

The comms chatter had grown quieter by the time he'd reached the circus since John had walked the perimeter of Reynauld's building and suffered no attacks, and then Grif and Alanna had begun to sneak inside.

"Alarms are disabled," Scar said. "Dive on in."

"Don't mind if I do," Alanna responded as the comms lapsed to silence again.

"You look troubled, son," Javier said, the dark concern in his eyes a comfort Tuck had fallen back upon too many times. The man shouldered too many burdens though—the weight of the troupe, his daughter, and all the devastation that had rained down on them as of late. The last thing he needed was to carry Tuck's.

"Just hoping we can solve your problem tonight," Tuck said. He'd never come out to say what he did to Javier who hadn't asked, but Tuck assumed Javier had a vague idea. The man was always as sharp as his whip, and Sophia could never keep anything from him.

Javier stretched out on the stands beside him, leaning back on his elbows as he stared up at the striped top of the tent. "You're still the same, Ace," he murmured. "Trying to carry everyone's problems as if they were your own."

Javi's words landed a little too close to the mark, mostly in regards to his mother. He'd tried to enforce boundaries and distance over the years, but he couldn't bring himself to just walk away.

"In this case, I'm in a unique position to help," Tuck said, tracing patterns on the rickety metal stand. He'd never actually watched a show, but he'd spent plenty of time hanging around in the Big Top afterwards with Sophia and the others, whiling the hours away. "And I haven't forgotten where I came from."

"After everything that happened with your mother, we understood why you needed to leave," Javier said, the declaration sinking into his skin a little like guilt.

Tuck opened his mouth and closed it again. He'd spoon-fed the same excuse to everyone—but the truth still lingered, the one he'd been afraid to mention time and time again to the older folks in the circus. But after all these years, maybe Javier would understand. "It wasn't just that," Tuck murmured, soaking in the familiar setting—the framework of the tent, the bright, splashy colors, the tightrope strung overhead. "Traveling from town to town but doing the same shows every night—I'd started to dread it."

The words hung in the air between them, a veritable slap in the face to every effort Javier had made through the years to keep their family together.

"I understand," Javier said, those words wearier than he'd ever expected.

Tuck blinked for a moment and rolled up from his hunch. "But you love this life."

Out of everything he'd expected, it wasn't for Javier to get the reason he'd left. This man had lived and breathed circus his entire existence. When Tuck thought about those who emblematized this life, their ringleader came to the forefront of his mind every single time.

Javier cracked a grin, the lines around his obsidian

eyes deepening and making him look more tired than normal. "It's all I've known, son."

That reality swept over Tuck like a weighted blanket. Maybe Javier did understand what he'd gone through.

"The old saying exists in the circus for a reason," Javier continued, weaving his fingers through the air as if he was creating his own invisible tapestry. "When you've seen the elephant, there's not much left to surprise you."

Tuck swallowed hard at hearing his father's old phrase spouted by the man who'd stepped into his place.

Javier said the words the same way his father had—as a world-weary man who'd seen too much. Tuck had a hard time wrapping his mind around the age-old mantra coming from someone as dynamic as Javier who'd led and inspired the troupe for years.

But he supposed the years had changed them all.

John came over the comms. "There's someone circling the building. I'm going to keep my pistol ready."

Tuck's veins buzzed with readiness even though he wasn't anywhere nearby. He'd been sucked into the conversation with Javier when he should've been making rounds through the campground to ensure no one lingered nearby. Instead, he was reminiscing with his former ringleader and friend. Still, it beat the earlier anguish that had tugged at his veins over all the complications this job had brought—including the one man in particular who dominated his mind.

"I should go through to make sure everyone's doing okay," Tuck announced to Javier, swinging his feet over the edge.

"If you want company, I'll join you," Javier said. "Make an old man happy, Ace. It's been too long."

Tuck's brows drew together. "Are you sure you don't want to catch up on some rest?"

"I'm not that old yet," he said with a loud, booming laugh, the sort that made him a perfect feature on center stage. Javier oozed charisma from his pores, and Tuck had looked up to him for years, as if he could even wield a slice of that. Instead, he'd been quiet and steady, the polar opposite of their ringmaster.

"Let's go, then," Tuck said, stepping away from the stands to head for the exit.

Scar's voice came across the comms. "Tuck, are you there?"

He stopped midstride. His senses pinged into high alert at the mention on the comms.

"Yeah," he murmured, trying to keep his voice low enough so Javi didn't notice. Based on the sharp look from the man strolling a few paces behind him, though, he wasn't as subtle as he hoped.

"You need to clear out now," Scar said, her tone urgent.

"What's going on?" Tuck asked, not bothering to hide the fact he was talking to her. Javier had already figured it out, so that ship had sailed. He began walking again, resuming the path toward the exit of the Big Top.

"Leo called and said you're in trouble over there," Scar said, the worried tone sending his alarms clanging full force at this point. "I'm not getting a good feeling about this."

"Maybe he knows something else about the Stockyard?" Tuck asked, his heart pounding a little faster. "Something they're planning?"

"I don't like the sound of that," Grif said over the comms. "Tuck, head back to home base."

Tuck chewed on the inside of his mouth, a bitter tang filling it. He couldn't up and leave the troupe to fend for themselves. If they were in trouble, he wanted to help—that was why he'd showed up tonight. The exit for the Big Top lay feet away, and Tuck felt Javier's presence at his side as the man kept pace.

"Tuck," Scar said over the comms again, more urgently than before. "Get out. Now."

Ice flooded through his veins. "Why?"

He could feel Javier brimming with questions beside him, but he needed answers just as badly.

"Leo sent over the files. There's a traitor in the troupe," she said. His shoulders tensed on reflex before she continued. "It's Javier."

Tuck forgot how to breathe.

The man who'd been leading the troupe for so long. The man he'd considered a surrogate father after Dad died.

The man standing right beside him.

He fought to keep moving, even though a full-body tremor rippled through him, and bile rose in his throat.

"What's wrong?" Javier asked—same charming tone and sharp inquisitiveness he'd always brandished.

Except now Tuck heard the bite behind it.

The concern—and not for him.

His blood dropped to Arctic temps, and the words dried on his tongue. He'd never been a proficient liar, and Javier had known him long enough to see right through his fumbling attempts. However, all he needed to do was stall until they exited the tent. He could whip out an excuse to head in a different direction or latch onto someone else as distraction.

And then get the hell out.

"Just a slight wrinkle in the plan for tonight," Tuck said. Not entirely a lie. His mouth filled with sawdust as his mind spun. This was worse than finding out Leo had lied. No, this reality threatened to unmake his past brick by brick, delivering more questions than he could ever hope to answer.

Was Sophia involved? Anyone else in the troupe? Were they all unaware of what Javier was doing, or were they in on it? His fingers and toes numbed from shock, and he couldn't help the crawling of his skin under the heavy weight of Javier's stare. He'd grown hyperaware of the space separating them, the proximity making his insides riot.

Was Javier working with the Stockyard or Reynauld?

Why?

The question echoed louder and louder in his head as his fingers twitched by his side, begging to go into action. His calves tensed with the need to run away as far and fast as possible. The man he'd trusted more than anyone was a traitor. Acid coated his mouth at the thought.

Steps away from the exit.

He had to make it out of here.

"That's a shame," Javier drawled, still in that even —*too* even—tone.

The unmistakable click of a safety switching off sounded beside him.

Tuck slowly turned his head even as his stomach bottomed out.

"You should've never come back, Ace," Javier said with a mournful shake of his head even though his dark eyes remained calm. Deadly.

The muzzle of a pistol stared Tuck down, and Javier's finger rested on the trigger.

CHAPTER 26

Leo raced down the highway at top speed, the wind whistling in through the open windows and turning the tips of his ears to ice.

His heart raced just as fast. From the moment his call with Scarlet had ended, he'd thrown on his shoes, packed his pistol, and run out the door. No plan in mind. No backup because Leo didn't even have friends to rely on now.

Yet Tuck was in trouble, and he couldn't sit idle.

The man had taken a bullet for him. He'd saved Leo's life when he'd been about to throw it away on Craig Baldwin. And even if all the potential between them had turned to ash in the wreckage of his betrayal, he'd come to care for the man more than he'd ever expected.

His chest squeezed tight as he glanced at the neon numbers on the clock for the thousandth time. The minutes were ticking by too fast and the miles weren't moving quickly enough. He couldn't shake the dread filtering through him like cyanide that he'd arrive too late.

That Javier would've already disposed of the problem.

Tuck was loyal beyond measure, and it was his own loyalty that would sentence him now.

Leo swallowed hard, glaring at the interspersed lights along the highway, an obsidian night stretching beyond them. He'd learned from an early age how terrible people could be, so Javier's betrayal didn't come as a surprise. What had been a revelation was the opposite. How Dan, Tuck, and the rest of the Outlaws had showed him a different side of broken people. One that had made him want to hope—at least, he had before his past caught up with him.

Leo's gaze narrowed in on the upcoming turn in the distance. The one leading to the Twilight Circus encampment.

He didn't even have a sketch of what he was doing here. Leo was a behind-the-scenes hacker who worked in a fucking office. Running with the Outlaws on this job must've infected him, because he would've never attempted this bout of insanity in the past. Growing up around the Stockyard meant he did the polar opposite of rushing toward danger. He'd hid, he'd bided his time, and finally, he'd escaped.

At least, that was what he'd believed.

His stomach soured at the realization that Baldwin had never been far away, aware of him the entire time.

Leo's tires screeched as he veered off onto the exit, the circumstances so different from the last instance when he and Tuck had come here.

As he soared down the road, he caught sight of the floodlights in the distance delineating Twilight Circus. Even post-show, the place still cut a presence that was darker and more consuming with the knowledge of what awaited him.

Maybe Tuck had just arrived.

Maybe Javier wasn't there tonight.

Maybe Tuck had swung in to check on them and had already left.

Right, he'd never been stupid enough to believe any of that. If life found an opportunity to fuck you, she'd screw you hard, fast, and dry.

He pumped the brakes to start slowing down as he closed in on the circus's campsite. The only hope he had right now was arriving in time to warn Tuck. And even that possibility seemed murkier by the second. From the moment the Outlaws had accepted the job, they were ten steps behind—whether from Leo's interference, or from Javier's, as he was now aware.

A sense of caution crept through him, and as he approached, he flicked off his headlights. He slowed to a crawl before he exited the road and drove over the beaten dirt of their parking lot. Calling attention wouldn't help anyone, least of all himself. A few cars remained, but for the most part, the lot was empty. Leo's gaze landed on a familiar Prius, and he made sure to park farther away from it in case they needed to make a fast getaway. The more directional options, the better.

The moment Leo switched off his engine, a wave of uncertainty washed over him.

What was he even doing here? Tuck had cut him out, and the Outlaws told him in no unclear terms to stay out of their business.

Except he'd heard the jolt of genuine fear in Scar's voice when he'd called. Plus, Dan was still enmeshed in all of this. Even if Dan didn't want to be his friend anymore, Leo couldn't forget the years of kindness from the man when Leo had experienced too little in his life. And Tuck…. Leo's betrayal had rocked him, so he couldn't even imagine what this one would do.

He swallowed hard, his throat parched as he patted down the pistol at his side, loaded and at the ready. The guilt over Tuck would bury him in an early grave if he didn't do this. He needed to at least try.

Even if he was just a broken man running from childhood nightmares—not a hero.

Never the hero.

Leo gripped the handle of his car door and pushed it open. The brisk winds slammed into him full force out here, a fierce reminder of the dwindling days of autumn. Chilly stars glared down at him, and with a waning crescent overhead tonight, the shadows positively crawled. Leo rubbed at his forearm, as if he could will away the frisson of fear that rolled through him as he took the first steps away from his car.

Even with the several floodlights still on, a vacuum

filled the circus at this time of night, voids at the entrance of every blackened tent opening threatening to devour. Leo swallowed hard enough that his throat clicked, the sound almost making him jump. He began to drift toward the closest tent even as he scanned the line of caravans parked farther out.

Movement bustled around several of the caravans, doors propped open and lanterns casting hazy glows over the area as troupe members sat around with each other, either perched in lawn chairs, leaning against the sides of their homes, or lying down on blankets in the grass. Completely unperturbed. Unaware of any upheaval heading their way.

He skimmed the faces, recognizing a few from the other night, but he caught no sign of Tuck. Or Javier.

Leo floated by one of the smaller red tents which was dark as pitch, and he shivered as he slipped past the entrance, as if something waited to drag him inside. Echoes of the noise and chaos from the day resonated through the area, a presence he couldn't shake, like energy still drifted through even after everyone had abandoned the grounds. Leo's hand crept to the pistol strapped to his side, the cool metal the comfort he clung to right now.

Every crunch, every whistle of the breeze, every faint sound of laughter that trailed through had him jumping.

He focused on the flow of the shadows, searching, searching, searching for any sight of who he'd come here for.

Leo rubbed at his forearm again, as if the chill he felt was superficial and not burrowed deep. He sucked in a shaky breath as his gaze landed on the Big Top in the center of the grounds, the red candy stripe looking purplish under the dark helm of night. Amber light spilled from the entrance.

Someone was still inside the tent.

If nerves had jangled inside him before, they hummed at a fever pitch now as he approached the entrance one cautious step at a time. Chances were, it was just more of the troupe members unwinding after the show or some of them cleaning up after-hours.

Or it wasn't.

He made sure to creep around from the side, not wanting to risk getting spotted as he inched closer and closer. Leo strained to try and hear any noise coming from inside, but the empty spaces around the circus grounds ached with quiet. One step. Another. His shoulders prickled, and he kept glancing behind him to make sure no one approached.

Leo reached the very edge of the entrance flaps, brushing against the vinyl, and peered inside.

The breath snagged in his throat.

Tuck stood feet away from the entrance, frozen in place.

Javier was beside him, but that wasn't what snared Leo's attention. The man was pointing a pistol in Tuck's direction.

Fuck. What to do, what to do? He glanced around the interior of the Big Top, no ideas springing to mind.

Give him a laptop and a tech problem to solve and he was unstoppable, but this?

"Why?" Tuck asked, the crack in his voice like shattering glass.

"I want out of this life," Javier said with a slight shrug. As if that could explain away sanctioning the murder of members of his troupe and all the damage he'd caused due to his choices. Leo's gut clenched as rage built inside his chest like a stoked furnace. It was people like this who gave humanity a bad rap.

People like this who broke anyone who showed the slightest bit of softness.

He'd learned that firsthand.

"So, you cut a deal with Reynauld? Got your own daughter's husband murdered?" Tuck spat at him, his hands balling into fists at his side.

"I've had a deal with Reynauld for years, a circuit I've been running for him. If you think this is his first time working with the Stockyard, I've got a bridge to sell you," Javier responded. "Contract renegotiations just spurred a necessity to step things up. The troupe wanted their freedom, Reynauld didn't, and I wanted enough cash to live comfortably and never move cities again."

Leo drew his Ruger, bringing it up behind the cover of the tent. His heart pounded hard in his ears, a thump, thump, thump that almost drowned out anything else. Any move could turn into a threat, considering the way Javier pointed his gun at Tuck.

Any surprise could backfire.

However, inaction would kill Tuck just as quickly.

Leo brought his pistol over and aimed at the far side of the tent. Direct shot was too risky with their proximity. Distraction, however….

He pulled the trigger.

The pistol let out a bark as the bullet zipped through the air, tunneling into the packed earth by the stands.

Javier whipped his gun in Leo's direction. "Who's there?"

Leo darted away from the entrance flap. The thump of footsteps sounded, and a second later, a heavy whump echoed through the Big Top. Leo peered inside again. Tuck had tackled Javier, bringing both of them to the ground in a cloud of dust.

Shit. Leo snuck inside the perimeter of the tent, sweat beading on his temple. He kept his Ruger elevated and pointed in Javier's direction even though he didn't dare shoot with the way he was tumbling around with Tuck.

Arms flew, dirt and grit puffed up from the ground, and grunts sounded, echoing through the prime acoustics of the tent. Leo tracked the glint of the pistol in Javier's hands as he struggled to slam it down while Tuck grappled for the weapon. Knees dug into ribs, elbows into sides.

The gun slipped from Javier's grip, spinning away on the ground, just out of reach.

Leo's heart pounded hard, and his feet began moving before his mind caught up. He raced across the space between them, ready to dive for the pistol. Except

Tuck and Javier tumbled toward it, grappling with each other as their arms whipped around, fingers straining to reach for the gun. Leo's soles slapped against the ground, and he gritted his teeth so hard his jaw ached.

He closed in on the pistol right as Javier's fingers brushed against the handle.

Too risky to try for the grab.

Leo kicked Javier's fingers and the pistol—hard.

The silver gun went sliding across the Big Top, stopped by the raised perimeter of the center ring.

Javier tugged his arm back on reflex, but the movement gave Tuck the upper hand. In a fluid move, Tuck swung around over top of him, and he slammed his fist into Javier's jaw with a crack that echoed all the way to the top of the tent.

Leo kept his pistol trained and ready. He wouldn't try aiming while Javier and Tuck were tangled up like that, but if the man attempted to run….

Javier kicked underneath Tuck, bucking like a wildcat despite his age. Tuck let out an "Oomph," but he swung again, his fist landing with another heady thump.

"What's going on?" a confused voice said from the opposite side of the Big Top.

Zeb stepped inside, his brow furrowed, followed by two other guys that Leo had been briefly introduced to when he'd visited with Tuck.

Leo found himself speaking up, his voice ringing clear through the acoustics of the tent. "Want to tell them, Javier?"

Tuck pinned Javier down, overpowering the older man with his forearm pressed against his windpipe. When Tuck whipped his head up to look at who'd spoken, their gazes met, and Tuck's jaw dropped.

"Leo?" His voice was hoarse, and those dark brown eyes were flush with emotion.

Leo swallowed the lump in his throat as he tried to force a smile. Better than the "you die too, traitor" reception he'd been fearing.

"Tuck, what are you doing to Javi?" Zeb asked, his gaze flashing as he took careful steps forward.

"Please tell me the rest of you weren't involved in this," Tuck forced out, sparing a glance up at the approaching members of the troupe.

A few of the guys shook their heads, and confusion painted every expression. Their hesitation bloomed in the air, as if awareness had begun to creep in that they wouldn't like the answers to their questions. Leo didn't realize he'd been holding a breath until he let it go.

If Javier had been the only traitor, maybe they could salvage this.

A scream sounded from behind him. He whipped his pistol in the direction of the noise only to see the woman who'd made the delicious goulash at the entrance—Margo. Her hand was pressed over her mouth, shock etched across her features.

Zeb lifted his hands in defense. "Look, man, I have no idea what you're talking about."

"Guess who's been taking an extra payday from Reynauld this whole time," Tuck forced through his gritted teeth. "Who's been working alongside him to make sure your contract remains with Reynauld Industries."

"No, Javi, no," Margo said from behind Leo, approaching on shuffled footsteps. She paused a few feet behind him. "You wouldn't...."

"He's wrong," Javier gasped out, clearly trying some flashy footwork to see if they'd follow along.

Leo kept his muzzle pointed in his direction. "Keep telling lies. Go for it," he growled, the bitterness rising in an angry streak through him. The troupe was supposed to be better than this. People were supposed to be better than this, yet time and time again, they ended up nothing but disappointments, paste imitations of his hopes.

"His caravan got burnt down though," Zeb said, jabbing a finger in Tuck's direction as he chanced another few steps, though he gave Leo a nervous glance in the process.

"I can explain that one," Leo spoke up again, drawing Tuck's stare a second time. His heart ached at the sight of him, even in the middle of this. He'd believed he would never see the man again, and while these were the worst circumstances possible, something in him was soothed to see Tuck up and moving.

He'd been terrified he'd arrive to find a corpse.

"Let him go," Margo said, tears welling in her eyes. "We can all talk this through. There has to be a mis—"

She stopped midword.

Red bloomed across her forehead after the bullet zipped through it.

A second later, Margo collapsed to the ground.

"Thanks for the heads up, Javier," a sickeningly familiar voice said from behind her.

There, standing in the entrance of the Big Top, was Craig Baldwin. And he'd brought friends.

CHAPTER 27

One moment Margo was standing, feeling, pleading—living.

The next, she'd hit the ground, a puddle of crimson beginning to spread around her.

Shock rocketed through Tuck's system at the sight, and his grip faltered.

That was what Javier was waiting for.

The man's knee slammed into the base of his ribs, and before Tuck could right himself, Javier was already hefting his weight to the side to send him toppling. The man might be older, but he'd been working in the circus for years and had more tricks up his sleeve than any magician. Instead of diving back in for the grapple, Tuck rolled away, pressing against the comms in his ear.

A bigger threat had showed up.

"The Stockyard's here," Tuck choked out.

What miracle he was expecting, he didn't know. Dan and Scar remained in the penthouse on the opposite side of Chicago, and Grif, John, and Alanna were all stationed in the city in the middle of the heist they'd planned on Reynauld. None of them were close enough to make a difference right now.

And if the Stockyard had arrived, a slaughter would follow.

Javier scrambled up from the floor, wheezing as he drew in choking breaths. The man's clothes were disheveled, his neatly oiled beard and mustache a mess, a far stretch from the perfectly poised man he'd known. If Tuck had really known Javier at all.

Seconds later, Javier was rushing toward Baldwin and the five bruisers he'd brought tonight. Apparently, he wasn't fucking around.

"Reynauld's decided the lot of you have caused him enough trouble," Baldwin announced. "Investment's not worth keeping."

Javier paled. "They don't need to die."

Rage bloomed inside Tuck like a fresh bruise. If Javier hadn't gotten bored, if he hadn't made deals with the fucking devil, maybe the Twilight Circus would've found their freedom years ago. He'd dragged them in too deep, and now the coward attempted to voice his regrets? Blood and bones.

Asher was dead.

Mugs was dead.

Margo was dead.

How many more of his former family would die tonight? His gut clenched as his gaze swung to Leo. What would happen to him? Leo Kennedy had been the last person on the planet he expected to show up at the campgrounds tonight.

The man might've lied about his past, but this—this action spoke louder than any words.

Tuck had been wrong in his judgement of the man, and the sight of him had his heart sparking to life once more.

However, Leo might've just signed his death sentence along with the rest of them. Tuck pulled out his pistol, needing something in hand to level the playing field because the six men from the Stockyard were toting Glocks and worse, and the troupe members who'd fast been approaching, drawn by the sounds of their scuffle, were decidedly not. They wouldn't stand a chance.

"They killed Margo," Hernando shouted, a raw anguish in his voice that drove straight through Tuck's heart.

She'd been the heart of their troupe for so long, the woman who'd made sure their bowls were full in the cookhouse and offered a hug to those who needed one, like a mother to them all.

Now she was lying on the ground, dead.

All thanks to Javier. Betrayal didn't begin to describe the crawling, creeping sensation that mounted inside Tuck, a corrosive bitterness that threatened to rise like the tide until it consumed him body and soul.

"Don't worry," Baldwin called out, his tone almost jovial. "The rest of you can join her in a moment."

Tuck's gaze locked on Leo, who stared Craig down

with an intensity he'd only seen emerge the other night. Unlike the other night, however, when Tuck had been consumed by the news he'd just learned, today he noticed what brimmed from Leo in waves.

Pure, unadulterated fear.

This was the man who'd terrorized Leo as a child. A fucking *child*.

The one who'd locked him up in a trunk for who knew how long.

Yet Leo had driven here tonight to try and help Tuck anyway. He stood here now with them, ready and willing to fight.

Tuck closed the distance between them in quick strides until he stepped up beside Leo. "Thank you," he said, the words heavy on his tongue with a weight he struggled to convey.

Leo's blue eyes flashed in surprise, the brief, genuine expression making him all the more beautiful. Tuck's heart squeezed hard. This man had imprinted on him for a reason—because he continued to surprise him, over and over again. Impressed him when so few did. Leo offered a smile—pure bravado—and a nod. "Couldn't leave you to face all the fun without me."

"How are we supposed to deliver shipments if I don't have a troupe to travel with?" Javier tried to argue with Baldwin, the tone Tuck once found charming now coming across wheedling. Pathetic.

Despite the way several of his former troupe members had crumbled to the ground, some openly weeping, others braced themselves, shoulders tensed as they prepared for a fight. Yet their numbers didn't matter—not when they were unarmed.

There were only two guns on their side—Tuck and Leo's—against six.

Those weren't odds. This was a massacre.

He needed to do something. Anything. The comms remained silent—no word from any of the other Outlaws.

His heart pounded hard, a droplet of sweat tickling as it trickled down his cheek. Those pistols were out and aimed, the men from the Stockyard ready to unload the moment Baldwin gave the word. Floodlights beamed down from the sides of the Big Top, a rig stretched across the length closer to the top, the stands in an arc around the center—the other exit beyond that.

"Not my problem," Baldwin said to Javier, lifting his pistol and aiming at Zeb.

"Run," Tuck barked out. Panic thrummed through him at seeing his old friend in the crosshairs. The time to act was now.

He glanced at Leo and tilted his head toward the stands. They needed cover first. His legs had already begun moving before he got a response. He flew to the stands, the prickle of awareness buzzing around him that those muzzles were trained in their direction. That at any moment, those men would begin firing, bullets whispering promises of pain. His shoulder ached with the reminder.

The stands rose in his shaky view, and he launched himself toward them. The crack of gunshots lit the arena, a bone-chilling sound that ricocheted through his entire body. Tuck sailed through the air, only to roll the rest of the way.

The second he righted himself behind the stands, Leo was skidding his way, crouched low to join him.

Screams echoed through the Big Top, and Tuck followed the noise. Zeb staggered forward, a red stain growing on his shoulder, and several of the others had already started heading for the exit.

The men from the Stockyard kept their muzzles trained on the helpless members of his troupe. Fuck. Fuck, fuck, fuck.

No time to waste.

He whipped his pistol up, lined a shot at the nearest bruiser, and fired.

The guy let out a grunt, his shoulder bucking back. Then the bruiser's muzzle swung Tuck's way, and he was squeezing the trigger.

The bullet zipped in Tuck's direction, whizzing inches from him.

His heart lodged in his throat. These weren't garden-variety thugs—they could aim.

This would be over in minutes.

Zeb had rushed forward, a low growl coming from him, and Hernando surged behind him in an attempt to stop the men from the Stockyard. The exit flap to the tent rustled as Sophia stepped into view, blinking as if she'd been woken from sleep.

"What's going on?" Her bewildered voice carried

through the Big Top, but when she paused to soak in the scene before her, she froze.

Tuck couldn't shake the acid in his throat that rose over how the family he'd once believed in had fallen apart. Over how they'd now be massacred. Bitterness gripped his chest tight.

"Don't leave anyone alive," Craig Baldwin commanded.

Tuck and Leo could shoot all they liked—they wouldn't be fast enough to save his troupe.

A wave of devastation raced through him, numb, consuming, and terrible, even as he lifted his pistol again and aimed.

They were all going to die.

Craig Baldwin brought his pistol up, focusing on Zeb again.

The sound of a bullet cracked through the Big Top.

Tuck tasted bile as he scanned the tent. His finger found the trigger, and he prepared to shoot.

The bruiser Tuck had already fired at dropped to the ground. His chest blossomed with red, pretty as a poppy.

"Aren't you supposed to be stealthy?" an achingly familiar voice said from the entrance of the Big Top, right behind the guys from the Stockyard.

"Yeah, but I wanted to make an entrance." Alanna said as she strode in, her pistol still lifted. Her gait was pure confidence, ponytail swinging behind her as a smile that couldn't be anything but menacing curled her lips. Grif and John followed close behind, taking aim as casually as if they'd embarked on a Sunday afternoon stroll.

Craig Baldwin whipped around, as did the other guys.

The Outlaws had arrived.

Tuck's heart lurched forward as hope flooded through him in a fierce torrent, and his grip tightened on his Sig Sauer.

"What took you so long?" Tuck called out, drawing Grif's attention. He tried to stifle the giddy lift in his chest of the sheer adrenaline that salvation brought.

They might not all die today.

Grif didn't even pause his stride as he fired a shot off into the Stockyard guy closest to him. The asshole let out a low grunt before staggering forward, and Baldwin squeezed his trigger a second later.

The bullet zipped toward Alanna who ducked and was now hurtling toward him.

"We got held up with that little project of ours," Grif said with a wink, picking up the pace to close the distance, aiming for close quarters. His gaze slid over to Leo at Tuck's side, and his brows lifted for a flash of a second. "We would've said more on the comms, but we weren't sure who might be listening in."

With the arrival of the Outlaws, a few of the guys from the Stockyard separated off from the herd, rushing in the direction of his troupe. That was going to be a clusterfuck in about two point five seconds. Tuck's heart rattled in his ribcage. Shooting from here would only get him so far, and if he rushed into the fray, he'd get lost in the chaos.

The beam stretching to the rig that spanned the entire Big Top lay mere feet away.

"I've got to get a better vantage point," Tuck murmured.

He whipped toward Leo, who still crouched next to him, those brows drawn together in concentration. This might be his one chance—fuck it.

Tuck crushed his mouth to Leo's in a bruising kiss. He drank in the heat, the masculine taste of him, the rosewood and sweat emanating off him, and for a brief, blissful second, he could pretend everything else had melted away—the problems, the danger, the imminent destruction. He could pretend that nothing had shattered between them, that Leo was his, and they were hurtling toward a beautiful future at a thousand miles a minute.

Then he pulled away, and reality returned.

"Stay safe," Tuck said, already racing toward the beams. His hands landed on the metal bars, and he began to scale them as fast as possible, bringing himself higher and higher with ease. Memories of launching himself to the top lunged to the fore, but they tangled with the reality that lay before him—of Javier standing beside the men who wanted to slaughter his troupe. Of Margo lying dead on the floor. Of Zeb on his knees, blood dripping down his chest at an alarming rate.

Of the Stockyard assholes who were rushing toward the members of the Twilight Circus who were still standing, prepared to gun them down before they made an exit.

Tuck climbed higher, faster. He loped up the side of the beam as if he was racing along a staircase, his movements fluid, familiar. He might not be in his tightrope flats, but he'd been scaling heights from the moment he learned to walk.

He zeroed in on the top beam, trying to shut out the chaos below. The crack of bullets ripe in the air, the echoing shouts, the muffled grunts, the cries. His heart slammed harder at each noise, fear rising like bile that each shot might end someone he cared about. Someone he loved.

Tuck gripped tight to the top beams, his upper arms flexing as he pulled himself up to perch at the edge. Up here, he could see the entire damn arena beyond. He'd witnessed this perspective a thousand and one times, but now it'd give him the vantage point to take out the rest of the bruisers who were trying to murder his goddamn family.

His feet dangled into nothingness at a height that might be dizzying to some, but up here, he felt centered in a way he never did in the chaos below.

Tuck sucked in one breath, then he pulled the pistol from his side.

On another breath, he scanned the brawl taking place below. Grif, Alanna, and John had entered the fray, coming in hard and heavy. They'd barreled toward two of the guys from the Stockyard for a little hand-to-hand action that was close enough to take guns out of the equation. The other two bruisers had thrown themselves in amidst the members of the Twilight Circus. Tuck aimed at the nearest one.

He drank in a third slow breath and fired.

The bullet ripped through the air, tunneling through the man's skull.

The moment he saw he'd landed his mark, he'd already started scanning the crowd again. Leo had slunk away from the metal stands, and it didn't take long to figure out where he was heading. Craig Baldwin had slipped away, creeping toward the entrance he'd come in from.

The man was going to run.

Leo wouldn't let him.

Tuck searched out the one person he hadn't caught sight of yet—the traitor who'd brought this hellish landscape down upon his old troupe. His gut roiled at the thought of Javier, of everything the man had cost the people who'd loved him. At the years of admiration Tuck had devoted to him, the deep, abiding trust he'd placed in the man.

Stupid. He'd been utterly stupid.

He spotted Javier ducking down by the arena to snag his pistol from the spot it'd slid to earlier. Javier bolted forward to where the Outlaws tussled with the last man standing from the Stockyard. His trajectory was clearly on the exit, but Grif blocked his way.

The pistol in Javier's hand rose. He was going to shoot Grif—Tuck's leader, his comrade-in-arms, his friend.

Tuck didn't think—he just squeezed the trigger.

The shot fired, and a half second later, Javier swayed on his feet.

The pistol clattered from his hands as he grasped his chest, which was now growing darker by the second with blood.

Tuck stared, unable to look away as the man who'd taught him how to breathe when he was walking the tightrope, the one who'd made sure he'd eaten enough dinner before a show, the one who'd told him the stupid joke about the tiger over and over to elicit a smile when he'd get in a funk after his dad died—as *that* man, that patriarch, collapsed to the ground.

Just another one of the corpses.

The only words that left Tuck's lips were the ones he'd heard Javier quoting time and time again. Ones he should've heeded long, long ago.

"You can fool most of the people most of the time."

CHAPTER 28

The moment the Outlaws arrived, the situation shifted from "fuck, we're going to die" to "maybe, *maybe*."

Leo crouched low behind the metal stands, so far out of his element he needed a fucking telescope to see where he belonged.

All night hacking sessions? Sweaty nightclub hookups? Slipping into a suit and pretending to be professional day in and out?

Check and check.

Getting in the middle of a gunfight between the Twilight Circus, the Stockyard, and the Outlaws?

Holy hell, his legs were shaking at this point. He swallowed hard, clutching the handle of his pistol with sweaty palms. Tuck raced off to the side, clearly aiming to climb up to the beam spanning across the Big Top. Reckless fucker. His lips still buzzed from the kiss Tuck had laid on him, and he clung to the feeling as if it could bolster him.

The bliss of that man's mouth on his, the consuming way he'd devoured him as if during those seconds, he mattered.

Leo should be regretting his choices by now, but after that look in Tuck's eyes, he found he couldn't.

Bullets zipped overhead, and another was buried in one of the troupe members who let out a loud scream, gripping at their hip. Grif, Alanna, and John swept in with a fury, closing the gap between them and the guys from the Stockyard to make guns pretty much useless. With all the chaos that had just arrived, no one was paying attention to him hiding behind the stands.

He could sneak out.

Leo had showed up. He'd warned Tuck, and he'd even gotten involved. It was a miracle he remained standing.

And yet his unfinished business stood in the middle of the arena, shoulders squared and his ugly mug twisted in a snarl at the newcomers. Leo's throat tightened at the sight of Craig Baldwin, a reminder of the hold the man still had over him.

Alanna swept in first, hurling herself at the nearest guy. She drove her head right into his torso with a thump, but before he could swing down, John had reached out to grab his arm and yank it back. The crack echoed throughout the arena, and the man let out a howl before he lashed out.

Leo's shoulders tightened in his hunch, his gaze

focusing on Craig who'd started taking steps away from his men.

His stomach dropped.

He was going to run. Craig was going to escape, and then Leo would never be free of the man's hold, his influence that spanned much further than Chicago like a living web crawler. Acid burned in Leo's gut at the thought. Craig maneuvered back another step. Then another. His men didn't notice—no, they were too occupied with the Outlaw onslaught barreling their way.

One moment Craig was standing there, and then the next, he'd melded with the tent walls, taking slow, measured steps toward the entrance. Leo found himself rising unbidden, even though he could feel the tug at his calves to run. To ditch the tent, to get in his car, and to just drive until he left all of this behind.

Except Craig would still be out there. And no matter how hard Leo tried to reinvent himself, how hard he tried to escape his past with the Stockyard, Craig would be waiting to drag him under again. The truth crawled under his skin, making him want to tear it off, and his throat grew tight as he crept toward the same damn exit.

Leo let out a low curse.

He couldn't let him go.

Craig wasn't looking his way. The guy was focused on one thing: getting the hell out.

This job had taken a turn for the deadly, and the leader of the Stockyard was smarter than most. He'd survived as long as he had by not hesitating to throw other bodies in front of open fire to protect his own hide. Or letting others take the fall—case in point, Leo's parents.

Leo's legs trembled, but he slipped along the perimeter of the tent with a quickness that surprised him, as if he was being drawn by a magnet. A gurgle sounded to his left as Grif finished off one of the assholes from the Stockyard. Others had rushed past to fight with the troupe members, stuck on finishing the job even though Baldwin was making his escape. Unsurprising, since he relied on grunt men who were too stupid to realize when the odds had flipped.

Craig had almost reached the tent flap—so damn close.

Leo continued to follow him with one smooth stride after another as he remained hunched. With the way bullets were flying around here, he wanted to minimize the chance of catching a stray. His heart pounded hard. What the fuck was he doing, going after this man? Craig Baldwin had put so many others in the ground, dropped their bloated bodies into the Chicago River.

He had stuffed Leo in a goddamn lockbox.

His fingers and toes numbed at the memory, and his breath suddenly lodged in his throat. His vision flickered once, going fuzzy around the edges.

Not now.

Leo forced in a long, slow breath, keeping his gaze focused on the entrance Craig had just slipped out of.

The bastard was going to hop in his car and get away. Leo maintained another steadying breath, and the feeling rushed back to his fingertips. With each continuing breath, his vision grew sharper, more stable. The past had been claiming his actions for years—crippling him, keeping him from pursuing anything real. But throughout this entire job with the Outlaws, he'd come to realize one thing.

He wanted more.

Leo wanted more than the half life he'd been floating through.

And that meant Craig Baldwin needed to die.

Leo reached the entrance and cast a glance back at the arena that was now filled with a flurry of limbs in action, scattered pools of blood, bullets cracking through the air, and even louder screams sounding. It looked like an artist's depiction of the Inferno. And yet he'd be escaping it only to face Lucifer himself. He slipped through the opening in the canvas and back out into the night.

The cool air caressed him at once, a crispness to the breeze that was so different from the sweat, dust, and metallic blood from inside the tent. He didn't rush forward even though his shoulders pitched in that direction, at the ready. Instead, he skimmed the grounds for a glimpse of Baldwin.

The multicolored tents were just shades of white and dark at this time of night, and several marred the way between here and the dusty lot, but it didn't take long for Leo to zero in on his target.

Craig was zigzagging between them, careful to stay out of view. Even with his bulky form, the man moved fast. However, Leo didn't need to guess his trajectory—and that gave him an advantage.

Leo had mapped out every detail of the grounds on his slow approach in, and that paid off now. His pistol weighed heavy in his hand as he surged forward, moving as quietly and carefully as possible. He might never be able to creep as silently as Tuck, but he exercised caution with each step to avoid snapping a twig or kicking a stray stone along the way. Craig hustled forward with an efficiency that didn't surprise him—the man had been murdering folks and escaping the scene of the crime for years now.

Leo couldn't let him get to his car.

The second Craig Baldwin drove away, there went Leo's freedom as well. And the man had already stolen so much from him—he wouldn't let him take any more.

Leo pushed himself harder, racing along in a straight line toward the lot, needing to close the distance. He could feel the steady thump, thump, thump of his steps reverberating up his shins. Unlike Craig, he wasn't worried about members of the troupe or other Outlaws spotting him. What that did tell him, though, was that the man hadn't brought backup. Hence the quick exit once their "easy job" got tough.

His palm was sweaty as hell, and with each forward step, he was sure the pistol would slip from his wet grasp. If it came down to accuracy, Baldwin had him beat. If it came down to who shot faster, yeah, he was fucked there too.

His sole advantage narrowed down to the fact that Craig Baldwin didn't know he was coming for him.

The shadows slithered across everything tonight, the pale stars and threadbare moon barely casting any light. He raced alongside one of the tents blocking him from Craig's view, picking up his speed here, operating on adrenaline alone at this point. The man wouldn't be able to see him, though, and vice versa. His mouth had dried, and his heart tap-tap-tapped in his chest like the clicking of keys on a keyboard.

Craig might look back.

He might spot Leo, and then bang, it'd be over.

Before he ever got to experience the life he'd always secretly longed for. The one he'd never allowed himself, in which he'd be letting people in. Trying to trust them for once rather than icing them out. His eyes burned. He didn't want to die.

But he couldn't let Craig Baldwin live.

He slowed as he reached the edge of the tent and peered past it.

Craig had reached the edge of the parking lot. The stretch to the lot was clear of obstacles, but that also placed Leo as a wide-open target. The parking lot was the length of a few small tents away, and he'd need to sprint to try and catch up, which minimized his ability to be quiet.

Yet the chance was already slipping from his fingers.

Leo gripped his pistol tight and lunged forward.

The wind swirled around him, and all he could taste as he raced forward was the bitter tang of metal, like all the blood that had been spilled inside the Big Top had permeated through him somehow. His calves pumped, and he pushed himself faster as he booked toward the parking lot.

Craig had already begun to run too. He veered to the far left, opposite to the side Leo had parked. If Leo chased after him, he wouldn't be able to follow him by car. Not a chance. Which meant he needed to close the distance here and now.

Leo kept hunched down, his center of gravity lowered as he barreled forward across the clearing, trying to stay in the line of the cars on the off chance Craig looked back and might catch sight of him. His heart threatened to burst out of his chest, and if he made it out of this alive, he was putting a moratorium on running for at least a month or six.

He reached the edge of the mostly empty lot and ducked behind the nearest car, a Ford Focus.

Craig zeroed in on a dark Pontiac Grand Am in the center of the lineup. Probably one of the junkers the Stockyard rode into the ground until they needed to turn it around for something new. Cars never lasted long in their line of work. People didn't either.

Leo gauged the distance.

If he ran to try and catch up with him, Craig would spot him in an instant. There was nowhere else to hide, and Baldwin would just lob a shot at him out the window of his car at the first opportunity. His fingers trembled, his entire soul buzzing, buzzing, buzzing.

Craig reached the door of the Grand Am and yanked it open with force.

He was going to escape.

Leo peered past the back end of the Focus and lifted his pistol, taking aim for the car door.

Only one option left now.

Craig practically dove into the vehicle, bringing the door shut behind him with an echoing slam.

Leo pulled the trigger. Again. And again. And again.

The bullets littered the driver's side door of the Grand Am. Craig looked like he was seated in the car, but the engine wasn't bursting to life. The car wasn't peeling out of the lot. Leo slipped past the edge of the Ford Focus, creeping forward step by step.

His nerves thrummed. Had he done it? He closed the distance. This many feet away from the Grand Am, the pervasive shadows made it hard to tell. Each inhale he took dragged cool, dry air into his parched mouth, and he struggled to swallow.

The door creaked open.

Leo tensed and whipped his pistol up.

Craig grappled with the car door, his movements erratic. Leo didn't hesitate and fired the gun. The bullet traveled straight into his chest, sending the man shuddering back. Dark stains covered his shirt, and from the distance Leo stood, he could hear the ragged, wet breaths coming from the man.

Craig looked up at him, those venomous eyes meeting his, a gaze that had once upon a time chilled Leo to his core.

This was the bogeyman who'd haunted him for years.

This was the man who tortured and killed without mercy.

However, Craig's eyes then flickered shut, he swayed, and he collapsed against the steering wheel of the car.

Leo stood there, pistol aimed, as he waited for Craig to get back up. He waited for the "gotcha" moment, because men like him didn't just keel over and die. They lived on and on in the pain they'd caused, and Leo was living proof.

He didn't know how long he waited, standing there in between the cars, the cold wind turning his fingertips to ice, freezing his cheeks, numbing the edges of his ears. Time was immaterial as he stared at the slumped-over body of the leader of the Stockyard.

Finally, he forced his feet forward, like wading through mud, before reaching the car. Craig still didn't stir. Leo nudged the man's leg with his shoe—no response. Another minute passed, but that didn't make the man any less a corpse than he already was.

Craig Baldwin was no more.

The leader of the Stockyard was dead.

Tremors shook through Leo's entire body, an earthquake of a release he hadn't expected rolling through him, cracking him apart from the inside out. Tears sprung to his eyes unbidden.

He was free.

He sucked in a shaky breath, his brain not quite able

to wrap around the concept after having lived so long in the shadow of the Stockyard with the fear that his past would emerge to drag him back under. However, now he could go wherever he wanted, chase whatever dreams he longed to. He could pursue something real and true and lasting without worrying about the past.

And maybe this time, he wouldn't fuck it all up.

Leo cast a glance back at the Big Top in the center of the circus grounds, the striped tent visible from here. His heart squeezed hard, and he lifted his fingers to his lips, brushing them as if he could still feel the remnants of that kiss. A few stray tears slipped down his cheeks, hot against the ice they'd become, as if all of the frozen parts of him were beginning to melt at last.

If he could've chosen anyone, he'd want someone like Tuck. Someone loyal and patient. Someone who grounded him, who protected him. Someone who in a short time had managed to see the real side of Leo that he'd always hidden from others. Except Leo had ruined them, and he wasn't naïve enough to believe showing up tonight had tipped the tide.

Leo slid his pistol back into the holster at his side and stepped away from the Grand Am, from Craig Baldwin's corpse. He turned from the circus grounds and began to stride toward his car on the opposite side of the lot.

First stop, his apartment so he could begin to pack.

Next stop… anywhere he damn wanted.

CHAPTER 29

Once the last guy from the Stockyard dropped, Tuck began to climb down from the rig.

He scaled slowly, sinking into each handhold with a meditativeness that belied the riot in his mind.

Javier was dead, and he'd killed him.

The blood of their former ringleader stained his hands.

Bile rose in his throat, and he fought with the full-body shakes threatening to overcome him. He'd taken the shot, and while he couldn't regret protecting Grif—the reality shredded him to pieces. He'd built a foundation with his troupe, brick by careful brick, a trust in the family who'd raised him. And after he'd lost his father, Javier had stepped in to offer a guiding hand, support when he'd needed lifting up, and advice when he was lost.

Yet he'd been more corrupt than any of them could've anticipated.

Tuck's feet settled on the ground, and he blinked. He must've floated the rest of the way down because he didn't remember the descent. Before he could turn to find the rest of his crew, to see what had happened to the other members of his troupe, Sophia's anguished wail pierced through the air like a siren. She crouched in front of Javier, her hands balled into fists, tears streaming down her face. Tuck's stomach flipped.

He couldn't go over there. He couldn't face Sophia and deliver the truth of her father's sins. They would come out soon enough, but Tuck had done enough damage tonight of the sort that couldn't be scrubbed out with bleach.

Hernando hunched over by Zeb, ripping cloth and creating a makeshift bandage. He looked up as Tuck approached. "We called an ambulance," he said, his voice shaking. "The paramedics should be here any minute."

A sour taste bloomed in Tuck's mouth with the understanding that statement brought.

If authorities were called, the Outlaws needed to be gone.

He soaked in the sight of the Big Top one last time—his Big Top. The big broad stripes of the tent, the center ring with its beaten dirt middle now spattered with pools of blood and crumpled bodies. The rig he'd climbed for the final time—not to scale the tightrope, but to take Javier's life. He saw Margo's body lying on the ground a few feet away from one of the men from the Stockyard. Lila, their contortionist, crouched next to

Felix, one of the clowns, trying to patch him up even though he was losing blood too quickly from a gunshot wound.

And Sophia draped herself over her father who lay there lifeless. Those vibrant eyes were clouded in death, his booming voice that had heralded show after show forever silenced.

Guilt clogged Tuck's throat. He needed to be out of here now, and not just because the ambulance was coming.

"Come on, man," John said, clapping him on the shoulder. "We've got to go."

Tuck nodded, unspoken words squeezing his throat tight as he caught Hernando's gaze. "Take care," was all he managed to say, even though so much more brimmed inside him. So many memories he wanted to share, losses he wanted to mourn, and people he wanted to apologize to—however, that chance was gone.

Instead, he broke into a jog after John, heading toward Alanna and Grif who waited by the exit of the Big Top.

"Where's Leo?" Tuck asked once he reached the others.

"Haven't seen him since he snuck out," Grif said, already leading the way toward the parking lot. "Looked like he had a bigger target in mind."

Craig Baldwin.

Tuck's blood chilled at the thought of what might've happened in a face-off between the two of them. Leo was untested where Craig was wily, and… his mind threatened to fully shut down if he let it head in that direction.

"What happened with grabbing the folder from Reynauld's?" Tuck asked as they cut a quick pace through the circus grounds.

Alanna flashed a vicious grin. "Fucker only had a couple of guards and a shitty-ass security system. We were in and out in no time."

"Reynauld Industries will be an on-fire dumpster come tomorrow morning when we turn the files in to the authorities," Grif said, a smugness ringing in his tone. He glanced at Tuck. "Your old troupe will be free, for what it's worth."

The grimness in Grif's statement tunneled straight through him. He'd just wanted to help. A bubble of grief rose in his throat, threatening to overwhelm him.

"We're on our way back," John said over the comms.

"So, I should place the takeout order?" Scar came on the comms to ask, her tone amused.

"Double of everything," Alanna replied. "I'm fucking starving."

They began to bicker on the comms, the normalcy of it all sliding over Tuck like an emergency blanket, as if he were huddled at the back end of an ambulance, shivering in the wake of everything that had happened. Except he was simply striding to the parking lot, preparing to drive back to the penthouse.

Because at the end of the day, this had just been another job.

His throat tightened, and he resisted the urge to retch.

Grif's hand clapped down on his shoulder. "John, Alanna, you head back together. I'll drive with Tuck."

Tuck nodded and began the short trek toward the Prius, numbness infiltrating. Along the way, one sight stopped him still. A Pontiac Grand Am sat abandoned in the lot, a man half spilled onto the ground from the driver's side. He and Grif veered toward the sight at once, a vigilant stiffness creeping into his shoulders.

It only took a quick glimpse to tag the man—Craig Baldwin.

The first bit of hope he'd felt all night pierced through his chest, a momentary gasp of light.

"Leo did it," Tuck murmured.

"Ballsy fucker," Grif agreed.

Tuck glanced around the parking lot in case Leo might still be around, but he didn't see his car in the lot. The heaviness returned, the reality that Leo would be gone for good now. Nothing remained for the man here in Chicago.

Even if Tuck wished they could've been something more.

Tuck trudged toward the Prius, but when they got close, Grif outpaced him, snagging the driver's side. That was fine. He wasn't in the shape to drive right now anyway.

All he could see was Javier lying there dead on the floor of the Big Top.

Sophia plastered to her father—utterly alone in the world now.

If he had never gotten involved, maybe it wouldn't have ended like this. He could've spared her the heartbreak, the devastation. Maybe the past needed to stay in the past for a reason.

Grif turned the engine on and was peeling out of the parking lot in a matter of seconds. Any minute now, the ambulances would be rushing in, all flashing lights and chaos, and they needed to be gone. Tuck slumped in the seat, a hollow ache where his heart should be.

The Prius sailed down the road, Grif hunched forward and focused, his silence intentional—clearly giving Tuck space. Tuck couldn't feel his fingers or toes at this point, too numbed after everything that had happened.

He'd just wanted to help Sophia. To see his old family again and bask in the joy he'd once felt in the circus. Instead, he'd witnessed them fall apart—torn to shreds by death, by greed. He still wasn't sure what Javier had been involved with, but from the sounds of it, he'd been doing favors for Reynauld for years and not just recently. His gut soured at the idea that the man he'd admired so much had been working for Reynauld even back then.

They zipped along on the highway, but Tuck's brow wrinkled as he checked the signs. "Where are we going?"

"Figured you could use a minute before returning to the anarchy," Grif said, a knowing tone in his voice that had Tuck swallowing hard. They might not all bleed their past around each other, but each of them carried scars. Each of them understood.

The scorched sky spanned ahead of them, and Tuck lost himself in the expanse, not bothering to respond. He felt hollowed out, as if someone had carved into him and splattered his guts across the floor. The metallic scent of blood still invaded his nostrils even though he hadn't gotten bloody. Hadn't soaked in the crimson pools that stained the ground there. Yet it had marked him, nonetheless.

The turn signal made a clicking sound that echoed through the car as Grif got off onto an exit, and within minutes, their destination was clear.

Lake Michigan glittered in the distance like a dark jewel as Grif pulled off to the side of the road by Promontory Point.

"Come on," Grif said. "Fresh air first, and then we can join the others for whatever takeout's left after Alanna's gotten to it."

Tuck's lips lifted on reflex, and he slid out of the car, the sounds of the closing doors echoing in the still night. In long, loping strides, they crossed the distance to the stone overlook by the water, thick, pale rocks that jutted out to greet the vast expanse. Grif found a long flat one and took a seat, his legs stretched out in front of him. Tuck plunked down beside him, the coolness of the stone shocking him through the thin fabric of his clothes. He hunched forward, bringing his knees up to rest his chin on them.

"So, Javier," Grif said, cutting through the quiet.

Tuck's throat grew thick. "So, Javier."

"I'm not going to feed you some garbage like, 'don't let this taint your memories' or 'at least the rest of them aren't like that' because it's useless," Grif said, offhandedly, as if he wasn't digging in right past Tuck's ribcage.

Tuck gripped his shins tightly as he stared out at Lake Michigan, watching the undulating water that glimmered under the minimal moonlight.

"When bad shit goes down, it tends to fuck those memories up," Grif said, his tone grim. That understanding struck to the core of him, a reminder of why he'd joined the Outlaws. He might've been raised in the circus, but he'd *chosen* this life.

"Yeah, it does," Tuck said, his voice soft. As much as he tried to remember the good things about his mom, all he could see was the struggle now. And after tonight, those sepia-hued memories of growing up in the circus were all spattered in blood. Acid churned in his gut at the realization that now—he truly couldn't go back. He hadn't planned on it before, hadn't wanted to, but the circus had always been an option.

Always a comment from Javier about if he ever wanted to return.

Turns out, the man himself never really wanted to stay.

Grif glanced his way. "You know, Leo saved your life tonight."

Tuck bobbed his head in a nod. Great, another regret. He was drowning in them today.

"You're our backbone, you know that, right?" Grif said, talking more than he had in ages. Tuck appreciated it because right now he couldn't summon the words. "You're grounded, you're focused, and you're loyal," Grif continued. "And you don't hesitate to help or sacrifice for those you care about. However, you're allowed to be selfish too. You're allowed to take something for yourself."

Tuck let out a bitter laugh. "The one time I tried that went great."

Grif picked up a small stone from his side and tossed it out into the lake, watching the pebble bounce before it sank into the depths with a plop. "It's not a zero-sum game, you know," he murmured. "Revenge… it can consume you—muddle your thinking. Just because he fucked up doesn't mean everything between you was false."

Tuck's chest squeezed tight at hearing those words from their leader. He knew the man spoke from experience after the way he and Dan had come together. If Dan hadn't chosen to forgive Grif for lying about his identity while on the job, for the deceit, they never would've found the happiness that consumed them both now.

And fuck, Tuck *wanted* that.

Leo had come for him tonight. He showed up when Tuck's world was falling apart, even though the odds were against him.

He'd risked everything. If that didn't tell Tuck the truth, he didn't know what would.

They didn't live in a world of black and white but in one of shades of gray as pale as the bleached rock he sat upon and as dark as the shadows in the cracks. The cool firmness of the stone beneath him seemed to trickle through as if he was finding his foundation again. As if he was rebuilding himself from the ground up.

Tuck glanced over at Grif and their gazes met. "Thank you," he murmured.

He'd chosen this family for a reason—because their loyalty was the same shade as his.

He was no longer Ace from the Twilight Circus.

He was Tucker Hennings, an Outlaw.

CHAPTER 30

Leo paused to wipe the sweat from his forehead and glanced around his nearly empty apartment. He'd just finished packing up his five thousand paperbacks, which had taken far longer than anticipated because he couldn't bear to part with most of them even if he only had so much space to work with.

The place looked odd littered with boxes. He'd been living in this studio shoebox for years, a slice of independence he'd treasured, and it had been his. However, it was time to move on. He had a couple of remote interviews everywhere from San Diego to Asheville, so he could go anywhere.

Despite the newfound freedom, he couldn't summon a smile about it. Not while his heart tugged at the thought of leaving, as if some sort of tether remained connected to this place. He should be rejoicing over the freedom from the Stockyard, but he didn't want to go. Still, he didn't know how he could stay, either.

Leaving Torres Industries behind wasn't hard—he'd already been trying to find a different job even though he still loved Vanessa. Leaving Dan behind… that socked him in the gut. Only a few days had passed since the massacre at the Big Top, which had hit the news. Part of him had been hoping maybe he'd hear from his best friend, but his phone remained silent. And leaving Tuck behind…. His throat tightened.

They hadn't even gotten much time together to explore their chemistry, the spark that had detonated between them, but Leo couldn't put it out of his mind. The loss of all the potential knocked him out at the knees every time he dwelled on it.

A rap sounded at his door, and he tensed on reflex.

He'd been keeping an eye out for news about the Stockyard, on what might've happened with the demise of their leader, but things remained quiet on that front. That didn't mean he should get lax.

Leo wiped his palms down on his pants before heading to the door.

He grabbed the knob, feeling a bit naked without some sort of weapon on after all the carrying he did the past few weeks. Who even was he? When he pulled the door open, the air evacuated his lungs.

The sight of Tuck socked him in the sternum hard enough to send him reeling. The man looked so damn good, all compact muscles beneath the slim-fit black clothes that showcased them. His curls were a bit windswept, and Leo's fingers itched to brush them back. But it was Tuck's eyes that had him arrested. Warmth blazed from them, a tenderness and heat Leo had believed he'd never see again.

"Mind if I come in?" Tuck said, leaning against the doorframe.

"Yeah, sure," Leo said, swallowing back the drool that threatened to erupt at the sheer sight of the man. "Though I don't have much furniture space available at the moment for entertaining."

Tuck stepped inside and ran his fingers through his inky curls as he soaked in the breadth of Leo's apartment, half packed up and in shambles. He let out a low whistle. "So, you're really moving on." Tuck wandered over to a clear space by the wall and leaned there.

Leo shut the door behind him with a soft click and closed the distance between them to take a seat on the arm of his couch, the cushions covered by boxes. He offered a one-shoulder shrug. "Nothing left for me here," he murmured, trying to not let the shards that reality sent piercing through him show.

Tuck glanced at him again, and their gazes locked. The relief of seeing him again was fast turning painful, his chest tightening as the space between them, mere feet, grew interminable.

"What if there was?" Tuck asked, rubbing his fingers along his jaw. Leo couldn't look away if he wanted to, a line forming between his brows as he tried to process what Tuck was saying. "A reason to stay, that is."

Leo lifted a brow, not able to form words right now.

Hope trembled inside him as he fought to shove it down, unable to handle another blow right now. Still, the intensity Tuck watched him with, the fact that the man had shown up on his doorstep… What could he be here for?

"I should've said this from the start, but I didn't want to scare you away," Tuck said, a firm confidence in his tone. "I'm interested in you, Leo. Not just for a fuck —though, goddamn, we're fire together. You're clever, tougher than I think most people realize, and braver than almost anyone I know. And the connection between us? I haven't felt so comfortable with another soul in my life. I know you don't do relationships, but if you're willing to try—I want that."

Leo swallowed hard, his eyes stinging. Tuck's words washed over him like a tidal wave, the immensity of them a crash and roar that left him blind and deafened in the wake. Tuck… wanted him? That couldn't be right. The Outlaws had cut him loose, which meant that killed any chances between him and Tuck, for good. And still, he stood here in front of Leo, telling him words he'd only dreamed of hearing from another soul. His chest spasmed as he bit back a sob.

"I lied to you," Leo said, the one thing surfacing at the moment. How could Tuck see past that?

Tuck pushed up from the wall and took slow strides toward him to close the difference. "And then you saved my life." He stopped in front of Leo and those callused fingers brushed against his cheek. Leo leaned into the touch, electricity arcing through him. "You're already forgiven. Dan, the other Outlaws—if anyone were to understand why you acted the way you did, we would."

His fingers trembled. He hadn't realized how badly he'd needed to hear those words until they'd hit the air.

Forgiven.

His past had been full of extremes—and even his perfection never brought him the love he'd hoped for. If he fucked up, that was it. He got tossed out on his ass, or worse, in his parents' case. However, this forgiveness washed over him like afternoon sunlight, rich, hazy, and golden.

Tuck brushed his thumb along Leo's cheek. "So, what do you think?" he murmured, a gentleness in his features Leo had been drawn to from the start. He'd known so little of it that he hadn't been able to recognize it at first, but the more he was around Tuck, the more he could see the care that emanated from him. "Want to give us a try?"

Leo nodded on instinct alone, but it took a second more before the words rose to his lips, shaky but true. "I want you, Tucker Hennings."

"Thank fuck," Tuck said, a grin sliding over his lips as he leaned in to steal his mouth in a kiss.

Leo gripped Tuck's shirt tightly, plastering himself up against this man. He drank in the taste of him, all coffee and sweetness, and the feel of him, heat, hard muscles, and the scratch of stubble. Tuck's hand slid down to his lower back, and the kiss fast turned filthy as Leo ground his stiffening cock against Tuck's thigh.

A low moan escaped him as he sank into the bliss radiating through him, something he thought he'd never feel again.

Tuck's stubble scraped against his clean-shaven face as the man devoured his mouth with long, hungry kisses that dripped through him like hot honey. Leo succumbed to the pleasure shuddering through his veins at each collision, desperate, consuming, like they'd never get enough of each other. His grip tightened on Tuck's shirt as he sucked in the scent of vetiver like it was a drug, the masculine musk all Tuck.

He'd missed this man with an ache that plagued him from the minute things had shattered between them. And yet this kiss—this kiss took those broken pieces he believed irreparable and began to knit them back together again. His heart pounded hard, the reality pumping through his veins that this wasn't a one-off fling. Tuck wanted him—and together, they'd try for a real relationship.

His first.

Joy dizzied his mind, and he kissed Tuck back hard, unable to believe this was real. At any moment, he expected to wake up in his bed alone, but the sting as Tuck nipped at his lower lip, the grind of his cock against Tuck's thigh, the white-knuckled way he clung to Tuck's shirt tethered Leo here in the moment.

Tuck reached around to squeeze his ass, pushing his thigh against Leo's cock. "Keep grinding like that and I'll be tempted to take you here and now."

"Yes, please," Leo murmured, a wicked grin spreading to his lips.

"I've been sent here to collect you for dinner at the penthouse though," Tuck responded. "I'm not the only one who wanted to see you."

Leo pulled back and relaxed his grip on Tuck's shirt, though he didn't let go. He lifted a brow.

"Dan's been dying to talk to you," Tuck said. "I wanted to come see you first to talk about us. But your best friend isn't going anywhere as long as you aren't."

A knot in Leo's chest loosened, and a giddy laugh bubbled up inside him. "Next you'll be telling me I won the lottery, and it's all strawberry ice cream for life."

Tuck blinked. "Strawberry's your choice of flavors? Damn, don't know if I can do this anymore, gorgeous. Think that's a dealbreaker."

"Are you kidding me? What's yours?" Leo shot back, unable to help the buoyant giddiness rising inside him like a balloon. He was standing here with his boyfriend having a conversation about ice cream. It was so simple, so normal he could barely believe it.

"Cookie dough," he said with a smirk. "You know, like a normal person."

"Fucking terrible," Leo said, leaning in to steal another kiss. When he pulled back, he hesitated, chewing on his lower lip. "Are you sure it's okay to head over? Last time…."

Tuck slid a finger under his chin to tilt it up until their eyes met. "Yes. We all want you there. Hell, Grif was the one who suggested it."

Leo blinked in surprise. That was the last person he'd expect to forgive him. However, if Grif had given the okay, he believed the rest of them would be fine. The man seemed to have a pulse on how to lead a group better than almost anyone he'd met. He leaned in against Tuck again, stealing yet another kiss. He still couldn't believe Tuck had come here for him.

That he was in a relationship.

"All right," he agreed after he pulled back. "Let's go."

LEO'S HEART POUNDED HARD AS THE ELEVATOR SOARED UP the floors. When he'd last been here, he could've sworn it was for the final time. The one thing that simultaneously grounded him and sent him floating into the stratosphere was Tuck's hand in his, their fingers woven together. A month ago, if someone had told him he'd now be holding hands with his boyfriend, he'd have said they were insane.

A lot had happened since then.

The elevator doors binged open, and he followed Tuck out to the familiar sight of the penthouse doors.

His nerves simmered as they approached. He still didn't know what to anticipate. Tuck had said this was fine—that everyone was okay with him, and yet... he half expected to walk in to those icy looks, to the acidic bitterness that had dripped from them upon discovering his past.

Tuck leaned in and pressed a kiss to his cheek. "It'll be fine," he murmured.

The gentle touch had him melting, not anything he would've ever anticipated liking. And yet from this man, he basked in the feelings erupting in him, brand-new and incendiary. Before he could even panic, Tuck had already opened the door and started to drag him along inside.

The strong scent of garlic and cooking meat wafted his way, making his stomach rumble. He'd been packing boxes all afternoon and hadn't bothered eating. All the stress of moving currently seemed like more of an annoyance than anything because now that he and Tuck were dating, he wasn't going anywhere.

Scar stepped into the foyer, a thick gray hoodie on. He tugged back the hood, and a grin surfaced on his lips. He extended a hand to Leo.

Leo tentatively took it, and they shook.

"I owe you a massive thank you," Scar said. "If you hadn't called and alerted us, who knows what would've happened to Tuck. And the intel you sent over was beyond useful."

"Oh yeah?" Leo asked.

"Reynauld had been running drugs through Javier from stop to stop, and the Stockyard had been involved for a long, long while." Scar slipped his hands into the pockets of his hoodie, his eyes open and clear—no accusations, no secret loathing. Leo swallowed hard, some of the nerves inside him settling. "Of course, with Javier dead and Reynauld behind bars, that's ended."

Tuck tensed, so Leo squeezed his hand a little tighter. Clearly, Javier's death had shaken him—that was something they'd need to talk about later.

"And the Stockyard's gone to ground with Baldwin dead," Leo volunteered.

Scar arched a sculpted brow. "Heard you had a little something to do with that."

Leo offered a half smile. "Maybe a little." His brow crinkled. "How did you manage to get paid for the job?"

"We didn't take the money from the Twilight Circus," Tuck replied, his shoulders hunched a bit. Leo gave his arm a light tug, trying to loosen whatever guilt he still carried.

Scar's lips quirked. "All the insurance money Javier collected on his caravan went mysteriously missing."

Damn clever. Leo grinned.

"I hear voices. Is he here?" Dan asked, peeking around the corner.

Leo couldn't help the bloom of warmth in his chest at the sight of his best friend. Who apparently didn't hate him. "Is that Daniel Torres in the flesh or an apparition?" he asked, mimicking his friend's usual line whenever it'd been a while since the last time they'd seen each other.

Dan flew toward him, and in seconds, he flung his arms around Leo, dragging him into a hug. Leo let go of Tuck's hand to return it, drawing his best friend in close. Not talking to Dan had just about killed him. After Leo had spent years on his own, Dan had pushed his way into Leo's life simply by being the cinnamon roll he was, and the idea that he'd hurt Dan, that he'd broken their friendship, had been unbearable.

"I'm sorry," Dan murmured, his voice hoarse.

Leo shook his head as they broke the hug. "No, I am. You deserved more from me, and I promise I'll try to do better."

"Dan, you better get back in the kitchen," John called, peeking around the corner. "Grif's going to burn your dinner." He tipped his fingers in a salute. "Hey, Leo."

"Damnit," Dan swore, pulling away from Leo. "Come on. I made adobo."

"Like your mom's?" Leo asked, already stepping in behind Dan. "I haven't had that in ages." He'd been dreading coming back here, thinking he'd never be able to face any of them again. Thinking he'd always feel like an outsider—he always had.

Except this group had a way of drawing him in, an effortlessness to the brazen way they faced danger and tragedy and laughed in spite of it.

Tuck's low chuckle sounded behind him, and he reached forward to thread their fingers together. When Dan glanced their way before turning the corner, his eyes widened.

"So, I'm guessing the two of you...," he said, not stopping in his stride.

"With the way you guys gossip, I'm pretty sure you all know what we've been up to," Leo snarked back, not quite ready to share the feelings welling inside him—if ever.

"Yes, we're dating." The way Tuck said it was definitive, confident, and damn, Leo liked that. He liked a whole lot about this man, as he was coming to discover.

"Holy shit, I never thought I'd see the day," Dan said, his expression alight with glee.

Leo rolled his eyes, clinging onto his sarcasm because a riotous part of him threatened to burst from all this joy. He didn't think it was possible—not for him, at least. Yet, here he was, entering the Outlaws' head-quarters… for family dinner with his boyfriend. The idea was so saccharine, he'd want to puke if not for the intense euphoria kicking around in his chest. Instead, he just squeezed Tuck's hand in his, a reminder that this wasn't a hallucination.

He'd killed Craig Baldwin, and now he had the chance to go for something real. And there had only ever been one person he'd wanted to pursue that with.

Leo stepped with them into the modern kitchen, all nickel accents and obsidian walls and cabinets that gleamed during the day. It emanated a warmth that had always seemed strange to him. The whole eating together thing made his skin crawl in the past, but after almost losing Dan, Tuck, and the rest of them, he wanted this more than he'd realized. Just the chance to feel what it was like to be something other than alone.

Alanna was carrying a large pot over to the main table, a massive lacquered beast that had chairs enough for all of them, and place settings too, because apparently they didn't eat out of their computer chairs like savages.

She glanced at Leo. "Oh, thank god he's here. I'm starving."

Leo swallowed hard. She'd welcomed him back as if he'd never left, just like the rest of them had.

"I thought you were burning my dinner?" Dan said, approaching the table to take a seat beside his boyfriend, who'd perfected tall, dark, and menacing.

Still, Grif softened around Dan, those icy eyes growing a little less chilled, and he patted the seat next to him. "Alanna kicked me out and took over." Grif glanced up at Leo. "Are you making an honest man out of our Tuck?"

"Fuck off," Tuck responded flippantly from beside Leo as he guided him over to the opposite side of the table. "As I said five seconds ago, we're dating, so get used to seeing him around here."

"Can you cook?" Alanna asked, "because I'm sick of the inedible shit half of this lot makes. You being the exception, Dan."

"Basic meals, yes," Leo responded, settling at the table. "French cuisine, no."

"These assholes wouldn't know what to do with French cuisine," Grif responded.

"Okay, how about we eat before the dinner gets cold?" Dan said, spearing some of the chicken with his fork.

"We were supposed to wait?" John glanced around,

already chewing the mouthful he'd taken from his plate.

Tuck's fingers found Leo's again, and he squeezed. Leo shared a smile with him, one that could barely contain the pure sunlight threatening to burst from inside him at the moment. They were crazy, all of them, and yet found himself relaxing, laughing with an ease he'd never found elsewhere. He sat by Tuck's side, eating dinner with his chosen family, and that should've sent him bolting.

However, he found himself feeling like doing the opposite. Tethers he'd never experienced before, connections he'd never dared to dream of, snared him, as did hopes for a bright future he'd never dared to reach for before. A little bit more dangerous, chaotic, and loud than he'd ever anticipated, but here amongst these people, with Tuck, he felt the first stirrings of the one thing that had been eluding him his entire life.

A home.

And he'd begin building it here.

EPILOGUE

SIX MONTHS LATER...

Tuck's entire body felt like one big bruise.

He wanted to wring Grif's neck. "Easy job," his ass.

But they'd stolen the information necessary to bait Hayes Tech, so mission accomplished. He stepped inside the penthouse, which was quieter than normal. The rest of the Outlaws had gone out to Polished Knives for drinks, but he'd wanted a night in. He strode down the corridor to his bedroom, trying not to wince with each step after the number of punches he'd taken tonight. How Alanna remained upright was beyond him, but the woman was made of fucking Kevlar.

When he got to the entrance of his bedroom, he stopped still, a stupid smile rising to his lips. "Hey, gorgeous."

Leo lay there on his bed, his laptop up and the screen's glow illuminating him in the otherwise dark room. If left to his own devices, he could get lost in that thing for hours. Leo blinked and glanced at him. He set his computer aside and pushed up off the bed and strode to greet him. "Heard you took a pounding and not the fun kind."

Tuck shook his head. "Fucking comms chatter."

Leo grinned. "I'm grateful for it. Not only highly entertaining and sometimes enlightening—did you know John has classical opera training?—but it also lets me know you're safe."

Tuck reached forward and dragged Leo the rest of the way to him, devouring his mouth in a kiss. Relief saturated him the moment their mouths met, and he sank into the taste of his man, the feel of the body Tuck had mapped out with his hands, his tongue, and his teeth.

For not ever having been in a relationship before, Leo took to it better than both of them had anticipated. He was exactly what Tuck had hoped for— remaining his chatty, sarcastic, and caring self—and Tuck lived for the quiet, small moments with him. Whether Leo was resting against his side while he hacked into something on his laptop or making a face at him over breakfast when Grif was being too broody for the day—the man brought a light and warmth into Tuck's life that he hadn't even realized he was missing.

Only one thing could make it even better.

Tuck pulled back at last, both of them a little breathless. "Move in with me."

"What?" Leo's brows drew together as he wrinkled his nose. "Did I miss a massive segue or something?"

"Most of your clothes are here, you sleep here most of the nights of the week, and you're at almost every breakfast with everyone," Tuck launched in, needing to get all the reasons he'd been collecting off his chest. He'd been thinking on this for a while, wanting it more than he could communicate, but something about coming home to Leo on his bed flipped the switch for him. "I know it's only been six months, and you like your space, and this is all new—"

"Yes," Leo said, cupping the side of his face as he gave him an affectionate stare. "I'll move in with you and your band of crazies."

Tuck's heart soared. "Fuck, I love you." He dove in for another kiss, this one gasping and fierce, nipping on Leo's lower lip before he pulled back again. He didn't bother restraining his grin this time.

"I love you too," Leo said, the words hushed in the way they'd been from the first time he'd said it, as if it might vanish if he spoke it louder. Tuck loved him even more for the bit of vulnerability that peeked out every time.

Leo belonged here, something that had been apparent from the first day they started dating. And the more time he spent with them all, the more they ended up dragging Leo in on jobs as a secondary hacker, although he preferred to stay off the field. But in this man, Tuck had found the partner he'd always been searching for, his equal in every way.

"Want to celebrate?" Leo said, waggling his brows suggestively.

Tuck let out a groan. "I've taken so many punches tonight, I don't think I could move if I wanted to."

"Who said you needed to move?" Leo smirked, the fucking minx. "Why don't you lie down and let me take care of you."

Tuck licked his lips, unable to help his grin. They just came unbidden around this man. "Lead the way."

Leo grabbed Tuck's hand, heading for the bed, Tuck mere paces behind.

Tuck's heart pounded hard as the realization crashed over him in a consuming wave—this was his life now, and he loved every second of it. After growing up in a tightknit family in the Twilight Circus, Tuck had created his own home here amongst the Outlaws. Something more permanent, more lasting than where he'd come from.

Yet a small part of him had still been searching, yearning for something more—until he met Leo.

He was the final piece Tuck had been waiting for—the first lick of flame lighting the path to his future.

YET TO READ THE REST OF THE SERIES? **MIDNIGHT HEIST** IS available. Plus check out Katherine's delicious MM small town romance series, Chesapeake Days, starting with book one, **STRONGER THAN HOPE**.

ACKNOWLEDGMENTS

First off, huge thanks to Cate and Landra, who listened to my incessant whining about the intense research required for the Outlaws books. I'm also eternally grateful for all the folks who offered feedback on this book—Jo Jo, Damon, Rob, and Nadine—you helped make it so much better. And a huge thank-you to Hot Tree Publishing for taking a chance on my crazy Outlaws as well as my lovely editors there.

I also want to shout out to the readers of this series —whether the folks who reached out and messaged me or the ones who simply took the time to leave a review. You all inspire me to dig deep and keep going in this grittier series of mine.

ABOUT THE AUTHOR

KATHERINE MCINTYRE is a feisty chick with a big attitude despite her short stature. She writes stories featuring snarky women, ragtag crews, and men with bad attitudes—and there's an equally high chance for a passionate speech thrown into the mix. As an eternal geek and tomboy who's always stepped to her own beat, she's made it her mission to write stories that represent the broad spectrum of people out there, from different cultures and races to all varieties of men and women.

WEBSITE: HTTP://WWW.KATHERINE-MCINTYRE.COM

NEWSLETTER SIGN-UP: HTTP://EEPURL.COM/DUIScB

facebook.com/kmcintyreauthor

twitter.com/pixierants

instagram.com/authorkmcintyre

bookbub.com/profile/katherine-mcintyre

ABOUT THE PUBLISHER

Hot Tree Publishing loves love. Publishing adult romantic fiction, HTPubs are all about diverse reads featuring heroes and heroines to swoon over. Since opening in 2015, HTPubs have published more than 300 titles across the wide and diverse range of romantic genres. If you're chasing a happily ever after in your favourite subgenre, HTPubs have you covered.

Interested in discovering more amazing reads brought to you by Hot Tree Publishing? Head over to the website for information:

WWW.HOTTREEPUBLISHING.COM